She Came from Beyond!

SHE CAME FROM BEYOND!

A NOVEL

Nadine Darling

THE OVERLOOK PRESS
NEW YORK, NY

This edition first published in hardcover in the United States in 2015
by The Overlook Press, Peter Mayer Publishers, Inc.

141 Wooster Street
New York, NY 10012
www.overlookpress.com

For bulk and special sales, please contact sales@overlookny.com,
or write us at the address above.

Library of Congress Cataloging-in-Publication Data

Darling, Nadine.
She came from beyond! / Nadine Darling. -- First edition.
pages cm
ISBN 978-1-4683-1152-5
I. Title.
PS3604.A755S54 2015   813'.6--dc23   2015009164

Book design and type formatting by Bernard Schleifer
Manufactured in the United States of America
ISBN: 978-1-4683-1152-5
FIRST EDITION
1 3 5 7 9 10 8 6 4 2

To Kenneth—my first, my last, my everything.

She Came from Beyond!

1.

I T HAPPENED BECAUSE OF THE SHARK, THE GREAT WHITE, THE FIRST one to survive in captivity. She was a baby, maybe four feet and tangled in a fisherman's net. Instead of slicing off her tail and fins for profit, the fisherman brought her to the aquarium, where they deposited her into their massive Outer Bay exhibit, already teeming with sunfish, tuna and the humorously graceful giant sea turtles that swayed and twirled like the hippo ballerinas of *Fantasia*, and she ate and swam as though it wasn't a thing. Then, of course, people came from all over the world to throw down their wallets.

A few days after the shark went on display I got an email from Harrison, a capture of his airline ticket to Monterey. And this:

HARRISON: Can you get off?
ME: That's a hell of a thing for a married man to ask a woman who's not his wife.
HARRISON: Very funny. Work. Can you get off? I can make the arrangements. Separate beds and all.

Seeing that shark seemed circular, I guess; what we had, too, was something submerged with teeth. Harrison and I tucked ourselves away in a dark corner of the exhibit hall and kissed so fervently it made the shark in question dash like mad in her tank, high, I would like to think, from the electronic currents emanating from our hearts and groins. She would be released less than a month later for hunting and killing a small hammerhead. The official release would read that her return to the wild was prompted by "the onset of aggressive behavior toward her own kind."

It was inevitable that Harrison and I would make love, yes, even though he'd booked the room with twin beds and immediately fell asleep in his the night we checked in, but the trip to Monterey was not about consummating so much as it was about sensing, testing the water, seeing what could be held in captivity and for how long.

I shook the small, leathery hand of a spider-monkey for a quarter on that trip. Harrison paid the quarter but he couldn't bear to touch the monkey. I, on the other hand, was sort of delighted by the opportunity. The monkey grasped the tip of my finger tiredly. The pleasure was not his. I was just another john with a shiny coin, impressing no one.

There was petulance, and some big Lifetime movie stuff ("I just don't want to be the other woman!" "You ARE the other woman!") and many rhetorical questions to be asked. Would a man, despite what one of my fathers insisted, travel across the country for a handshake? What about a handshake and a steak dinner? And what about two handshakes and a pat on the ass? If a man traveled across the country and no one shook his hand, had he really traveled any distance at all? The twin beds did not become one; we made love in one and slept in the other, and while we made love, the clean, unused bed seemed somewhat judgmental, with its dust ruffle and tight, smooth corners.

The morning after at breakfast, I asked Harrison why a person who sensed he would be unhappy with his mate would even get married in the first place.

"What, now?" asked Harrison.

"Get married. Why?"

"Oh. I don't know. It's just what people do. You get to a certain point in your life and it's what you do."

"That seems a little . . ." and then I struggled a bit with which word I wanted to use. Communist? No. Really, it reminded me of a girl I once knew from Israel who had mentioned that she, and everyone else apparently, was required by law to join the army at eighteen. Even the girls. And she wasn't even torn up about it. I love my country, she'd said, and then she grew up and stumbled off to the Army, some kind of marriage based on some kind of love. The idea of all of it horrified me, as I'd seen Treat Williams, undignified and clumsy as I, be duped into going to war just so his friend could be a hippie for one more day at the end of the movie *Hair*, and then his hippie friends sang about spiderweb sitars at his grave and joined a large group of people holding flags angrily outside the White House. It was implied that the holding of the flags, and the singing and the anger are what ended the war, but not until after Treat Williams low-crawled under barbed wire and irritated his superiors and then was killed. That is what marriage sounded like to me: a low-crawl under barbed wire, a death.

"Yes, I know," said Harrison, "the thing is you don't think about it. I'm sure you know what I'm talking about. There are things, even now, that you wanted as a kid and understand will never happen."

I nodded, but I didn't really know anything like that. Twenty-nine was a very possible age to me. I still fully expected to win the cover model contest for *Seventeen* magazine, even though it was only open to girls sixteen- to nineteen-years-old. I just assumed they would bend the rules a bit for me.

"People don't want to die alone," said Harrison. "If you get a sunburn, who will put aloe on your back?"

"I don't know. Myself?"

"People don't like putting aloe on their own backs, Easy. This is a society of people who are dependent in their application of ointments."

"Yes, but it hardly seems a reason to marry."

"It's not just aloe," said Harrison, reaching for my hand across the table. "It's iodine and Bactine. And another person to drive on a road trip. And sometimes at Christmas there are sweaters."

"I think more than a wife you need a helper monkey and a bus pass."

"Monkeys lack the skills to choose holiday sweaters. And then there's the whole diaper issue."

"Yes, sure. You need a woman with full function of her bowels and a full medicine cabinet."

"Don't forget the driver's license," said Harrison, and then he leaned over into the waiter's path and asked if there was a full bar in this place.

Full, full, full.

LATER WE WOULD WALK CANNERY ROW AND A WAX MUSEUM WOULD educate us all about John Steinbeck, his dislike of women and his prickly delight mixed with his annoyance for "Chinamen." It was a dirty sort of cave-like exhibit with a roughly tattered rope separating the customers from the waxen scenes. A crackling audio of Steinbeck himself, sounding like a song that I'd fancied enough to tape off the radio, something with a withering summer drumbeat by Stevie B or Naughty by Nature, speaking wearily about the hot California sun. Oh the toil and the alcoholism and the thinly-veiled domestic violence and the pathos. The pathos. One by one as the scenes were named, a single light appeared above it, and the figures with the horrible marionette visages would take on some momentary animation, or would at least seem to. I would remember them striding painfully forward and turning their heads like a true life version of the movie *Westworld*, in which Yul Brynner decided that being a robot cowboy slave wasn't all it was cracked up to be and instead went on a theme-park-wide killing spree. I would grind my chin into my chest for some reason— the dirt, the film, the lack of irony—and Harrison would grip my upper arm hard and say fiercely into my ear, "the next time you show the back of your neck, I'm drawing blood from it."

His marriage was like all marriages, at least all the marriages that I'd ever known about—bereft, complex, weirdly sacred. I remember that around that time I'd heard a lot of people go on about how a marriage was a marathon and not a race and also many other things that a marriage was or wasn't. It wasn't a talent show. It wasn't a popularity contest. It wasn't a life sentence. It was a marathon. But maybe, I thought, there were always going to be girls like me at the marathons of other people's marriages. Maybe there were girls like me holding cups of cold water and wearing way-too-small shirts and reaching their arms into the participants as they were running past, seeing what they could grab onto and how long they could hold it.

2.

I HATE HOW IT HAPPENED, BECAUSE THE WAY THAT IT HAPPENED IS really ordinary. Sometimes I tell people that I was a stripper and Harrison was there the night before his wedding and, well, things just happened. Take a seat right here, he said, and that was all I needed to hear. I quit the stripping game, even though it had been my first night and Harrison had been my first client. I had had no bruises on my thighs, blue or yellow as team colors, and my hair had not smelled like beer and sweat. I was a stripper from Central Casting, basically, all beauty marks and painted lips, as delicate as the geisha doll that my fisherman uncle once brought back for me from Japan. That was a story that was good enough to tell people. Everyone assumed it must be exotic, and it pained me to disappoint them. It made me wish I'd thought more about a possible audience to begin with.

But it was the internet, of course, where I spent hour after hour on an entertainment message board called Cool News arguing with fourteen-year-olds about plot points and spoilers and dream casts. It was owned and operated by a fat guy who liked movies, and that was good enough for me. I really enjoyed DEFENDING THE GENRE, and going on and on about whose best work was behind him and what was stolen from whom and what was derivative of what. This required no actual skill other than having seen a lot of terrible movies and having a subscription to *Entertainment Weekly*, and there was an anonymity to it that very much satisfied. I could be a horny, horrible boy or man and then in a swoop of schoolgirl skirt, reveal my womanhood, a move that would end any conversation, no matter how apt the argument. Being a girl trumped being Kevin Smith or even James Cameron, because I was in receipt of the one thing greater than a lucrative job in the business: an actual vagina.

As I say, it was not a bad time.

I'd moved from my hometown of San Francisco and had settled in the bland hamlet of Troubadour, Oregon with my best friend Sybil, dog groomer extraordinaire, and her husband Richard, while I maintained my role as local celebrity on the cable access show *It Came from Beyond*. It was a bad movie/live skits/robots-made-out-of-car-filters sort of deal, and I had been playing the much put-upon eye candy since I'd turned twenty-four five years earlier. The general premise was that the host, who called himself Roy Rocket, and his robot pals were trapped in a spaceship and "traveled" from terrible movie to terrible movie, all of which had titles like *Origin of the Bear Creek Zombie Bride* and *Lady Nightmare*, where everyone cracked wise (with moderate success) over the film as it was being shown. Lame puns and instantly obsolete references to Crystal Pepsi and *Melrose Place*. This was interspersed with live-action bits, and that's where my tube-top-wearing bread was buttered.

I often played versions of the exploited women in the movies that were being skewered. The skit for which I will best be remembered was Bess Crocker, the giant leading lady of the '50s gem *Radioactive Sorority* who'd spent most of her time on film crashing around in front of a green screen in stockings, a girdle and a pointed bra that made her breasts look like the snouts of some large, feral rodents. I crashed around in front of my own green screen dressed thusly, playing up my school spirit and drunkenness as I gripped a giant, empty bottle with three X's printed cleanly on its label, shouting, "Kappa Phi, bitches! Radiation! Whooo!" I also did a version of Sandy Bach, the titular *Giantess!* and dressed in ripped hot-pants and a too-tight bodice as I batted down papier-mâché galaxies and a large model of a penis-shaped satellite bounced inelegantly against my thighs. I played a lot of huge, pissed-off, scantily clad ladies. Once I mentioned to Hoke the cameraman that the sheer number of these movies suggested man's dreamlike fear of women bearing down on their lakes and cities, destroying dams, urinating on national landmarks. Hoke saw it differently.

"Men just want eight-story boobs," he said. "It's that simple."

When I wasn't some out of control BBW, I played the breathlessly stupid Lola Starr, a "space teen" with a mad crush on Roy Rocket. As Lola I was forever yearning for Roy's affections, Elly May-style and with a similar wardrobe. I wore a lot of mules and wedge sandals to become Lola Starr. I heaved a lot and braced myself against things. There were long ponytails involved, whipping back and forth like fire hoses out of control.

It was a pretty good job; it opened quite a few doors for me. Sad, pointless doors that led nowhere, like a display of doors at a place that sells doors. I starred with the dog from *Frasier* (one of them, anyway. They lived and died with all the fanfare of guppies, those dogs) in a commercial for an online college. I judged chutneys at the Troubadour Chutney Festival. My co-stars and I were even the guests of honor at some low-rent Comic Con deal in White City, a town that used to be an internment camp. Like forty people showed up, including us, but we got to sit at a panel and drink bottled water and everything. And a guy asked me if I would sign a naked picture that my face had been Photoshopped onto. I got thirty bucks for that, which happened to be exactly twice my appearance fee.

THE BOYS ON COOL NEWS WORSHIPED ME, AGREEING WITH MY EVERY point regardless of its obscurity or stupidity, and wallowing in that was a comforting, happy thing. It mattered little to them that I was about to be ousted so close to my thirtieth birthday, in some unthinkable *Logan's Run*-esque twist, for a twenty-one-year-old au pair. I was getting too old for the game, my colleagues, older, adhering to no game's rules, had told me gently, and the show was moving in a different direction. A younger, taller direction with red hair. My final shoot was behind me; I'd get paid meager royalties when filming with the new me commenced in February.

So, yeah, I took my positive feedback where I could get it. As far as I knew, there existed no other venue for ladies that were too old to be considered sexy on cable access shows with eight-dollar production values, and I wasn't even sure that the niche was there before me. How old was Elvira? A hundred? She still had to be doing something, I reasoned, even though the last time I had seen her image had been roughly fifteen years earlier as a sun-faded standing cut-out ad for Coors Light, and even then the cutout was about ten years old. It was at a flea market somewhere. The guy running the umbrella hat stand seemed to think he was married to it.

So this evening I was up by myself very late, eating brown sugar cinnamon Pop Tarts right from the silvery foil—no toasting, I hadn't a moment to spare. The entire day, and most of the previous week, I had been on a certain hellish diet that consisted mainly of cabbage soup. I would eat it cold from the big stockpot in the fridge, chewing dutifully the floating, cylindrical veg, the carrots too hard, the celery too soft. I would hit a breaking point every third or fifth day and whirl Tasmanian Devil-like through the kitchen and pantry, consuming anything even remotely edible in my path. Pasta dry from the box, stale Fruit Loops with minor bites to the bottom corners and surrounded by jimmy-like droppings, slices of half-thawed white bread that smelled intimately of the freezer and its elderly contents— food as a sort of penance. If I was subjecting myself to these calories, I wanted at least to suffer for them.

Mildly chewed crumbs dusted across the keyboard in the very early morning, and I had settled into a comforting thread about zombie films. Fast vs. slow zombies, the new *Dawn of the Dead* vs. the old *Dawn of the Dead*, ironic zombies vs. non-ironic zombies. I mentioned that I had once seen an Italian film called *Island of the Dead* in which an actor dressed as a zombie had engaged an actual living shark in an underwater fight scene. It was crackly and fever dream-like, the poor shark biting the same rubber zombie arm that was shoved in and out of his maw like a toothbrush. Of course I had seen this film; I was a student of the world!

A commenter who called him or herself Brain_Damage67 was very quick to correct me: "That movie's called *Zombi 2*, not *Island of the Dead*. There was a film called *Island of the Dead* that came out in 2000, but it was garbage. Malcolm McDowell was in it. And Mos Def. In the end it wasn't really zombies but a kind of cannibalistic fly. So."

It was the "So" that I could not abide.

I was not used to being posted to unless I did the posting first, and certainly no one had ever had the gall to correct me to my own avatar. Brain_Damage67's avatar was of Han Solo in his white shirt and black vest, looking like some delicious intergalactic maître d', aiming his pistol behind his back with Fosse-like flair. My own avatar featured me, of course, lest anyone forget with whom they were discussing *The Watchmen*. It was from the episode in which I was dressed as Ann-Margret in *The Collapse of Planet Cat*, in barely more than fuzzy cuffs and a collar. It was taken about a year after I was hired, during what I like to call my golden abs period. In that year I did no wrong. My producers parodied a lot of bad Raquel Welch movies during that time, sometimes more than once.

But of course, I had taken notice of Brain_Damage67. But of course. It was my domain. I heeded every ripple in the water, every *Big Lebowski* quote, every argument for or against the Jack Nicholson Joker. It was my job, and after getting the boot from ICFB! I'd begun taking it very seriously. Like *RoboCop* seriously. I'd noticed a certain swagger in this Brain_Damage67, even without taking the Han Solo avatar into account. He eschewed network television, praised Brit-coms, referenced books that none of us had ever heard of, or, upon being made aware, would ever read. He didn't need the place and he didn't need any of us. Even me—ME—he'd sized me up and looked away, perhaps to his Millennium Falcon.

I didn't know what to say about the zombie/shark matter. He'd been correct, of course—I checked—plus he'd one-upped me with Malcolm McDowell. So, I simply did not answer at all. I stood and stared at the computer for a while, and no one needed to know that. As far as everyone knew, I could have left the computer for personal, or even sexual reasons. Perhaps I even left to thwart and hogtie a burglar. I brushed the crumbs from myself and went to bed. Case closed, as easy as when, at age four, I had become frightened by the art on the cover of one of my fathers' KISS albums and simply slid it beneath the clean towels on the tank of the toilet. Gone. Perhaps it was still there twenty-six years later. Of course I had no idea.

But Brain_Damage67 didn't stop. Once he'd corrected me, he

couldn't stop himself correcting me. You spelled Yaphet Kotto's name wrong. Yaphet Kotto wasn't even in that movie. You're means "you are"; it's not the same as the possessive "your." It was relentless, brutal as boot camp. I did my best to avoid him completely, but his hubris had weakened my stranglehold on Cool News. I wasn't a tawny, unattainable knockout in a cat's collar, I was just a thirty-year-old woman who couldn't spell Yaphet Kotto's first name. And at the end of it all, he emailed. The email was Hjrice67, a Gmail account. He wanted me to know that he'd watched a compilation video of my skits on YouTube, and that he thought I was really funny. He thought I had fabulous timing. I wrote back that I'd never heard them referred to as "timing" before. LOL. LMAO. ROTFLMAO.

He suggested we IM.

HJRICE67: You should have your own show. Will *ICFB!* let you out of your contract?
LOLASTARR: Oh, they'll let me out of my contract all right—let me out of it two months ago!
HJRICE67: what are you talking about?
LOLASTARR: It seems I'm too old to don the sacrificial hot pants.
HJRICE67: bullshit.
LOLASTARR: there's always someone younger, stupider and cheaper, that's a sad fact of this sad world.
HJRICE67: that was the subject of my thesis actually.
LOLASTARR hooboy.
HJRICE67: What?
LOLASTARR: I think I'm in big trouble, is what.

My housemates, Sybil and Richard, fought all the time, in a way which was both horrible and kind of a relief, because seeing marriage as a big scam could really let a person off the hook in advance, as far as trying was concerned. What was the point in trying if the person you loved more than anything was constantly reminding you about that one time you went to Hooters or didn't give them an orgasm? Or the fact that you own a Spice Girls CD?

Really stupid shit. I was on the computer most of the time, or in my little bedroom on this stationary bike from around 1974, and I always had my headphones in, listening to hilarious R&B from the nineties, a time in which a man could wear suits made of green space-age taffeta and still bang any woman in the club, and still I heard every word of every fight.

"Oh, Lord, this again? Can you wash your own underwear if you're not gonna bother wiping your ass?"

"Hey, this is a vacuum, ever seen one? It uses suction to clean dust and crap off the floor. Yeah, you know it, you bought it off the TV for two hundred bucks in the middle of the night and then it arrived! In less than two days! Because you paid for the extra shipping! And then it sat in its box next to the door for a month!"

"You think this is a game? Is this a game to you? I'm so sick of your games!"

If it was a game, man, it was a horrible game, like a big, boring version of *Jumanji* with additional screaming and alcohol. The fights between Sybil and Richard lasted about forty-five minutes in general, and ended with one of them knocking on my door to ask if they could hang out in my room, like a kid after a nightmare, too scared to go back to bed. Sybil, usually, but sometimes it was Richard. Sometimes he would lie on my bed and smoke and read something deep like *Naked Lunch* or *Gravity's Rainbow*, and I could never tell if he was actually into it or just flipping pages. He laughed a lot, though, and never tried to explain what was so funny.

I PICTURED HJRICE67 AS COMPACT, THIN, WITH LICKS OF BUTTERMILK blonde hair that flopped over his eyes, and those eyes would be a certain shade of amazing green, like the green on a package of Mystic Mint cookies. He would be my height—short for a woman, tiny for a man—with graceful musician's hands. Very shy. A thrift shop dresser. Everything organic. He would say things that would make other people uncomfortable, just to make them uncomfortable. We would be able to watch Troma films and see the hard, ugly art of them.

All he'd told me was that he lived north of Boston, in the blue-collar fishing mecca of Providence. Of course by then I had made a point of not believing anything typed. I'd met too many lesbian travel agents claiming to be male clairvoyants. It was a tough game, a game of *Clue* with no clues. In the end you were left fingering the outside of that tiny envelope, not sure if it was a noose in there or a candlestick.

And he said that he was forty-one, which I actually did believe because I could not for the life of me imagine someone pretending to be forty-one. It is one of those ages that just drowns in the weight of itself, of its blinding reality, too old to be exciting, too young to convey any gray-at-the-temples distinction. Forty-one seemed an odd, trying age for a graceful musician, but I took that in stride. I'd found that small people tended to age exceedingly well, like small dogs. It was the big dogs in life, tongues lolling, the areas under their eyes slick with mudslides of unidentifiable gunk, that showed wear the most easily. Everything in their environment hurt them.

He would often IM me after work and tell me about the disgusting things he was eating.

> HJRICE67: God. This whole pint of Ben & Jerry's: chocolate ice cream with white chocolate chips and a hidden core of pure caramel. Disgusting. One sitting.
>
> LOLASTARR: "a hidden core of pure caramel" you say?
>
> HJRICE67: yep. Right to the bottom of the container. Like this deadly tornado of caramel. Just waiting there like quicksand.
>
> LOLASTARR: when I was a kid, I chose a book about quicksand from the Scholastic Book Club. It told about what to do if you were ever trapped in it, how to survive. I was a pretty nervous kid.
>
> HJRICE67: well, you looked for solutions, at least? Can you remember how to save yourself from quicksand? Seems a fairly handy thing.
>
> LOLASTARR: I actually do not remember at all. I think it may have involved a vine, or something? I think it would be more situational. You know, vines

might not always be available in the worst case
scenario.

HJRICE67: Not in the worst case scenario, no.

LOLASTARR: I actually think that one of the solutions
was just to scream really loudly.

HJRICE67: Geez.

LOLASTARR: the thing that I remember really clearly is
that if a horse is trapped in quicksand it will fold
its legs up and sort of float to the edge of the pit
and just jump out.

HJRICE67: That's all very well and good for horses, I
suppose.

LOLASTARR: I think the main point of everything was
to not panic.

HJRICE67: Yes, well, that's generally the main point of
everything.

Finally, in the cruel, *Sweet Valley High* plotline that was my
life—Richard revealed to Sybil that he was having an affair.

Apparently it was the girl who worked the front desk at the
Golden Auto where he worked. Days later Sybil and I would don
ridiculous disguises and stake the woman out from the Carl's Jr. next
door. She was a bit soft, not a fatty, with frizzy hair and an overbite.
Sybil did a speech about how "this was the woman that my husband
chose over me and our unborn babies" and cried bitterly into her
onion rings.

And Richard made things worse by not really wanting to
make things better. He was full of logical, painful excuses for his
indiscretions. He was lonely. He didn't feel valued. He didn't feel
desired. He felt taken for granted.

"Well, welcome to the real world, Boy-O!" shouted Sybil, her
face a dark Pollock of mascara and tears, "because that's the way
you're supposed to feel!"

We moved out, as angry women of the world, to an apartment
complex/project called The Aloha Terrace, and we took the computer.
This was how I was able to regale Hjrice67 (who I now knew as Har-

rison) with my bright tales of humorous poverty. Sybil and I cloistered ourselves in our one-room apartment and judged men for a while. That was fun. We discussed the things that they were good for (sex, nothing) and watched things like *Married . . . with Children* to back up our defense. Well, of course! Men hate women! They just want cold beers and orgasms! Nothing of value was valuable to them.

To make Sybil feel better, I purchased naughty novelties from the adult superstore and erotic bakery; we wore penis hats and ate penis cake. We mocked and cannibalized, as though this would some-how make up for everything, for the stupid kids we'd been only weeks before with our *Glamour* magazines and quizzes and secret storybook endings. Who among us had not assumed that Sybil and Richard would be rocking back and forth on their patio ages from now, their gaggle of babies unleashed to a benevolent world, fingers clenched against the cold lies of everything, that maybe nothing mattered in the end, ever. Now Sybil and I lived our sad lives in our sad apartment, listening to cats and humans fuck loudly and incessantly, hijacked the minute we opened the apartment door by sad ladies who wanted to remind us where the fire exits were.

> LOLASTARR: I think it maybe used to be a very nice place to live, actually. The colors, the original paint seems very cheerful. Like sherbet.
> HJRICE67: Oh, the slums are generally the most color-ful places from an architectural standpoint. It's to get people's minds off bettering themselves and re-volting against the system. No offense.
> LOLASTARR: It's not exactly a slum. It's just more . . . I guess, working class.
> HJRICE67: is there water in the pool or just a bunch of trees?
> LOLASTARR: just a bunch of trees.
> HJRICE67: yeah, it's a slum.

Harrison and I knew very little about each other, and there was comfort in that. He knew that I did comedy with robots at one time, and that my friend and I were living out a Norman Lear sitcom in Southern Oregon; I knew that he was forty-one and lived and worked in the north shore of Massachusetts. He knew that I was single, I guessed, and I guessed that because I felt that I exuded singleness. I never talked about men in a wanting or possessive way, certainly not in the shoot 'em all and let God sort 'em out manner in which I lived my life with Sybil. Harrison and I lived 3,000 miles from each other. By the time I dragged my sorry ass out of bed every morning at times he was just leaving work for the day. It seemed natural for me to assume that he, too, was single. It seemed illogical that a married or, at least, attached man would have so much free time to spend on the internet.

In hindsight, of course, I realize that I was just taking my own irrational, insecure musings about marriage and applying them generally, scooping up fistfuls and hurling them in all directions like so much domestic confetti. Innocuously, I had always imagined that my future marriage would be tight and concise, punctuated only with small hilarious fights that always managed to right themselves in thirty minutes or less. Maybe I imagined myself wearing a flouncy skirt through this marriage, and saw myself often serving my husband glasses of beer and cheese sandwiches. For a man to choose a computer (the Pet Rock of the nineties!) over his bride, the woman with whom he had stood before God and done the whole bit about sickness and health like a kind of forever-binding insurance, seemed incorrect and only a very small part of my brain would accept it. This tiny portion of my brain would slump in its chair in its cramped little cubicle and speak to me in the worn, weary voice of Droopy Dog. *Don't you think it would be best to ask, Easy? Easy? This is getting pretty serious, Easy. Don't you think you should at least ask? Easy?*

And of course I didn't want to ask. Harrison and I had played this game so far with an incredibly even keel. We joked and half-flirted, neither one of us committing to anything, and I was damned if I was going to be the one who made that awkward. *Oh, that was so funny, the thing you said about Gymkata. I know! Why would a primitive village of mostly zombie immigrants have a pommel horse right in the middle of town?! Do you have a wife? Just curious. About wives. LOL.*

I very discreetly brought the conversation to Sybil, very hypothetically. I asked, "So, if a person was chatting with another person online and they suspected that this other person might be . . . let's say *attached* in some way or another . . ."

"Who are you messing with, you whore?" said Sybil, who'd worked a double shift at the groom shop and was in no mood for my tentative bush-beating. She didn't even look up from counting that day's tips.

"Nobody. Jesus."

"Oh, really? Then what is all this?"

"I don't know," I said. "Magazine survey."

"Whatever," said Sybil. "Just answer 'B' to everything, and call it a day."

"Thanks," I said. "Thanks, that's helpful."

LOLASTARR: what are you doing this evening?

HJRICE67: having supper with my parole officer, why do you ask?

LOLASTARR: No reason.

HJRICE67: why so glum, chum?

LOLASTARR: I feel pretty pensive, I guess. You know this whole Internet thing.

HJRICE67: you don't have to capitalize it, Easy. I won't tell anyone.

LOLASTARR: I've kind of been up my own ass about this for a while. You know that thing that people are always using on the internet, IRL?

HJRICE67: In real life, yes.

LOLASTARR: the distance between the two, between the internets and IRL, has really been getting me down. Did you ever see the movie *Hollow Man* with Kevin Bacon?

HJRICE67: Skinless gorillas, Kevin Bacon using his power to undress sleeping interns, sure.

LOLASTARR: Well, it occurred to me like a year after I saw it that that movie was actually about the internet. Kevin Bacon was invisible, and he didn't have to take responsibility for anything. He could do anything and not get caught, do you know what I'm saying? He could trespass on anything or anyone and then just disappear, and once he had that ability he discovered all these dark things about himself, that maybe he wasn't the most moral of people when he didn't have to be.

HJRICE67: I don't really feel like this is about *Hollow Man* anymore.

LOLASTARR: I just don't want you to think that I don't take responsibility for this.

HJRICE67: for what?

LOLASTARR: for this friendship.

HJRICE67: I'm not asking anything of you and you're not asking anything of me, and that's what is so good about this, the fact that you're the only person in my life who doesn't expect me to do anything.

LOLASTARR: okay

HJRICE67: well, okay.

And it just sort of hung there that way, a cliffhanger of okayness. I remember it ending there, but it probably didn't. We probably made some jokes about things that were easy to joke about, and we probably behaved in a way that was very superior to everything else. After that we ducked and hid our faces, the only faces we had to show.

THINGS FELL OFF FOR A WHILE. HARRISON AND I STARTED LOGGING ON TO Cool News at times when it seemed logical that the other would be asleep or working. I would sit down at the computer at one in the morning, 4:00 a.m. to him, and read the comments and quips he'd left earlier, each a small revelation, a tiny joy, bright and snug as an Easter egg. I would never answer, but instead always behaved as though I were being watched. I flounced a lot. I side-eyed. I committed to nothing. IRL I sniffed and ate horrible, unmonitored things, such as fifty-percent-off cinnamon rolls right from the box, their cream cheese frosting, a glycemic time bomb on the tongue. My fingers were stained constantly— orange by Cheetos or white/yellow by Smart Food. I watched infomercials with sugar-crashed weariness, floating in and out, in and out to testimonials about juicers, baby food makers, and little plastic devices that enabled one to make perfect sushi, every time. Even sushi for kids! Using Rice Krispies and Fruit Roll-Ups! I would slip into dreams of flight, of preparing to fly. Glass ceilinged terminals with motorized walk-ways and such sun, such blinding white sun, and I would wake to the applause of a studio audience who now truly believed that they could finally drain pasta without ending up in the emergency room.

Richard came by, and I opened the door halfway and peered out. This was partially because I did not want him to see the cinnamon-scented filth in which Sybil and I lived, and partially because I was still wearing his clothes.

"She's not here, *Rick*," I said, too nastily. He'd always hated any variation of the name Richard, explaining that they all seemed like rings in a personal pervert hell. Rick, Ricky, Dickie, Rich, Ritchie, each more infantile and suspect than the last, like a police lineup of guys hanging around a library bathroom. This time he seemed not to mind at all, or to even notice.

"I'm just bringing the mail," he said, easing a thick stack of envelopes secured with a black hair elastic through the crack in the door. He was dressed for work in his blue coveralls and steel-toed boots from Wal-Mart. He'd shaved and his hair was combed neatly, and I wasn't certain why these small details seemed so threatening to me personally. Maybe without responsibility men were free to comb their hair more often. Maybe adultery was good for the complexion. I had wanted him to hurt the way my friend was hurting, and the way that I had hurt in empathy, living in such close quarters with the moist-eyed cautionary tale of her.

"Pay your own bills, for Christ's sake."

"I always do, Easy. This is mainly just the demand notices from *Teen Vogue*. I'm not paying those."

"Whatever," I said, and when he stalled for a moment I felt for sure that it was my Gloria Gaynor moment to Defend All Women. "She's not coming back, you know."

"Yes, I know." Then he yawned, "Thank god we never had children."

Thank god we never had children, said partially as a yawn.

"Yes," I answered, quickly and dumbly, "Thank god, *for her*!"

"Yeah," said Richard, not caring enough to be defensive, in a bland and tired way, "The guys from your show have been coming around and calling. I think there's a letter or two in there from them."

"My show?"

"Yeah, that . . . thing. That show you used to be on, that outer space thing. I told them you didn't have a phone anymore and I tried to remember the address of this place. I remembered the name but I couldn't remember the apartment number. I think I gave them 33."

"No, that's a shut-in," I said, "one of them, anyway." We had a few. One was a guy too heavy to leave his apartment, another thought that UPS trucks were monitoring his activity. One lady had a shit-ton of dolls in her apartment and was always having tea parties with them and playing the soundtrack to *Man of La Mancha* super loudly. The Aloha Terrace really catered to the mentally ill and emotionally bereft, which is why Sybil and me were drawn to it in the first place. Also, they were the only place in town that didn't threaten to check credit histories.

"Yeah. So," said Richard. "They said get in touch with them, that it's pretty urgent."

"Do I owe them money?"

"Maybe, I don't know. The one guy with the comb-over . . ."

"Isaac."

"Yes, Isaac. He said something about when filming was starting."

"They probably want me to fucking sign off on something," I said, bare toes working angrily at the greenly defeated shag of our carpet. The door had opened wider as we talked, a thing I noticed in a weirdly tidal way, as though it had moved on its own.

"Yeah. I don't know. Just thought you might want to know."

"Thank you."

We stood there for a second, pregnant with strangeness. I wondered if he could look at me and know I'd eaten his penis in effigy as an inappropriate cake, if he could see the butter cream phallus in my eyes, laid out and quivering on our coffee table like some kind of ritual sacrifice. I wanted him to say something to me about his relationship with Sybil, to be vulnerable enough to do that even though I myself had lumped him in with such men as Scott Peterson and the old guy from that one bird show who'd brought his gun to a diner while eating with his wife and then denied shooting her. It seemed circular to me, even though I had never known Richard very well, only in the casually over-sharing way that a wife will discuss her husband in front of other women. I knew that once he'd gone to the doctor to get "black wax" drained from both ears. I knew that Sybil often popped whiteheads on his back, and that his semen was bitter when he ate pulled pork, sweet when he ate cantaloupe. It occurred to me standing there that I did not know his middle name.

I said, "Sybil is not doing well."

"She was never doing well."

"She misses you is what I'm saying. She's not doing well."

He paused and looked away, blowing out air. I saw him choosing to be kind. "You don't really know anything about my marriage."

"I know that my friend is hurting. I know that you took vows, and I know that those vows did not include a receptionist at a fucking body shop."

"Well," said Richard, "then you really don't know anything about anything else, either. If Sybil is mad or she has anything to say to me, have her come around. She knows where I live."

"It's like you don't even want to work things out, is the worst thing. You never gave her the chance to forgive you."

And at that Richard didn't seem to be thinking that kind was the best way to go with this. He kept his cool, I will give him that, which is more than I could say for most men faced with their wife's ignorant best friend berating them in a slum hallway while also wearing that man's clothes.

"I do not choose to forgive her, is the point." He said, "and this is not a conversation that I want to be having."

He did this little half salute with two fingers against his forehead that seemed both sad and funny at the same time, and then I was sorry I had called him Rick. He was a sad person at the periphery of my life; he'd let me stay in his house for almost nothing, he'd trusted me with his computer and stereo equipment and even his car. He'd always had a very communal snack policy, even where ice cream was concerned.

As he was walking away I leaned my head out and said, "I will make sure to get all your clothes to you," and to this he only half-turned, not stopping.

"Keep 'em!" he called, over his shoulder like a summer blonde. The clothes, it seemed, were like his wife, part of something old and smothering as burlap and in shedding them he was shedding everything. There was no place in his new life, it seemed, for three wolves and a moon, or an Old Navy pick-up truck, or cargo shorts with poorly treated bloodstains at the crotches.

He took the stairs and not the elevator, his work boots clicking off the steps like the happiest of music.

3.

SEEING RICHARD HAD MADE ME MISS HARRISON. THE IDEA OF A clean man coming to the door with mail, aside from the mailman, had just tugged me in all sorts of directions, and I settled sadly with my stack of mail by the door until Sybil came home smelling of Dawn—which made a poodle whiter than anything—and wet dog.

"Richard was here," I said.

"Richard is here?" said Sybil, clawing fingers through her hair like a homeless woman who's heard that Brad Pitt is in the area. "Where? In the can?"

"Was. He was here."

"Oh," said Sybil, looking off mournfully in the direction of the bathroom.

In the weeks since they'd split it had been easier to configure a case against my old friend as co-conspirator in the demise of her own marriage. She'd often been cruel to Richard, pointing out his lack of hair and earning power, the shit stains in his underwear and the wadded white tissues she would find in the bed several times a week in stiffly blooming puffs, all of which happened while I was in earshot. She had disliked any sort of real romance or emotion, choosing instead to turn it into a joke or ask him whether or not he was high. They never got the other's input on their whereabouts; they'd walked in and out on each other as roommates. Once, Sybil had even suggested that she and I share the master bedroom and Richard take my smaller room at the front of the house, enticing me with such bonuses as a mini-fridge and all night Patrick Swayze marathons. In the end, it had been me who'd pulled the plug on that particular dream. A line had been crossed that had nothing to do with me, and sharing a room with Sybil would have felt too much like rolling about in the crime scene of a marriage, trying on all the clothes and scenarios like some ghoulish Goldilocks.

I loved Sybil, of course, it was just that I could understand not wanting to be married to her.

"What did he say?" she asked now, her face horrible with expectation, and I could only shrug and hold out our mail in a fan like lottery tickets.

"That ass," said Sybil. She scanned the letters quickly and then whipped them to the ground as though they were on fire. I actually half expected her to jump up and down on them.

The letter on top was from Isaac Barris, his sticky alphabet-like primitive little huts too influenced by the forces of nature. As Sybil tromped off into the kitchen to swear and splash cold water on her face, I opened the envelope and read:

> *Dear Kiddo,*
> *How have you been, lol? I have been trying to call but it seems you guys don't answer your phone lol. I should come by but you know our last conversation wasn't on the best of terms, haha.*

He spoke that way, too, inappropriate laughter scattered like oversized croutons. It made it really hard to talk to him in any venue, even over the phone. In fact, just reading his letter made me want to wash my hands.

> *But I could use the walk, lol!*

That was deliberate. I had made light of his weight problem when we'd last spoken but, in my defense, he'd just uttered the words, "Well, there are crow's feet and then there are crow's feet."

> *We sure miss you a lot down here, despite the things that were said or thrown, and you may wanna sit down, lol, because have I got some news for you.*

It Came from Beyond had been picked to run primetime Thursdays on the Syfy Channel, and although the budget would be bigger, it would continue to shoot out of Troubadour to save money. (*"Plus I'm too fat for Hollywood's standards, lol!"*) Most shocking of all, my fans (my nerds, *my people*) had come to my defense with a letter-writing campaign to the president of Viacom. It was my old ass they wanted dancing inappropriately with men dressed as Japanese Monkey Aliens, not Helen from Marketing's twenty-one-year-old second cousin with implants. Mine. And as much as my joy was tempered with the fear of having stuffed every cream-filled thing within a thirty-mile radius into my mouth over the previous six weeks, I felt proud of myself and looked forward to bleeding money out of Isaac until he squealed like a pig.

> *"I know that we've had our differences, Easy, but this is such a fantastic opportunity for all of us! The quality of art we can create! Can you even imagine?!"*

He closed with his phone number and a bit about me getting my "game-face" on for an upcoming convention in downtown Troubadour, which I guess meant that my eating habits had not been a secret around town. I often left O'Bannon's with a roast chicken under one arm and an Italian sheet cake under the other. It was cheaper than therapy, and I did not have health insurance.

Sybil poked her head in from the kitchen, eyes punched-puffy from crying. "Wanna binge tonight?" she asked, holding out a fistful of bills like a sad and scrubby bouquet. "I did two St. Bernards and got a bunch of tips."

"I can't, man," I said, thinking of a convention, the mournful pageantry of it, Klingon weddings, group solitude, ironic t-shirts as far as the eye could see. "It's bad for business."

I LOST A GOOD DEAL OF WEIGHT AFTER SIGNING WITH *ICFB!* FOR THE SECond time. Actually, an unreasonable amount of weight, something like twenty pounds when there had only been maybe six to lose, and it had wizened me and made me more than a little goofy, and I came off more as Hunter S. Thompson in the desert than Ann-Margret. I reacted strongly to sudden noises; a headache curled constantly in my left temple like a grub had left my eyes wild, broken as yolks. Still, the people from Syfy had all but cheered when they saw me, resting, I guess, on the notion that they should have kept a twenty-one-year-old in the wings.

THEY SENT ME TO BE TANNED AND WAXED ON SYFY'S BILL; IN THE END I was baked and bare, defenseless as a squab. I had long drool-strips of blonde in my hair, and platinum extensions, and they'd put me on some kind of eye drops that had turned my lashes into rough, spiky fern-like entities that threatened to pierce my eyeballs like toothpicks through cocktail onions.

I took my advance and moved out of The Aloha Terrace, and, of course, Sybil was distraught. Two deserters in two months was too much for her, even though I left all the pathetic furniture and a bit of cash, to boot. For me, it was a sad (but easy) decision. As much affection as I had for Sybil, the kooky *Laverne & Shirley*-ness of our relationship had really strained its boundaries since we'd moved into The Aloha Terrace. I had not known, for instance, that she liked to walk around naked after work, often while having long, animated conversations on the phone. She, conversely, did not know that I sometimes listened to death rock and cried. These were uncomfortable topics to broach. We parted ways with tentative, awkward humor, like when you have to tell a salesman that after three hours and countless pairs of loafers you couldn't afford to spend four hundred dollars on shoes, and then ask for a balloon from the children's department.

I put a down payment on a four-bedroom cottage in the nicer part of Troubadour, near where the library was before it was turned into a cockfighting ring. It had once been a library, anyway, and that subdued my raging ego like a tonic. I still don't know what I assumed I was going to do with three extra bedrooms at the time, keep a harem? But I was sad and starving and never prone to good decisions, and I'd decided that the house should be mine. It was blue and white and pretty beat up and even before stepping inside I had made peace with the fact that it would stay that way. The front yard was enclosed with this horrid sort of *Blair Witch*y fence, just slabs of unfinished wood pieced together in the most haphazard way like a train track of toothpicks. It was damn near folk art. It made my heart undulate strangely in my chest like something broken or breaking, a wiggly tooth connected to a doorknob by floss.

It was three short blocks to The Troubadour Center, with its anchor shops of O'Bannon's supermarket on one end and Señor Squawk's on the other. Señor Squawk's was a Mexican restaurant overseen by a colorful parrot in a sombrero. I guess he was left the restaurant in a will, or something. All's I know is that if you guessed how many sunflower seeds he could eat in one sitting you got free nachos. And they had margaritas you could bathe in. So, yes, that factored deeply into my house scouting decisions. I enjoyed the idea of a leisurely walk down to the Troubadour Center to eat burritos under the watchful eye of an obese bird, even though Troubadour did not have actual sidewalks, just a few littered feet of dirt that separated the homes from traffic and turned into a brownish slop from October to April. Even this was enchanting to me. For some magical reason, when it rained, magnet numbers and letters would rise to the top of the muck and settle there like night crawlers, and then you'd pick them out and carry them home, where you would clean them up and affix them to your fridge and rearrange them constantly looking for signs from God or your future husband or the mole people or whatever. And sometimes a person would push a couch out of his or her house and just leave it there where the sidewalk should have been, and that was good luck, to see that. But it was only good luck if you were walking, since of course to see a couch while driving by seemed no great feat. You couldn't see the wine stains, say. You couldn't appreciate the weave of the upholstery.

I was in love with my house and with my town. Of course I guess I should've known that something big was going to happen. A girl can't just love a town that hard without something getting in the way of it. That just isn't how shit works.

N

IN MY NEW CONTRACT I HAD A MANAGER/PERSONAL ASSISTANT/MAKEUP artist named Sally Brawn, although after meeting her I, like everyone else, called her Sally Balls. She was always dressed in red, which seemed a natural defense of sorts, and she had a chemically vanilla scent about her like a car freshener, the kind of smell meant to mask other kinds of smells. It reminded me of living at Aloha Terrace with Sybil and not being able to afford the coin-op wash machines downstairs. We would often Febreze the crotches of our panties and jeans, which sometimes resulted in a nasty sort of yeast infection we enjoyed calling 'poppin fresh.' Sally Balls scared me in the way that most people I assume would have me killed for money scare me. It was as though the entire cast of *It Came from Beyond!* had drawn straws to choose their managers and I had been the one to come up Sally, who had seven ex-husbands, who picked her teeth with her press-on nails, who, at least once that I know of, drank Brut when no other alcohol was available.

She'd driven me to the convention center in her red VW Bug, speaking angrily on the phone the entire time with her latest ex-husband, Ferdinand. I had once made the mistake of mentioning that I liked that name, as it reminded me of the children's book about the bull. Sally had reacted badly to that.

"That numb shit left me for a seventeen-year-old, did you know? I walked into my bedroom in an eighty dollar peach-colored La Perla bra and panty set for his forty-fifth birthday and he's bulldozing a child from behind in our marital bed. Does that sound like any sort of kiddie book to you? No? Well, that's what I fucking thought."

I was often not just taken aback by the things she said but paralyzed by them. I would shake my head in a small terrified way, long ponytails swinging, lips retreating between my teeth like the polyps of a sea anemone. Just as I had done with most of the gym teachers I'd known in my lifetime, I sat very still and hoped not to be called upon.

She was too thin and the skin of her face too tight and her clothes hung on her. She often wore sunglasses of comical size. I sometimes considered her look to be "foreign burn victim about town," although I could never bring myself to say such a thing out loud. Once I thought that she'd read it off my mind and I panicked; she'd sort of lunged at me for no discernible reason. Later, I'd find out that she'd gotten the idea somehow that I might have swiped her wallet. She had no grounds to go on of course, she just didn't mind looking a fool, or drawing blood, where money was concerned.

I WAS DRESSED IN MY OLD SPACE TEEN GET-UP—JEAN CUT-OFFS SO SHORT the whites of the pockets hung down in some kind of half-mast sur-render and a blue, white, and black checked plaid men's button-down shirt, buttoned down. Worst of all, modesty dictated that I wear these orangey tan-colored tights beneath my cut-offs, the kind that the Hooters girls wear, and then hard-soled booties to mimic bare feet. Actual bare feet were out of the question; a sommelier, of all people, told me that once a guy who knew a guy had told him about a guy who'd stepped on a hypodermic needle and contracted hepatitis B, and I was fearful enough to take heed. I was being paid obscene money to be shamed and made uncomfortable; my brain could digest it if I thought about it as some wacky kids' game show, the kind where you dive out of a big plastic nose into a vat of green ooze and win a state-of-the-art water gun, or whatever.

My first photo opportunity of the convention was with the Japan chapter of the *ICFB!* fan club, who appeared to be three small well-kept gentlemen, apparently instrumental in getting my job back. No sooner had I canted my hip and pointed my ray-gun jauntily, I was barraged by several dozen Korean men, all of whom had previously been in the bathroom, I guess, grasping and pinching and bumping into me with boundless energy like some bastard, robotic three-hole-punch. I can only imagine the finished photos looked like something out of a banned issue of *Hustler* from the sixties, something rubberized, sterile and non-consensual.

"You did good out there," said Sally, her teeth clenched around a cigarette she should not have been smoking inside, "you took it like a man and that's all anyone can ask from a woman."

The shock of that, that bustle of hips and elbows combined

with my own casual starvation, had brought me close to white-out conditions, and I backed up against the nearest wall to slide down the length of it. Enclosed in a milky sort of iris I could see Sally's pointed red pumps, one pushed down enough to reveal a nipple-like corn-pad adhered to her big toe. I muttered out something that didn't remotely sound like what I'd wanted to say; what came out had very long vowels, or maybe I was just hearing them that way, drawn-out for the hearing-impaired or intoxicated.

"Yes, you rest," said Sally, sounding very far away, "I'll come get you when the Intergalactic Panel convenes."

It occurred to me that I was in the only place in the world where such a statement might be as likely true as it was a hallucination, and I thought about granola bars and slept.

SHOES. A BROWN SORT OF BLACK AND SHINED TO A HIGH GLOSS, WHICH made me think of glazed donuts, which in turn made me think of happiness.

"Can I have an autograph?"

I moaned low, my head in my hands like a soft bomb. It was imperative to not be a dick, I knew that, no matter how dick-like my first reactions may have felt.

I tried out some words, "There's a scheduled time for that, sir. It's called the Intergalactic Panel."

"Sounds like the last word on panels."

"Yes. Yes. Ow. It will be starting very soon, sir, so if you don't mind, this backstage area is for the talent . . ."

That was met with a laugh like cigarette-clogged cabinet doors swinging solemnly.

"What? You don't have the same appreciation for your American fans that you do for the ones from Korea?"

"I value all of my fans, sir," I said, blinking. While unconscious, I'd dreamed of being a child; the time my family house-sat for my aunt and uncle in Weed, CA. They'd had the first VCR of anyone we knew, a Betamax. A year after they bought it, my uncle would scold my fathers lightly for buying the four-head VHS they'd read about in *Consumer Reports*. I dreamed that while my dads swam in my aunt and uncle's Doughboy, I'd stayed in the house and attempted to eat an envelope of my aunt's cherry-flavored Kool-Aid, and it ruptured and was unsweetened, besides. In my dream, one of my fathers had called me out of the house and poolside, and I was standing there, hennaed blood-red across my face, torso and hands, maintaining my innocence.

"THERE WERE LOTS OF THEM IN THE CABINET," I SAID NOW, THINKING that there had been. Reds and oranges and purples, all seducing me with their haughtily powdered variety.

"Lots of what in the cabinet? Are you okay?"

I nodded stiffly. Or maybe I shook my head, or did nothing at all.

The face that appeared before me did not belong to the freshly-shined donut shoes; it was Isaac in his space coveralls. He'd grown a mustache and some kind of goatee; it gave him the appearance of a horrible beaver-faced man, and I flinched.

"Gotta get goin', champ! This is the big leagues." He smelled like too much aftershave and not enough mouthwash. There was a shuffling, a stalling of time, and a hand was offered. I was pulled to my feet.

"I'm taller than I remember," I remarked, looking down. Then there was a paper cup in my hand and I was drinking.

The man who'd offered the hand and the cup was Isaac's height but thinner, and his blue spacesuit was actually a blue hooded sweatshirt and jeans. He had a wool hat on, the brim rolled several times in a jaunty, nautical way, and his eyes were a kind of gray green blue that seemed to change in front of you like those weather maps they have, storms closing in and enveloping, warm fronts creeping up like fingers of surf against the shore, and I couldn't tell if I was feeling better or worse.

"You look as though you could use a cheeseburger, Madame," he said, and then I knew it was Harrison. In the short time we'd chatted, nothing had been so romanticized, so fetishized, as the humble cheeseburger. We'd detailed our demands like letters to Santa Claus. No tomato, ever, but sometimes lettuce. Never mayo. Bacon, of course. No sweet potato fries. No whole-wheat bun. Preferably American cheese but never a blue, and not a cheddar sharp enough to overwhelm the taste of the meat. Medium, which was illegal in some states, like California, the orange and tan-oil scented place of my birth. Imagine, I had written once to Brain_Damage67, a burger like a gun or a Chinese throwing star, banned as a book from the sixties. Maybe I had named an actual banned book, which would've meant that I had gone to the trouble of researching a banned book, because even then I was half in love with him.

"You all know me," said Harrison, "you know what I do." A line from *Jaws* for Christ's sake. It was too much, like being at the hard end of a beating. I kept shaking my head and nothing kept happening.

He stuck out his hand to Isaac and said, "Harrison Rice," like the old timey-est of product placements. Harrison Rice comes out fluffy and perfect every time! Never clumps like some of those "foreign" brands! And what the hell kind of background did it signify? Long Grain-ian? Brown? Jasmine?

"Isaac," said Isaac, sounding unsure, "and this is Easy."

"Speak for yourself," I said. "When is our thing?"

"The Intergalactic Panel?"

"Yes, yes, whatever you say."

"It's, like, now."

It was then, vision clearing in a gradual way like kicking through underbrush, that I realized that not only was I not backstage, I was smack-dab in the middle of the *Babylon 5* auction showcase. I was bracketed by life-sized dummies of Na'Toth, some kind of alien, snake woman in a long robe and Londo Mollari, who looked like a bird-headed kabuki guy dressed in one of Michael Jackson's middle career soldier get-ups.

"Jesus," I said. My fingers worked towards my mouth, as if to guide a cigarette.

"They shall be judged by the company they keep," said Harrison.

"Will you be here later?" I asked, half to Na'Toth.

"I don't see where else I would ever want to be," he said, and looking at him I felt the same joyous fear I'd felt at seventeen after getting a strangely oversized "blue" Chihuahua as a birthday gift. He hadn't been any kind of blue, of course, more a kind of brown that had shots of indigo if you squinted long and hard enough. My delightful ideas of stuffed squeaky hamburgers with eyes and fancy dog sweaters were tempered with the horror of ownership, of being responsible for something's life. That *Fuck! I have a dog!* feeling returned to me now, looking into Harrison's meteorologically blue eyes. It was part finality, part acceptance and two parts bus ticket.

"I will see you after the panel," I said, each word a slow, careful bubble from my mouth, a fragile little hiccup, "back here by the lizard woman."

"Okay. I'll have a corn dog waiting for you."

And he would, I just knew it. He was not the sort of man who lied about corn dogs. Things like that you can tell right away.

AFTER, I PUT ON PANTS AND WE WENT FOR A WALK THROUGH THE VARious booths and exhibits, the portioned off little Monopoly houses that made up the convention.

"It's not one of the better ones," I said, simply parroting something that Sally had told me in the car, although once I had my bearings I could see that she'd really had a point. For example, the obese singer who'd won an early season of *American Idol* had a booth of his own, looking like a cartoon walrus in a three-piece suit.

"Well, that just means that you get to be the star of it," said Harrison.

"I don't know. Maybe. It sort of seems like being the star of a house fire."

The auditorium had last housed an all-child performance of *Equus*; the walls were still awash with fake blood and bridles, painted in spots to look like the library in Dr. Dysart's office. The titles were meant to be viewed from a distance, up close they were jumbled together thoughts and words. Something About Psychology. Sexual Horse Obsessions. And, oddest of all: Pickles, Envelopes, Non-Fat Milk.

"The old grocery list as art deal," said Harrison. He had a gap between his front teeth, which seemed an unfair advantage. This, what we were a part of, was what they call a meet-cute, and I am generally opposed to them. Most people do not meet in line for the world's largest roller coaster, or whatever. Most people do not collide with someone on an ice skating rink and then decide they are in love and should marry. It just doesn't happen. People meet at work, or at a bar, or through other people. People meet online when they are lonely and need things and that is what happened to us really, truly when we met, so, anyway.

We eased past a booth filled with elderly golf stars demonstrating a handheld video game system based on elderly golf stars. They seemed to very much disapprove of our walking by without stopping. One turned to the other and threw his hands up widely, as though to say, you see? I told you this was a dumb idea.

"God, you have to want it more than that," said Harrison.

"Troubadour has a very large number of seniors," I said, "and they all vote. The rest of us fear them more than a little."

"Jesus, what the hell are you doing here?"

"I'm a homeowner," I said. It was my new thing to say. It saved me, I thought, from revealing too much of my true self, which, as I knew in my deepest heart of hearts, was more than half dumb-ass.

"Yes, but why? Why someone like you?"

I shrugged a little, pleased that I'd pulled the wool over someone, at least for the time being. Harrison knew that I was originally from San Francisco, that I'd attended the School of the Arts, that my parents had owned a frame shop on the corner of Market and Castro, and he seemed to think that all of those things combined to mean something. Maybe that I had been surrounded by art and opportunity, or maybe he'd just seen *Fame* too many times.

"Troubadour is my town," I said, and it was. It seemed a doctor's note for being unemployed, living in that town. It even sounded sad. Troubadour. "They say that it was founded by folk singers, and that that lasted a while until the loggers came, and then the loggers chased them away."

"Bull. Shit."

"That's what they say. There's no library, though, so one can't be sure."

I sighed a little, lover-like.

Nearly sixty miles over the California border amidst the hot, dry breezes that blew through Southern Oregon's Forfeit Valley, in the shadow of the immense blue swooping skeleton that was once the nation's largest water slide, lay the sad, still town of Troubadour, as insignificant a place, as foul and accursed, as has ever graced a map. On some of the finer maps, actually, Troubadour was not included at all. On some of the finer maps, actually, Troubadour was showcased as a tiny gray gap between the town of Prospect and the town of Twee. Some of the more upward thinking cartographers came up with the splendid idea of selling this space to elite members of the public with something to say and a great deal more money than sense. On maps such as these instead of a tiny gray gap between the town of Prospect and the town of Twee you might find the message Black Sabbath Rawks!! or Edith Ann Walliker Will You Marry Me? Love, Toby. P.S.—Black Sabbath Rawks!

The town itself was constructed like a child's valentine, visible glue, letters backward, glitter held in place with scotch tape. There was a market and a hardware store, a laundromat and a small, under-staffed hospital. There were very few jobs and even fewer men who wanted to fill them. Most people got their money from out of town, from sympathetic monocle-wearing relatives, by selling their blood or plasma, by writing letters to celebrities and pretending to be sick children, or through telemarketing scams geared towards stealing from the elderly.

There were spaces between buildings, between houses and shops, wide unexplained unpaved gaps where nothing collected or grew, like long awkward pauses in conversations. The entire town was like a condemned building full of runaways, a beat-down country where children will jump into rivers polluted with rotting meat and human waste for American coins.

It was a block of ice in the winter, a flat, hot rock in the summer. You could walk the distance of it in a quarter of a day and when you reached the scorched outskirts, be overtaken with a stoned kind of fuzziness, feeling like a person at the edge of the world, of any world, the sun puddled down to slurpy watercolors at the horizon. Then you turned around and there was Jack in the Box.

I had such admiration for Troubadour, the kind of town with no need for a functioning elementary school but which welcomed two rival Fatty Arbuckle museums, oddly enough, since no one could get a clear answer to whether Mr. Arbuckle had even ever pissed in our town. We had a TV station and a local news team, though in the hotter months no one really showed up all that often and the station took to playing two movies over and over all day, the creepy-ass cartoon version of *Animal Farm* and the animated French film *Fantastic Planet*, which is a lot of tiny naked humans as pets of giant blue things with gills and red eyes. It was about animal rights. Or human rights, or something. Maybe it was one of those deals where it was actually about nothing, and every person who saw it added their own parable, like a big stewing pot of mistrust. Seeing those films back to back was like sliding backwards into a dark well and worrying that you won't fall fast enough. I can't explain it otherwise if you haven't watched a sinister cartoon pig playing cards at a table, chewing at a cigar and contemplating Communism. Your eyeballs want to vomit or commit suicide; you have to retrain yourself to speak to other humans. During cooler parts of the year the news team would mainly go on and on about their days, or complain that things were more expensive than they once had been.

"Four dollars for a little carton of blackberries is a lot of money for blackberries," was a common complaint, "and yet try and taste one in the store! You might as well rob a bank so far as they're concerned."

Once a local man called in with a marriage proposal and his girlfriend said no on the air. That made the news team laugh quite a bit. Then they talked about it again on the following day.

They grow pears in Troubadour, and meth. The pears get a lot of play around Christmas but the meth business is hopping all year round. Great double-wide trailers abound, hissing and trembling vaguely, like things you would not want to step on in the dark. Men in headscarves stand guard, chewing with their arms crossed as though they are waiting to be filmed or maybe are being filmed already. It's a tough-luck town; people don't expect such hardship without a reality show.

To me the lovely streets of my birth city, long and willowy as the arms of a supermodel, where you could turn any corner and take a picture that would make a valid postcard, was perhaps too good for me, or for anyone. In the five years I'd lived in Troubadour, I'd gotten in two fights with two different women about the same brand of coconut pie at the same big-box store, and that is what made it my home. My self-serving ambition-less life was just a drop in the bucket. And I had a job. And owned a home. I was actually thinking of running for mayor.

"It's one of those situations where you could do a whole lot better but I'm not sure you could do any worse," said Harrison, and he'd only seen the airport.

"I just love really hard," I said, sounding stupid, sounding like the type of girl who says that she loves really hard. "I won't give up on a thing just because it's a parody. It's not Troubadour's fault it's a parody."

"You looked great up there," said Harrison, gesturing to the long table covered in coffee-ringed butcher paper that had been our Intergalactic Panel. He had a nice, smiley face, sort of Irish. He reminded me of Sean Connery, my mad crush on him after seeing *Darby O'Gill and the Little People*, all dimples and crinkly eyes. And he reminded me of Sean Connery, and my mad crush on him after seeing *Time Bandits*. I'd taken his hair loss very hard.

"That's a piece he's wearing," Dad said at the time, gesticulating with his beer can, and I'd covered my face with my hands, not wanting to believe.

"It's not hard to look good in front of people who want you to do well," I told Harrison. "They don't want to look stupid themselves, usually. Or they want a job. Shit, that's how I got my job."

"No, sir."

"No. No, I was discovered reading a magazine at a soda counter, or maybe it was that there was an audition and I was the only girl who showed up."

"Well, half of it is showing up, I've heard."

"Half seems low," I said. I squinted at him. "You showed up. From across the country. I don't know whether to be terrified or flattered."

"Don't be too flattered," said Harrison. "I have a client in Weed, California."

"Oh," I said.

"No. No, that's a lie."

"Oh?" I said.

"I actually have family right over the border in Weed, California."

"Oh?"

"Actually . . . I have in-laws right over the border in Weed, California."

"Oh."

I can't say for sure how I looked then, probably worse than I had when he'd found me splayed on the floor of *Babylon 5*. As much help as I got, as much female spackle and scaffolding and mystique, I always saw myself as one of a trio of horrible dolls, the kind that an emo kid might attach to her backpack, all lank hair and lost eyes and white/purple skin. No matter what I was in at the time it was always one of those dolls looking back at me when I washed my face before bed, a bad doll with too-short bangs. A bad doll that smelled like smoke and patchouli and library books.

"Well, you must've known," said Harrison, finally. I'd checked out. I was looking across the room at Isaac, who was calmly signing a man's bare ass.

"I'm not a fucking GPS," I said. "How the hell would I know where your in-laws live?"

"I rented a car. You . . . you wanna get out of here?"

And I did, I honestly did, no matter the company. I wanted to get out of there more than I'd wanted to get out of that water park where I threw up when I was eleven on a trip with the obese Girl Scouts. More than I'd wanted to leave my aunt and uncle's house in Weed when it had been discovered, along with my red-stained lies, that I had raided the pantry.

WE WENT TO CHUCK MCCLUCK'S ON THE FAR END OF TROUBADOUR
Center, which was also home to the town's crab-infested movie house
and about two or seven shops that sold cold medicine, bongs and exotic reptiles. Chuck McCluck's was known, oddly, for its variety of
burgers. There was not a chicken item on the menu, not even strips
or nuggets for the kiddies. It was one of those restaurants that doesn't
have enough of a theme to be national, so the proprietors get nervous
and start throwing random shit up on the walls, say, a framed picture
of Al Capone next to an old bicycle wheel, like fidgety hostesses at a
dinner party blurting out that the woman next door had a miscarriage
just to make conversation. The booths were upholstered loudly with
multicolored stripes like serapes, but the lamps that hung low over
each were a kind of fake Tiffany meets lava lamp. Harrison had ordered us both burgers with the never-ending fry bowl, a concept that
seemed overly optimistic to me. Overly optimistic and due for a lawsuit. The burgers arrived in front of us in tissue-lined plastic baskets
that looked like the little sand sifters that children play with at the
beach, and my stomach sort of clenched at the sight.

"Two corn dogs, a burger, and a never-ending fry bowl?" I
said. "Nice little jump-start for the eating-disorder."

"Don't joke about things like that," said Harrison, chewing
grimly.

"Well, since you're the guy paying for the binge, you don't
have too much of a say in the matter, now do you?"

"I know that this is a hell of a way for you to find out."

"Yeah, no. I mean yes. I mean no." The carbs and the sugar
had sort of liquefied my system; looking at Harrison was like trying
to listen to a radio through someone's fillings. I couldn't really tell if
I was mad or not. What had been implied? What was at stake? We'd
never cooed to each other over the phone or email, or texted naked
pictures of ourselves to each other. We'd talked about ice cream and
quicksand, big whoop.

"Well, I wanted to have this conversation with you face-to-
face."

"That doesn't really make it any easier for me."

"Yes, I know. It's not my desire to make this easy on you. This kind of thing, it should be hard."

"Nice. That's nice of you." The girl in the couple at the booth next to ours was covering her face because it was her birthday. A small congregation of waitstaff made their way slowly to her table, clapping solemnly, surrounding a sparkly cake held flat like a coffin. The boyfriend was saying, "It's okay! It's okay! Are you mad?"

"She doesn't know."

"What?" I said, thinking that he meant the birthday girl. She certainly must know it was her birthday, I'd thought. Unless her boyfriend was just fucking with her, a thing that I actually would have kind of admired. Once Sybil and I paged Richard in Sears when he was in automotive and we were in apparel. Later, in the car we'd laughed and laughed while he angrily chewed his caramel corn.

"My wife doesn't know I'm here."

"Oh. Okay." What was being implied, I wondered, even now, this minute. If this were a TV movie he'd be asking me to kill his wife so that we could be together. Was that what was happening? I didn't really see how I could kill somebody's wife and not ruin my career. Didn't he know that I was a homeowner?

"She's not even in the state, she's back home. I came down to refinish and paint my in-law's porch. They didn't want to pay to have a guy do it."

"So you flew three thousand miles."

"I have a lot of frequent flyer miles. I mean, it was a ruse anyway. Fuck their porch. I wanted to see you." He paused and rubbed at the back of his neck. Without his hat his hair was closely shorn, a military smudge. "I saw the banner for the convention on Cool News and I clicked on it and there you were."

"That was an old picture," I said, even though I had no idea which picture had been used for the banner. I could only assume that it was old because Syfy hadn't sprung for our new action stills yet. A few days before, a woman had snapped a picture of me as I was walking out of Starbucks and then she'd looked hard at me, spit between her teeth and said, "you aren't Johnny Depp!" as though I'd told her

I was Johnny Depp. Maybe that was that picture they'd run in the banner, how should I know?

"After we stopped being friends, I got pretty depressed. I missed you. I realized that I had really looked forward to our chats, and without them I just . . . without them I couldn't pretend that there was a point to anything anymore."

"Yeah," I said.

"I guess what I wanted was to come here and meet you and have there be no chemistry, and then to be relieved and finish that fucking porch and just go home. But then that didn't happen, you know?"

I did know. The natural couple-ness of us couldn't be denied. It was a thing that just rolled, in the way that it had when we'd only chatted on the Internet. We played perfectly together. We both smelled what the other had cooking. And he was handsome in a way that I didn't expect to be into. He was fetish handsome. He looked like the type of man that some rich lady might pay to throw her on a bed and pretend to rape her, terrible, amazing things like that.

"You think they're gonna eat all that cake?" he asked. The crowd had thinned at the table beside ours and now the couple sat silently with their heads down, eating.

"Maybe. They look like they need it."

"Yes. This was a last-ditch effort, I can tell."

"You've been on the receiving end of them for some time, yes?" Twice the lady had come by to refresh our fry bowl, and I just kept getting testier and more ceremonious about it, like a character out of *Who's Afraid of Virginia Woolf?* The next time I would clutch my drink and fiddle with the cross around my neck and bray something like, "so, no one's ever heard of a never-ending SALAD bowl?!"

Harrison smiled in a very boyish way, caught. He had dimples as well as the gap between his teeth so most of what he did seemed very boyish and charming and sort of offhand, as though instead of me he were talking to fucking Leeza Gibbons, or something.

"We took my wife out for her birthday not long ago and I almost proposed to the waitress. I was projecting. I saw you in our waitress and I laid it on pretty thick. Also, alcohol was involved."

"A projected proposal? Your wife must've been thrilled."

"She didn't really notice. If you've been with a person for a great deal of time, you start to just have this angry roommate kind of relationship with them, and they don't care. No one cares. Everyone can see it but them."

"A long time."

"Maybe . . . eighteen years?"

"Yowza. Where did you meet?"

"A bar."

"Yes. That is where people meet."

"It hasn't been good for a very long time."

"Well, you certainly talk the talk," I said. A waitress, not ours, walked by and I grasped her pleadingly by the hand, "Please give me a big frozen thing that's full of booze," I said, "I don't care what. A margarita. An ice cube tray."

"I'll let your waitress know . . ." she began with forced brightness, staring concernedly at her hand still clamped in mine.

"No," I said, "you."

I pulled a twenty from the pocket of my jeans and crumpled into her hand like I was stubbing out a cigarette, "please."

"Okay," said the waitress, her lower lip between her teeth. She pocketed the money and walked away.

"And you," I said, pointing across the table like I was drunk already, "you have three minutes to say something to me that will not result in that drink in your face. Maybe less than three. That was a twenty."

Harrison blew out hard.

"I'm not a bad guy," he said, and I shook my head, three fingers up like a gang sign.

"I saw *The Phantom Menace* thirteen times in the theater," he said, "every Sunday by myself for thirteen weeks."

"No, you didn't," I said.

"I did. It was in the paper. They ran an article that read, 'Local Man Enjoys Movie.'"

"Knock it off," I said. My fingers were down, though.

"I had seats. There were these two seats kind of set off from the rest and I took the one on the aisle, just in case some fat or smelly man were to sit there. I was concerned about being overwhelmed."

"By the obese and non-hygienic."

"Yes, but after the third week it wasn't really a thing. No one wanted my seats. It lost the thrill. The waking early, the carb-heavy action breakfast, the night before planning."

"And yet you still kept going for ten more weeks."

"I like a good rut sometimes," he said. He looked beautifully tired, the way they paint princes to be tired in picture books. He looked as though someone had made him up to be tired.

My drink arrived, fluffy and toxic green in a plastic glass roughly the size of a manhole.

"It's meant for four people," the waitress said, her day seeming to have brightened. I noticed that she had only added one straw.

"Don't worry," I said when she'd gone, "I couldn't lift this thing to chuck it in your face. I guess I could hurl handfuls at you." I didn't, of course. I drank the damn thing.

No one came to refill the fry bowl after that. By then word had gotten out, and we had to pay our bill at the cash register.

"We are already so controversial," said Harrison.

I hiccupped a few times, nodding.

AT CHARLES CARAWAY'S, NEAR THE ELECTRONICS SECTION, I TOLD HIM I was adopted.

"I'm adopted," I said, "if that makes any difference."

"If it makes any difference how?" asked Harrison. We were strolling aimlessly through the departments, marveling at how they switched without segue. Lawn care became lingerie. Crafting became calligraphy. I'd wanted to go because it was my secret wish to be locked inside for a night, and I'd whispered that to Harrison drunkenly, perhaps more drunkenly than I'd had to. I would watch movies and try on clothes! I would eat chips and try on makeup! Harrison had implied that I could've very easily done any of those things in the comfort of my own home and I'd slapped his arm, angry that he'd ruin such a thing for me.

"I don't know," I said now, about being adopted, "I guess I wanted you to know that I wasn't somebody's first choice."

"You're right. This changes everything."

"Don't be an ass. It's a mystery."

"Why your parents didn't want you?"

"Yeah. Yes. A mystery has always surrounded it. My dads are very vague about it."

"Oh, Jesus. Did you say *dads*?"

"Oh, homophobe, are you?" I said. Before me there was a bed big enough to shoot skeet across and I leaped onto it. The spread and linens were a sort of Laura Ashley floral, super loud, in red and orange drop cloth colors. I laid with my hands clasped over my belly, playing dead.

"Of course not," said Harrison as I closed my eyes, "it just sounds so cliché. Two dads. San Francisco. Lived in the Castro."

"Well, it's all true," I said. The lights played heavily at my eyelids, flashes of veins like bare, reaching branches.

I opened my eyes and he was standing above me like a sinister god or sinister preacher, someone who wanted me to believe something so he could laugh about it. Then he walked away slightly dragging a foot, the side on one hand against his chest, laughing in an off way, smile crooked and wide.

"STOP," I said, sitting up, but he did not stop.

"You can't pretend to be retarded in Charles Caraway's," I said, *sotto voce*. I did not want to say retarded, but I wanted him to stop, and I felt as though saying mentally challenged would only make him do it more. I unhooked a pair of pink bedroom slippers from a display within reach and hurled them at him.

"Stop. Fucking stop. This isn't the East Coast."

The East Coast, I imagined, was filled with dark haired young toughs and loud women in tight pants, and someone was always eating or fighting loudly. And huge stock pots of pasta were sometimes thrown. And the gum snapping and street fights. It seemed a hard terrain; one couldn't attempt a visit with an open heart. It reminded me of Nina Simone singing Bob Dylan's song about the "Tom Thumb Blues," the part where her (his) brother visited from the coast, looking "so fine at first but left looking just like a ghost." Everyone said re-tarded there, even though they knew better. They said it because they weren't supposed to, to see who wanted to make something of it.

The slippers hit Harrison and he stopped. He came and sat down on the edge of the bed.

"What country did they adopt you from?" he asked.

"Shut up."

"It's just that I can't imagine they were adopting out too many healthy blonde babies to gay couples in the seventies."

"It was the late seventies," I said, "and I was less blonde then. My mother may have been Adrienne Barbeau." He made a face at me until he saw that I wasn't going to make one back.

"From *Swamp Thing*?"

"Yes. I may have been the product of an affair."

"La de da."

"My father may have been Ben Vereen."

"From *Roots*?"

I nodded.

"You don't—forgive me—look too much like a . . . *Ben Vereen*."

"I'm telling you what I was told," I said, "after that I have nothing to tell."

I'd found out about my maybe biological mother and father from an inebriated Jim Nabors, who had been friends with my dads while I was growing up. Before then I hadn't really gotten any of a read off of him. He would come say goodnight to me and maybe sing a song about a bird or a girl who took his money and ran to Venezuela, and then he and my dads would have supper and drinks in the parlor. I'd liked him, I guess. He was Gomer Pyle, there wasn't much not to like there.

When I was fourteen or so, my dads' friend Sweet Olsen died of pneumonia, which of course meant that no one wanted to say that he'd died of AIDS. A bunch of people came to our flat the night after the funeral and brought cheeses and Bundt cakes, feeling bad sorts of foods that could easily be toted in or out of a house, carried in the crook of an arm like a football. And tons of wine. I filled and emptied the recycling bin three times that night; the neighbors, all gay monogamous couples with at least one child as well, regarded me with kindness, as though it had only been a matter of time before one of the conservative queens I called father started hitting the bottle with a vengeance. Jim came to the wake, and sang "Ave Maria" and "Galveston" and "You'll Never Walk Alone," and he was so shit-faced and leaning so hard on our china hutch by the time he sang "The Impossible Dream," I thought he was going to bring the damn thing down with him, Belleek songbirds and all.

Afterward, he came and hung out with me and kept patting my hand and calling me Tammy. He told me about a show he did in Indiana at a retirement home; one of the residents died during his performance. Jim felt the power of the Lord taking this man home to heaven. He said it was the best gig he'd ever been a part of. Then he wanted me to know about the time he did *Grease* with my Mama.

"What?" I asked.

"She is such a professional," he said, "and the voice. The voice from God."

That is a strange thing that people sometimes say, especially strange if it's a religious person saying it. Isn't every voice a voice from God if you believe in God? Surely he didn't put his back into making a few and then just slack off on the rest, what would be the point in that? Wouldn't that ruin everything benevolent and awesome about God, who carried losers on the beach for the hell of it and whatnot? Did he only love bitches with the hot voices and asses he chose to arbitrarily give them? That hardly seemed fair. It seemed a good case for atheism, actually.

I said none of these things, of course. I stared at Jim Nabors and waited. His eyes were closed in telling, as though the story was a delicious broth to be savored. He described my mother's eyes and tush, also possibly ordained, not to mention that comedic timing. My mom had played Rizzo. This made my face and fingers tingle with blood. Even as a kid I'd known that I hadn't sprung from the starched and pressed womb of a Sandy.

"What had your dads told you about your birth mom before that?" asked Harrison, and I had to think a minute. It was not the kind of thing that came up a lot, and it was also a thing that I'd pretty much preemptively accepted. I had two men who cared for me and loved me and gave me an allowance; I had come out of a woman's vagina and that woman was no longer hanging around.

"They just told me that she couldn't keep me. There was some rustling in the background about the baby not being her husband's . . ."

"Escandalo!"

"Well, my parents *are* gay, after all."

"Yes."

"But that was it, really. They never made it a thing and I was pretty lazy. I never thought to make it a thing."

"Until Jim Nabors came to a wake at your house."

"Mmmmm."

"Wow. And how does Ben Vereen come into all of this?"

I shrugged a little, over it. *C'est la vie! My dad is Ben Vereen!* "Apparently, he and Adrienne had both been stranded in Dunsmuir, CA, in the middle of an almost unheard of snowstorm. Their cars had both broken down. They'd sought refuge at a little bar called The Rusty Bucket. There had been rooms upstairs."

"Oh, tale as old as time," said Harrison. "Just a drop in the rusty bucket."

"People get lonely," I said, "and full of alcohol, and what else is there? That's where babies come from."

"Did you ever ask your dads about it?"

"Not really. It seemed pointless to pursue. I was a happy kid, for the most part. I was much loved."

"Well, that's . . . sweet," said Harrison after a moment. He tasted the word, as though not certain of its appropriateness in this context, like a man adding cumin to something, to a flan or shoe.

"But surely you understand marriages, being married."

"That was an odd segue."

"Yes, sorry," I said, "I have problems with those." It was the truth. I was a great blurter of things that had no association to whatever was being said, and yet I tried in vain to find some common denominator, some connective tissue, so that I could change the subject to something more palatable or less awkward, and it always ended up calling attention to itself in a really horrible way, like OJ Simpson falling into a wedding cake and then burning his hand and then falling off a boat in that *Naked Gun* movie.

I was caught, I guess between wanting to know everything and not wanting to know anything at all about Harrison's wife. I was a product of the talk shows and soap operas of my youth, things that had entered insidiously into my brain after school as I enjoyed a juice bag while finishing up my homework. My main dad, Sam, worked the shop and my other dad, Chad, looked after the house and me during the day. He would watch the TV from a spot just inside the kitchen doorway, probably shoving a flour sack towel into a juice glass to dry it, and murmur softly at whatever goings on were going on, judging in an old-fashioned kind of way, which was hilarious and sad to me, even then. No one ever got it worse than the women who'd wrecked a home. No one. Not even the incest couple. The home-wreckers were always dressed in short, shiny things, and they wore them as their skins, as though they might as well be sitting there naked. It was they for whom the most damning of the boos and catcalls were reserved. Nothing they said could redeem them. They did everything but sport those twiddly little black mustaches.

"Ought to be ashamed," muttered Chad, who I called Pops. Sam was Dad. I introduced them as the Hardwicks, and just let people hammer it out for themselves. I got asked which one was the lady a bunch of times. The people asking weren't trying to be offensive by and large; it was all that they knew to compartmentalize things. It was just human, very human.

"It's one thing," Pops would say to the television whores, "to have a little fun. It's one thing to want to try something new once in a while."

He didn't know that I knew about Dad's cheerleader magazines in the laundry room under the toboggan. His female cheerleader magazines. I'm not sure what I was even doing down there. Laundry? Smoking? Anyway, I didn't try out for cheerleading the following year.

"I WILL TELL YOU ABOUT MY WIFE IF YOU WANT TO KNOW ABOUT HER," said Harrison. He lay back as well and turned to me, going up on one elbow. "I don't hate her. She's not a bad woman. I'm not one of those guys who goes around saying, 'oh that horrible bitch' or whatever."

"That's good," I said. I didn't know if he wanted points for that or what. I had yet to understand that in affairs everything was points and degrees, all based on a system that was somehow both unknowable and innate. These were things that people understood but could not ever speak of, like racial slurs or head lice. Harrison wanted to be on the good side of the spectrum, where you could acknowledge the pain of others and still want what you want. It seemed a little too diplomatic in a baby-kissing sort of way. There was no way I could see that everyone could walk away unscathed, a better person in the end. Someone's shit was ending up on the front lawn. Someone was getting bedroom slippers hurled at them.

"In a way, she's like Adrienne Barbeau is to you. Everything that was ever good was good so long ago, and you start to question things. Like, did they even happen? Like, maybe I was so lonely that my scale of happiness was not what it would have been otherwise. I was in the Army . . ."

"Yes?" I said, interrupting. "Did you shower with other men?"

"Yes," said Harrison, "why?"

"I don't know." I didn't know. Whenever I pictured the army I pictured death and showering. And push-ups. My only real connection with the military was from watching the cartoon of *G.I. Joe*, a depiction of a fifty-year war in which no one died. And reading was the best thing you could do. The worst, drugs.

"You just want to talk to anyone. You're so lonely. You just want something to look forward to."

I nodded, thinking numbly of Sybil, the way she'd circled our apartment in socks and nothing else, embracing a case-less pillow, singing "Easy to be Hard" from the movie *Hair*. She would really get into it, no matter how high I turned the TV up, and throw the pillow to the ground when she got to the part about "especially people who care about strangers." I had never known Richard to care about strangers or social injustice, but whatever. Being separated from him, and more so being the one who was dumped, she remembered the relationship as much better than it had ever been. These were two people who, by the end, would rather leave the house than pass each other in the hallway. The question wasn't "what did I do?" but "what the eff took so bloody long?" It reminded me of the time I rented *Saving Private Ryan* and watched the beginning Normandy scene through the narrow v's of my fingers. The idea that anyone had lived through that seemed to defy any logic, just these defenseless sacks of tissue flailing and falling, limbs dangling. I would come back to the house every evening wondering who would be there. It wasn't a judgment so much as an alliance to the odds. No person could withstand so much for so long. People broke down and then they left.

"I played Adrienne Barbeau once on the show," I said, "it was when we did a send up of *Queen of the Amazons*."

"I've seen it. They did a good job with your wardrobe on that one."

My wardrobe had been a parody of hers, which had been a tiny sort of native thing/bikini that appeared to be made out of beef jerky. For humor's sake, mine was tinier and made from actual beef jerky. BBQ with a kick of Tabasco, sewn right over my knickers.

"I've always wondered whether or not she saw it. I looked very much like her in that costume."

"Yes."

"It was my Gypsy Rose Lee moment. Having jerky sewn onto my underwear and staring into this full-length mirror like, 'I'm a girl, Mama! I'm a girl!'"

"You were very funny," Harrison said kindly.

"I tried very hard. Sometimes I don't try at all. Sometimes it's like, 'oh, fuck you. Give me my fucking pasties and I'll go out and get my money and we'll all just go home.' But I wanted her to see it and think well of me."

"She probably saw it. She's always seemed really down to earth."

"Yes," I said. I got most of my fan mail, honestly, from prisons. Generally death row. The inmates always said that they were praying for me, in addition to the other things they wanted to do to/for me. I rarely got letters from regular people, maybe a kid who was staying up too late or something, once in a while an old woman who wanted me to put some pants on. Most people didn't value me unless they were locked up somewhere, waiting to die.

Harrison and I lay there quietly for a moment, as though locked into a twin coffin. I imagined being married to him and watching him sleep, seeing the light fall through the blinds onto his back and neck, segmenting them with light. I imagined him without the theft and wondered if it was the same, the same attraction, the same cosmic pull. I was not above the idea that it was danger that drew me, the idea of being desirable and new. He didn't treat me as though I were normal and a bit ordinary, a girl like the girl I was, who often read mail right at the mailbox in a wife beater and sweatpants with the waistband rolled down enough to reveal her tramp stamp, a heart with wide angel wings, wearing sunglasses and smoking.

"I guess that you are pretty bored," I said.

"Now? Not a bit."

"At home. In your life."

"It isn't what I expected," he said, "but it's the thing my brother did and all of my friends. I don't know what else I was expecting. I guess it was one of those self-fulfilling deals."

"Well, this isn't where I assumed I'd be at twenty-nine," I said, a little piquedly, "I went to an *arts school*."

Harrison snorted out a laugh. He sounded like a boar with some kind of septum disorder. I laughed, too, then because we were on a bed in the middle of a store in spitting distance from the automotive department, and because we were in love and acting as though we could talk our way out of it. And my head hurt from it, and from sugar and wheat and grease and booze, the hard cocktail of love. I patted myself down for cigarettes.

"You can't smoke in here, Miss," said Charles Caraway himself, who had been getting closer and closer during the past hour, biding his time, clearing his throat threateningly. At my pat down, he'd made his move.

"I'm not smoking," I said, "I was just touching myself," and beside me Harrison went off on another round of laughter/animal noises.

Charles Caraway stood there, arms crossed over his middle

like a fat little mall cop. He was wearing a sweater with a lot of swirling colors, an old Cosby deal, it looked the way carsickness feels. He wanted us to know that we were not welcome there, that we would not spend the night, that night or any night, and that we were suspicious people. The kind of suspicious people that don't buy anything.

"I'll miss this old girl," said Harrison, patting the bed as though it were a carousel horse or suitcase, something that had given its life for the happiness of others. He turned to the salesman and said, "it was just two days away from retirement."

"Yes," said Charles Caraway, suddenly less angry than bone-tired, and he took off his glasses and rubbed the bridge of his nose, "you're very clever. You're both very clever and attractive; can you please just show it off somewhere else for a while?"

Harrison and I considered each other for a moment and I nodded, satisfied. I don't know what else we could've wanted from the man other than for him to acknowledge our specialness, the grating *dreck* of it. We slid off the bed and left. Through cosmetics and grocery and garden and out into the night.

BEFORE HARRISON LEFT WE DROVE PAST MY HOUSE, THE HOUSE THAT was almost mine, the one I paid for in cash, a huge stack of bills that made me feel like a rapper or a cartoon duck. I liked seeing it. I liked walking past at night and imagining myself asleep inside, locked inside safe against zombies and prowlers and all other people, really. Just sleeping forever like some lazy princess.

"It's nice," said Harrison.

"It's the only house I ever wanted," I said, and it was true. There were far bigger places, like the mansion buffered by two stone lions out by my gynecologist's office, but this house had swagger. It looked like the home of a disco woodcutter or a faded comedian possessed by the devil. Such a heady mixture of flash and rural like some crude mixed drink; unpasteurized milk and agave syrup, maple and the jellied eyes of some endangered bird.

"When are you moving in?"

"Sometime after shooting starts. I'm staying at the Monte Carlo right now. It's under the overpass."

"Let me give you a ride there," said Harrison, and I looked at him through the slant of streetlight, a sweet, funny man in a nautically rolled hat and a blue hooded sweatshirt. His eyes looked very clear. He was a very nice man.

"I will get out here and walk," I said. "It's not far."

And it wasn't far but I'd had a lot to drink and so had the rest of Troubadour. It was a maze of small homes, streets with names of old fashioned girls like Mae and Bessie and Eppie. There was the Troubadour Center, a small gas-smelling park that housed a homeless shanty town, and then my hotel, a sunken red painted little jewel beneath the swirl of the off-ramp. It was Troubadour's version of the Hotel Chelsea, I liked to say, and very few people knew what I meant or appreciated the irony. Harrison did both, the bastard.

"I don't want you to worry about me," he said. I slammed the passenger door and leaned back a bit through the window, "I've already made up my mind. I'm a very strong person." He didn't seem to believe these things but he said them well, anyway, like a child angling for a pet.

"Don't pull your back on that porch," I said, "Backs are tricky, I've heard." Then I knocked twice on the hood, but he didn't leave. He sat there parked, watching me as I walked away.

4.

I SPENT THE NEXT MONTH IN A TIRED, PISSED OFF STATE, SMOKING TOO much and starting shit just to start it. I began cracking my knuckles the way I imagined prisoners cracked theirs, as though I had nothing to lose, as though doing so would enrage police officers. I ate infrequently, and when I did I ate too much, steaks the size of toilet seats and chicken wings with thick brown-red sauce that collected under my acrylic nails and in the corners of my mouth like rust. I vomited out my lines. When it was time to move into my house I stood on the lawn smoking as the movers hauled my stuff inside along with the garish new shit I'd bought, horrible oriental rugs, ginger jars, a fake elephant's foot for my umbrellas. And I didn't even have an umbrella, was the thing. I imagined that this must've been the way that Keith Richards reacted when he found himself in love with a man who was already married. I imagined that he bought ginger jars up the ass. Rooms filled with ginger jars, great big fuck yous to life and society and the media and whatever. Yes. We were just alike, Keith Richards and I.

At night I would lock my doors and lie down on my new bed, actually, intentionally, the same model on which I'd lain with Harrison, and watch the ceiling fan, the eerily spinning daisy of it, and I would tell myself that I was better off this way. My art was fulfilled this way. I was cute and drunk and my teeth hurt all the time, and I couldn't figure out how you could miss a person you didn't know. It seemed a cosmic jerk-off, a painful alien blip, their follow up to anal probing.

One night I heard a woman chasing after a man after the bars had closed. I imagined her as blonde, raw-skinned and large boned, thick around the waist, wearing jeans and a flannel over a camisole. Some kind of too-high sandals that showcased cracked heels and scarlet painted hammertoes. She was pleading with the man, the likes of whom I could not picture.

If you ever loved me . . .

I love you, I'll always love you.

I don't know why any of this is happening . . .

Can you give me a minute; can't you just give me a single minute?

To which the man called back, you've been asking for a minute for two and a half hours!

And she began pleading faster, as though his acknowledgment, such as it was, came like a gulp of water to her.

I listened to the two of them for blocks, until I couldn't be sure whether or not it was really them, or the sound of a car mixed with the wind and the monotone of my own breath. I was so very still, feeling propelled, slingshot by my heart out into the world and lonely, complicated as math. How was I not that woman, with her sunburned skin and painful cracked heels and broken, yearning heart? How was I not that man, a tired, disembodied voice, a long silhouette fading?

SPURRED BY GUILT AND THE SAD WASHING MACHINE OF MY GUTS, I CALLED Troubadour Bath and Groom and asked Sybil if she'd have an early supper with me at Señor Squawk's. She agreed, somewhat testily, and at first I attributed her bad mood to a tough day at work. She was always having tough days at work, although when you considered it was in her job description to express the anal glands of dogs, you couldn't really blame her.

"Isn't is so fun here?" I asked, too brightly. "Isn't it just a scream? The bird and all?"

Señor Squawk perched tiredly at the hostesses' desk, its demeanor half misery, half methadone. It seemed to be suffering from any number of skin and feather-related conditions, and the fact that he was wearing that sombrero served only to make the bird's existence more sadly absurd. It would have done really well in a production of a Beckett play, just hanging around and reminding people that time is an illusion and death close at hand. I asked Sybil if she wanted to guess how many sunflower seeds the bird could eat to win those free nachos.

"No," she said. "What do I care how much a dying bird can eat?"

"But, how can you *not* care?"

"It's pathetic," she said, ripping her napkin into long strips and placing them beside her in a pile like droopy noodles. "This place is pathetic. One time, a girl I know from work came here with her husband and they did that sunflower seed challenge and the goddamn bird ended up vomiting on their table. Or, whatever it is they do. Re-gurgitate."

"It vomited on their actual table?" I asked.

"Yeah. When they . . . when you take the challenge, a guy dressed as a magician brings the bird over with a little gold bowl of sunflower seeds and everyone stands and claps and makes a big deal over every seed it eats. ONE! TWO! THREE! Like The Count, or something. So, anyway, the bird wasn't feeling it. It ate like nine seeds and then it just BLAAAAGH."

"Why would the guy who brings the bird over be dressed like a magician, though? That doesn't make any sense."

"That's the part of the story that doesn't make sense to you, Easy? That's the part?" She sat back and pushed her napkin strips away.

I said, "What's up your ass, man?" Maybe she'd never been the most fun person in the world, but I'd never known her to get all antagonistic about a vomiting parrot.

"I work quite hard, actually. I work for my money. We can't all lie around in furry panties to pay the bills, you know." She drummed her fingers after that, then softened. "It's very lonely in our apartment. In my apartment. Very quiet."

"I'm sorry."

"Are you? Are you sorry that the woman with all the Marie

Osmond dolls has started inviting me to her tea parties? And that I've thought about going? And bringing wine?"

"She and the dolls would probably like that very much," I said.

A waiter came around and Sybil ordered like three entrees and a big thing of potato skins, explaining that her hours had been cut and she was short on cash. She could eat for days on a leftover Mexican feast. I ordered a diet selection, something called The Slim Ole. It was strips of grilled chicken and swampy-smelling guacamole and hunks of tomato that looked like infected gums served in a lettuce cup. The waiter told me that I could enjoy it with a fork or "as a wrap," as though crushing this abomination in on itself would somehow create a sophisticated dining experience. I ordered a big margarita, too, because it was beginning to look like a big margarita kind of day.

"I can give you some money," I told Sybil, and she spat back with, "I'm not a prostitute!" So, I ordered another drink.

"What is this even about?" asked Sybil.

"I wanted to tell you about my . . . situation."

"Oh, god, are you pregnant?"

"No. No, why would you say that?"

"I don't know," said Sybil. "Seems linear."

"It's about a guy. That one I used to talk to on the internet. Harrison."

"Yeah?" said Sybil. "So he's married?"

"Jesus Christ. How did you know that?"

"Because you're pretty basic, Easy. You have about two speeds: Anorexic and Adulterer."

"What about Alcoholic?"

"Well, give yourself some time. Is this why you invited me out? To give you some kind of pardon?"

I looked at her; she looked like hell. Thinner, but sick-thinner, and bumps of cystic acne pressed out of the skin around her jaw like knuckles. The eyes that stared out at me were haunted and mad.

"I just don't have a lot of people to turn to," I said.

"And why is that? Is it because you fucking disappear when

anyone seems as though they might be starting to need you? Is it because the people in your life are only as attractive as your options?"

"Look . . ."

"No, you look. You invited me out, we've been here for like
forty-five minutes and you haven't asked me about me, about my life,
about Richard. He's filed for divorce, did you know that? He's moved
that *person* into our house. She's *sleeping* in our bed. How do you
think that makes me feel?"

"Bad."

"Yes, bad. Terrible. Completely lost. Then, after moving out
and abandoning me in my time of need, you drag me out to this . . .
ESTABLISHMENT and try to get a mea culpa for fucking a married
man."

"No," I said, "it's not like that. I just wanted to know what
you thought."

"I think it's a bad idea. I think that you shouldn't do it."

"Well, okay. Thank you. Thank you for your opinion."

Sybil motioned for the waiter; I ordered another drink. She
asked him for a bunch of those Styrofoam takeout things and started
loading them up with food very meticulously, all the different entrees
very neat in their little white suitcases.

"I can't stay," she said, not looking up.

"I'm going to be here for a while," I said, and then, "you
know, nothing's written in stone. We haven't even kissed. He emails,
he calls. I don't answer. It's not like anything's happened."

"Define *anything*," said Sybil, her cartons stacked high. The
waiter brought her a plastic bag to carry them. "I'm not trying to pile
on, here, but you're going to have an affair with that man. It's not
like you can stop yourself. It's not like you can stop pretending that
you don't have a choice."

"I have a choice. I've made a choice. But, I like him. *I like him.*"

"That's not even kind of a valid excuse," said Sybil. "I don't
know who you think you're fooling. You just prance around and magical things happen to you. Your stupid job, your stupid charmed life."

"Hey, I was a goddamned orphan!"

"Right, right. *'Adrienne Barbeau is my mother. Now I'm*

beautiful and sad and theatrical and I need to fuck all the married men of the world to feel better!'"

"I don't know what I ever did to you," I said, a stupid thing to say, a thing that made no sense, and she stood carefully under the burden of her leftovers and paused for a moment, considering me.

"Thank you for my food," she said.

"Don't mention it."

"For you, for your sake, you should think about your karma."

I snorted into my drink. Karma. Fucking karma. The way that the sum of all of a person's previous lives factor into the quality of their future lives, right? No, at last just another way for women to shit on each other.

"I'll do that," I said.

She nodded and left; I stayed around for a while and drank and watched that queasy bird.

At home, after several attempts to jam my key into the doorbell, I dropped my coat and slumped in front of the computer.

An email from Harrison: A capture of his airline ticket to Monterey. He wrote, "Can you get off?"

BEFORE MONTEREY, I VISITED MY GYNO, IN THE GOOD PART OF TOWN, near the nice houses with the stone lions and asked them to put me on something that wouldn't make me gain weight. They acted as though that shouldn't be my biggest concern.

"I'm on TV," I said. "It's a big concern."

"Have you thought about condoms?" asked my nurse-practitioner, a mere slip of a girl with red hair and a ring through her nose. I probably had like five years on her, and there she was, with enough of a degree to get paid for looking inside my vagina.

"I rarely think about condoms," I said.

"I mean, you know, I'm just asking because of the gaining weight thing."

"I don't know," I said, "every man I've ever been with has always said that condoms make it feel like nothing."

"Makes what feel like nothing?"

"The vagina, I guess. The act of sex."

"Well, you tell those men that if that's how they feel, they should just masturbate. You should tell them, 'it's a small load, do it yourself.'" After that she was very proud of herself; it was punctuated with a curt little nod of the head.

"Yeah," I said.

'Yeah, but it's situational,' was a thing I often answered to things that had no appropriate answer. My old answer to these things was, 'well, these are complicated times.' These are phrases that got me through a lot, but even their considerable weight was no match for the thing that the RN wanted me to say to boys who didn't want to wear condoms.

"The only thing that is a hundred percent certain is abstinence."

"Yeah, well, I've gained weight not having sex before, so I'd like to try something else."

Then she told me about the diaphragm, which sounded like some crazy blast from the past, like you might find it in an old box with a lava lamp and a rotary phone. It sounded like a hat for the uterus.

"Oh, wow," I said.

"They are not very popular today," said the nurse, and then she made this small shooing wave with her hand, as though she was SO DONE with the people of today, "but they are effective if you use them correctly."

"That's a pretty big 'if.'" I said.

"Oh, it's not really complicated, but it can be dislodged by certain penis sizes or heavy thrusting."

"Dislodged?" I said. I did not like that word in this context. It was fine for talking about a kernel of popcorn that needed extracting from one's teeth, but I rejected the idea of a massive, veined cock like a bottle opener that meant to pop a hat off my uterus.

The nurse nodded, her bottom lip hitching up, understanding my needs.

"If you're uncomfortable touching your vagina and vulva, it's probably not the best idea for you to have the diaphragm."

"I don't really have a problem touching my vagina and vulva," I said, waiting for something, maybe laughter or cheering. It amazed me how out of context everything felt, even in context. Being part of a television show, or even enjoying TV, had made me so aware of the absurdity of every single moment that I always half expected it to be acknowledged in some real, satisfying way, with big reaction shots and landlords who heard everything and understood something non-sexual to be sexual, rushing in to preserve someone's chastity while wearing ascots and loud slacks. I had no patience with the real world, where people swallowed their lines and stared blankly, horrified of being singled out and mocked.

I got out of there with three months worth of birth control pills, as it was the thing that required the least amount of effort. I could not sit there, legs spread to aching, and have my uterus fit for a hat. I did not like the nurse enough, or I might have. As it was, she was not the sort of person that I wanted to share that much time with. She would not make stupid jokes or ask me how I was doing or even talk about her boyfriend's cat and its various medications. She would camp out quietly between my legs and go about her business without ever looking up, like some little old German man tinkering at a pocket watch, and I couldn't have handled it. The moroseness of it, a girl toiling away in the salt mines of my vadge.

And so I would find myself in the coziest of inns after a puddle jump to San Francisco and another to Monterey, staring at two twin beds that seemed to chide and challenge concurrently, dressed in something dashingly concise like a peacoat over dark jeans and boots, like a girl who didn't even know how to be out of clothes, ever. And Harrison was there, also with a black coat and jeans and that rolled hat, which in my mind had already reached mythical proportions.

"Do you have anything?" asked Harrison.

"No. No, I was tested." I wished that I had copies of the tests to give him, that's how good they were.

"Good, but that's not what I meant."

"Oh," I said, and then, "OH. Yes, I went on the pill . . . they put me on the pill."

"When I invited you to see the shark?"

"Yes."

He seemed surprised or just happy, and it occurred to me that this thing, this conversation, was not a thing that would ever be less awkward, for me or for anyone, regardless of how old I was or how many times I went through it.

"Because I have condoms but I would rather not use them. They aren't my favorite."

"The RN told me you would say that," I said, remembering. I didn't tell him the joke about the "small load," though, as it seemed uncouth.

"You've taken a pill?"

"Yes," I said, and I had, I'd taken it the day I'd picked it up at the pharmacy, and then I'd gotten a headache and gained two pounds in the following two hours. And I didn't take another. I hadn't wanted to be fat and in pain. I'd stopped and the weight, and the headache, went away.

Things happened very quickly, the way they do, and the novelty of making love to a married person fell away and was replaced by making love to a person I really liked and I didn't, as I had planned I might, think about a wife, round as a ball of yarn, sitting home waiting for Harrison to call. I didn't think about their wedding or how it may have happened; I didn't edit wedding pictures in my mind with frilly script and black and white or sepia tones. When Harrison yanked my head back by my ponytail and bit my neck, I didn't imagine him on his knees before another woman with a little jewelry box open like a hungry Pac-Man. And it was my name that he said, not someone else's.

After, I stood at the counter in the kitchenette in my panties and ate a rotisserie chicken with my fingers in the bland, buzzing light of a dying bulb. There was a small, dirty window through which I could watch the goings-on of the gas station/mini-mart/Greyhound stop across the street. I'd actually stopped inside the mini-mart after we'd first checked in, and an Asian man had watched me carefully as I looked around for creamer, and I'd wanted so badly to win his favor for some reason, I bought a strawberry car freshener in the shape of a tree and a tiny eyeglasses repair kit. The creamer I would find later at a Walgreens downtown when Harrison and I went for a walk. It had been funny, he'd seen a sign for French Laundry and assumed it was the world famous restaurant; he waved me off when I'd told him that the real one was in Napa, then we got closer and saw that the sign was attached to a dry cleaners filled with Mexican workers. "This should be a running joke with us," he'd said, "the first time we went to French Laundry."

I didn't say that maybe people weren't meant to pick and choose running jokes, that maybe a running joke just kept popping up and finally a couple just stopped fighting it and decided that it should be funny. That it should be like a shared psychosis, a flying dog in the room that only they could see and chose to chortle about. I did not say these things. We bought creamer and went back to the motel and made love and then I stood nakedly eating chicken watching people waiting for the bus, getting on the bus, getting off the bus. Harrison came up behind me and put his hands on my waist. He wanted to know what I was doing all the way over here.

"Chicken," I said, my mouth full of chicken.

I didn't mention that I was also standing to give the semen a chance to drip out, in the event that taking one birth control pill two weeks before having sex was not as effective as I might have hoped.

"You can eat chicken with me," said Harrison, his hands sliding up to cradle my breasts, and I shuddered a little. The bright opposition of the scene, sex vs. not sexy was too much for a moment and I felt wrong, the subject of some random fetish website, topless women covered in chicken grease, badly lit.

"Are you all right?" he asked.

"Yes. Yes," I said, shaking my head. I turned on the warm water and peeled open a little soap wrapped like a chocolate so that I could wash my hands.

We went and sat on the un-rumpled bed and I hugged a pillow, suddenly modest. I am not good at bare-breasted conversation; as Susan Sarandon once said, "It's hard not to be upstaged by your own nipples," and I have always believed that with the greatest of conviction.

"It's normal," said Harrison, "whatever you're feeling or thinking about."

"Okay."

"I mean, I don't know. I've never . . . what I mean is I need you to tell me what I'm thinking and feeling is normal."

"I'm sure it is," I said, and then, "I don't know. Does it involve daggers?"

"Well, not daggers, the plural. Maybe a single dagger."

"Of course a fucker like you would be married," I said. "Of course a person like you, who I like and who is not boring and who is cute and wears a hat like you do, of course you're married. I guess I should count myself lucky that you aren't crazy and don't have a shitload of kids."

I was overcome for the first time by the unfairness of it, by the fact that it might be me getting the shit side of the deal. There had always been a satisfaction to it, I guess, even knowing nothing real about Harrison's wife. It was a general feeling of being chosen, and I won't even say that that feeling was alien to me, it was just good. You hear so much about the kind of woman who will mess around with a married man and there are all those daddy issues that are implied, all that father acceptance and whatever, and of course none of that ever panned out with me. I just liked not being too old to prance around in jean shorts and get paid for it. And in my deepest heart I knew that I deserved to not be too old to prance around in jean shorts and get paid for it.

I lay back and Harrison lay back with me. I was touching his head and face, the hair cut equally close on both, a bristling braille for the fingers, and we were kissing. It had been a very long while since I'd kissed on the mouth, as I adhered to some odd solidarity with the *Pretty Woman* in believing that actual intimacy was the final frontier, a place of red rocks and little to no oxygen, and then the pillow was gone and what we shouldn't have done we were doing again, harder.

And before I drifted off, my panties still wedged into me like a slingshot, both beds a deep crater like the resting place of a bomb or a very fat man, Harrison murmured into my ear that he had two children, a fifteen-year-old and a thirteen-month-old. It was one of those times I have sometimes when I am worried even though I understand that I must be dreaming, because what would be the alternative? I couldn't be grounded for failing an algebra class—I was nearly thirty. My parents could not ground me—I was a homeowner. Dad and my stepmom were contentedly raising my five-year-old brother, Harry, and my four-year-old sister, Peony, a name my stepmom had been inspired to select maybe from a Disney movie or maybe from a bottle of shampoo. There were better, younger, cuter ponies to bet on, and I knew this because I had attended all the weddings and births; I'd held the babies and seen their worth broadcast across my father's face, the kids themselves weighed down with their parents' happiness. Certainly I could not be in love with a married man who had two children, a teenager and a still-baby. What would be the sense in that? What could I do except for rise early, get on a bus, and leave the sharks and boys in Monterey sleeping, a never opened carton of creamer stuffed in my pocket like some poison or lube, like nothing.

5.

BACK IN TROUBADOUR, THE QUIETNESS BECAME NOT QUIETNESS. It buzzed and fluttered, like a desperate thing trapped. I would wake at terrible hours with no breath, the heat pressed into my skin like palms, and I drove to O'Bannon's and returned home with two air conditioners and two fans and set them all up to point directly at my bed, to surround me in an ominous half-circle, like rapists. I dreamed of rapists. Of burglars, or prowlers, and then I caught on the word prowler and played it over in my head until it wasn't a word anymore but a sound. It was an antiquated, silly word, like using 'rubbish' instead of 'garbage.' Who prowled anymore? Who would break into one's house just to tiptoe around, comic as any mime? It seemed a useless word, unless one used it to call an animal, a particularly prowling animal, such as a cat.

At the Forfeit Valley Humane Society, I adopted a cat I called Prowler and a dog I called Noah. The dog was a handsome one, a kind of mutt with lots of Fox Terrier in him, black and white in the most random of ways, as though he'd walked home beneath scaffolding. The guy told me that my dog had been shipped to Oregon from Puerto Rico, where he'd taken up with a homeless man who'd eventually sold the dog for a sandwich. After that, Noah had been picked up by animal control. I listened to this, nodding soberly. I hoped that Noah had been too young to realize that he'd been traded for a sandwich, even a really good one, as it seemed a really difficult thing to battle back from. In fact, having anything chosen over you, a wife of fifteen years, a turkey club, seemed equally devastating, and the dog and I regarded each other with quiet resignation. I asked if the dog was good with cats, and the guy pulled a striped tabby from a carrier like a magic trick and set it down in front of Noah, who sneezed and thumped his tail. The cat glared at him for a second and then proceeded to lift a leg and bend effortlessly backwards to lick its own anus.

"Seems okay," said the guy.

So, I got the cat, a boy that I'd assumed, because I'd been told, was a girl. The guy had told me that the cat's name was Samantha, and that girls were generally less clingy and more independent, less likely to form great attachments.

"Name your sources," I'd said and when the guy responded with confusion I'd put my hands out like I was being arrested and said, "Nothing, nothing, whatever, nothing." And then Samantha was a boy, and was always going to be a prowler anyway as part of an ongoing argument I was having with myself so, so what? Sometimes I would call him Samantha shittily, a means of verbal abuse when he failed at something in front of me, when he tried to make the leap from the back of the couch to the computer desk and missed, when he clumsily tightroped the length of the kitchen counter and banged into a canister of flour with his considerable carriage: "Oh, nice work, SAMANTHA."

After trips to the vet and pet supply warehouse to the tune of four hundred dollars, I sat silent in a living room chair with the blinds drawn, a cat and dog staring expectantly at me.

I thought about texting Harrison to tell him, not just because I missed him—and I did miss him, with the groin-aching intensity of a fourteen-year-old girl—but because he was the only person I could think of who would appreciate the fucked-up nature of my life and truly understand it. We were not people who loved hard and crashed cars, did needle drugs; we were the ones who adopted pets, who, even after five days, still jumped coming out of the kitchen because we'd once again mistaken the six foot cat-condo for a person standing near the doorway. He'd texted and called and emailed a million times since Monterey, until I ended up just changing my number without even listening to his voice mails. He'd contacted the studio, but I'd told everyone that I had a stalker so they mainly shut him out. I was afraid to hear his voice, or see his name or to read what he had to say about the lesser works of Dean Koontz. I didn't know what would happen to me if I were to hear him drop the G on some word, or go hard on his A's and all the rest. I had a homewrecker's heart, keen as a country song, every other minute I was weak, mewling. I needed an intervention and treatment, and my treatment was silence.

I called Dad in California instead and he reacted in very much the way I assumed he would, disappointed and loud. It was very much the same as being a child, and that was comforting in its own sad way, like standing in front of him after screwing up in some big or small way, faced with his tasteful firing line of disappointment. He took a moment, excusing himself and half-muffling the receiver as he sighed and consulted my stepmother. The only time he brightened was when he asked if I needed money and I answered no. He told me that he loved and missed me, and that I sounded terrible. He started complaining about me even before he'd completely hung up, and then I was left holding on to my end with the eventual dial tone, wondering about the end of the sentence, and what *was* my problem, really.

I SPENT A LOT OF TIME AT TROUBADOUR ELEMENTARY, WHICH HAD SAT empty and bereft since the late sixties. People with children did not frequent Troubadour; the air was thick, the water was sulfurous. The school remained a sad sort of Pete's Dragon or the stump of *The Giving Tree*, with no children to climb its play structure or trample through its long hallways. The doors stayed open, though, for sad men who needed a place to smoke pot or sad women who needed a place to think. It was not unlike the ghost town of Pripiat after the meltdown in Chernobyl, the clips I'd seen of empty cribs, bumper cars, and day cares littered with the colorful drawings of children. I would walk reverently, as though through a church or hospital or library with the late day sun careening in through the high windows to dapple against the scuffed floors and lockers. I would jiggle doorknobs and one would open, revealing a music room and rusted stands, broken chalk. The sheet music to "If Ever I Would Leave You," from *Camelot*. Once I found a box filled with bullets on a table in the teachers' lounge. My favorite room was on the south end of the school, the remains of a library with a tree growing in through the wall. Sometimes I stayed there for hours, singing the songs of *Camelot*.

Everything around me was a syrupy refrain, some faint music played badly and possibly plagiarized which licked at the edges of my consciousness like the surf. I was tired of everything and my house smelled of the things that I sometimes ate and the nothing that I usually ate. My cabbage-filled soup that exuded its farty smell when the pot was pulled from the fridge and the lid was lifted, failed to satisfy. I prepared it once and deposited the whole batch into the toilet (for once not through natural causes) the next day, my head high and away like a horse's to keep from retching. As it got hotter, I wore and ate less and slept more. We parodied *Battle of All Cave Women* and Sally Balls, in makeup artist mode, wanted to know what I was allergic to, a question I answered in part by staring dumbly at her.

"Your under-eye bags are worse than they've ever been, and believe me, they've never been great."

"I don't know," I said, sullen as a teenager, a thing that loosened my tongue enough to take my life in my hands by talking back to Sally. I was wondering why I had to have so many tell-it-like-it-is people in my life. Part of me had vainly hoped that when the show got picked up by Syfy I would have a harem of well-dressed people who were assigned to blow smoke up my ass. I'd assumed that that was a thing that happened, even on basic cable. I mean, the internet had sort of gentrified things, right? Everyone was famous, right? It didn't seem too much of a stretch for one person to tell me nice things about myself. One person, what would that cost? Maybe Isaac and I could both take this person at different times of the year like a timeshare. I wore the disappointment of things around my neck like a noose or a boa, and accessorized with sunglasses.

"Well, you need to use product!"

"I DO use product. I fucking USE product. GEEZ."

"Well, then you aren't using the right products," said Sally. She took out the Preparation H and came at me with it raised like a dagger.

"Not the applicator!" I said, backing away, "a clean finger, fine, but not the applicator." I did not know if that was just some ass ointment from her house or what. It did not seem at all in my best interest to blindly believe that Syfy would spring for a new bottle of Prep H specifically for my under-eye puffiness, especially when they wouldn't even pay someone to treat me like I was all big.

"Fine," said Sally, dabbing. "You need to take better care of yourself. There's no excuse for a kid your age with no husband and kids to look like this. What do you work, seven hours a week?"

"*No*," I answered. "I work *a lot*."

"Well, fifteen, whatever. You have a lot of time and money to waste on yourself. Get a fucking tan. Get a base tan."

"You get a fucking tan, Sally. You get one."

"I'm not trying to be an asshole."

"O . . . K."

". . . I just want you to sleep better, or eat better. Hell, do something better."

I whipped my head away and then back, furious until I got a look at Sally's face, frozen with Botox, smooth as a random princess Halloween mask. Her eyes were sort of . . . kind, though, and in the end that was just too much for me. I opened my mouth and then began to sob.

"Oh, Jesus!" said Sally as I fell against her in my poorly fitting furs; she held me strangely the way a man carries a sack of flour after his grocery bag has ripped through. Her hands simultaneously patted and pushed and she kept starting half-assed apologies or explanations. Well, I never meant to . . . I only wanted to . . . I didn't know that you would react so . . .

And then I was telling her, half-naked in the makeup chair with ass ointment under my eyes as men carted giant prop dinosaur bones back and forth in front of us, and the telling was in great heaves and over-enunciated words: MARRIED, MONTEREY, MOTEL, MARRIED, MARRIED, MARR-IED.

Sally sat back and sighed knowingly as though that was her lot in life, to address the skin and lifestyle problems of cavewomen. She lit up a cigarette and one for me, which I accepted and inhaled gratefully from until my lungs ached in the most beautiful of ways.

"Hey, Sal, you know you can't smoke in here," said a ball capped carrier of dinosaur bones, and she pointed her cigarette at him like a finger before slowly following its path with her head.

"You know what you can't do, Roger? You can't cure a certain kind of eye cancer. No one can. It took my father in '76, and there was nothing that anyone could do. You can smoke in a building, though, and you can ignore us and do your fucking job."

Then she turned back to me and told me it was going to be okay. Roger huffed something, a kind of word or swallowed emotion, and returned to the hefting and placement of large bones.

"Did he drop you?" asked Sal. She had her hating face on, I noticed. Hearing about a cheating man seemed a good excuse to unleash some anger on a bunch of other men on her shit list, ex-husbands and freeloaders and no-good boys and spoiled celebrities. There was a certain kind of shameful joy that seeped from the pores of women when they heard about situations like mine. Everyone had a story, or, like me with Sybil and Richard, a friend who they'd nursed back to her feet; every woman felt a sisterhood with other women who'd been wronged, a deep abiding fierceness against the man who'd ruined her. Until something happened. Until they understood.

"Not really," I said. "He just told me that he had two kids. One is sort of a baby."

"Oh, lord," said Sally, rearing back from it.

"It was after we . . . sealed the deal."

"Well, that's a hell of a thing."

"I never asked, though."

"So that makes it okay?"

"No. I don't know. It's not okay or not-okay. It just is."

"You kids," said Sally, exhaling angrily to my entire generation. "You make allowances for everything."

And I didn't say anything to that because she'd held me and let me wipe my nose on her shoulder. Also, technically, this kindness aside, she still seemed like a very dangerous woman, and I didn't want to push my luck.

"Well, it's over, anyway," said Sally, and I wanted to know

why. Of course I knew why I thought it should be over, but I was open enough to be diplomatic about it, I guess.

"Well, that's for the best, really. You know, the wicked step-mother legend didn't start itself," she answered. She'd pushed me back into the makeup chair and was doing her best to fix the damage that my ugly crying had done. Eventually she just sighed and swiped the whole bit off with a wipe that smelled faintly of lavender. "I've had my share of stepkids and they've all deplored me, especially the girls, not that I didn't give them reason. You're soft. Those kids would skin you alive."

Isaac came by then to ask me if I was off book and then he saw my face and swore under his breath and asked me if I'd been drinking, and Sally exhaled smoke and did some eyebrow things to let him know that she would tell him all about it later.

"It's not the worst thing that ever happened to a person," she said when he'd left, and of course I wanted to know what was.

She thought about it and said, "Well, that one gal that got her face and hands and eyes chewed up by a chimp—that's pretty bad. You can leave the house without a veil and you can watch TV, still. If you still have a face you are okay, if it isn't burned or eaten off and you can just walk around without anyone talking shit to you."

And I guess that she meant that to either be more or less pro-found than it was, but she was wrong.

I did my bits and vomited during one of them, the one where I was doing push-ups on one of the robots and everyone asked again if I'd been drinking. I can't even drink water, is what I said. I told them that I'd hit the Costco in Grants Pass and gotten this big thing of Popsicles and like four melons and that was what I was eating be-cause it was hot and I was sad, even if I could still leave the house without a veil and watch TV. And I mentioned that I might be allergic to my cat and dog, even though I'd never been allergic to anything before (even though I often fell asleep spooning Noah the dog as Prowler the cat dozed like a meatloaf at my hip). I suggested that maybe it was a sadness-induced allergy to many skeptical reactions. I suggested that my heart needed to work so maybe my lungs were tak-ing over and breaking down and then Isaac asked me what I'd been smoking. And would I agree to a drug test? And I said, whatever, I'll take one, if you're going to be dicks about it. And I was fine, of course, and pregnant. And congratulations, asshole. Stop smoking. And drinking. And stop with the coffee and Red Bulls, and take these vitamins. And congratulations.

6.

I WAS SIXTEEN WHEN MY FATHER LEFT MY FATHER FOR ANOTHER WOMAN. Or just a woman. There was no fight or anything, which is to say that Dad didn't fight. He came in and told Pops that he wanted to talk and Pops turned off the TV and followed Dad into the kitchen, where Dad told him that he'd met someone else.

Is it (name of mutual male friend) or (many names of mutual friends)? Pops wanted to know.

Dad assured him that it was no one that they'd known as a couple.

Well, I want you to stop seeing him, said Pops. I didn't see any of this, I just heard it, but I have total recall of how it looked in my mind at the time. Pops would be wearing black sweatpants and a big, frumpy t-shirt from some chili cook-off that happened a zillion years ago. This was always of interest to me, the t-shirts that were kept like random scalps or tattoos, why was a chili cook-off saved while a book fair or a box social left to fall by the wayside? What was the elimination process? So far as I knew, my dads hadn't had any more fun at the chili cook-off than they'd had at the box social. In fact, I could not think of one incident in which they'd had more fun than they'd had during another incident. At least they'd been talking when Dad told Pops about his lover in the kitchen that night; they should have thought to have shirts made.

It's not a *him,* said Dad.

Silence.

And then: Is this some kind of joke? Some kind of sick joke? Some kind of joke?!

And then a knife was taken from the drying rack or the block or somewhere, because Dad asked Pops to please put the knife down, and then Pops squeaked something indignantly about how it didn't matter because Dad didn't care if HE DIED RIGHT THAT MINUTE.

Dad, who I imagined was wearing a gray sweatshirt from some company where his brother had worked several decades before and a pair of baggy old guy jeans (my future stepmother Lisa would manage that problem later—as she was twenty-four and from Venice Beach and cared about such things—with great creativity and her employee discount from Hot Topic), did little to assuage Pop's emotional freak-out. He was at the past-done place; he'd shut down to the point where nothing could hurt or even surprise him. Of course I don't know what brought any of that on. I mean, I know what both of them eventually told me, super biased horrible fairy tales that exploded like some marital triple-A in the microwave, like some Rosh Hashanah with added malls and hybrid cars and pathos. No one shared, no one communicated. No one gave anyone a chance. And MY dreams, MY goals, and he never cared about what I *wanted*.

It was much worse that it was a woman, for some reason or reasons that I can't really explain but understand completely. It was a more significant betrayal because Pops couldn't up and become a woman, or at least a woman who was born a woman in a woman's body. And that was funny, because I was raised to believe that we were all souls in different and unique carrying cases, each with equal hearts and equal blood, and if you loved one person you loved them all in some way because we were all connected in our strange beauty and joy and loss, like a Lego set of the universe. But not Lisa. To Pops, Lisa was a beast (he even sometimes referred to her as "the whore" while insisting that I not disrespect her, or any adult, as it was wrong) who has stalked his happy family and decided to ruin it, just because. Sometimes when he drank he would talk about straight women the way that I'd heard others talk about driving Asians or groups of black and Puerto Rican boys hanging around outside of the supermarket. This was troubling, I guess, because I was straight and a woman, and because I had nothing against Lisa, with her squealing laugh and multicolored hair and her every sentence ending high like a question mark. (Oh, of course she's from California, just like every other brain surgeon, said Pops, and Dad said, you're from Napa Valley! And Pops said, NAPA IS NOT CALIFORNIA!)

The confrontation ended with Dad leaving, and Pops retired weeping to the couch, and I should have gotten up and done something but didn't. Dad called me an hour or so later from a motel out in the avenues and wanted me to know that I wasn't being abandoned. I told him that I didn't feel abandoned, but then I asked if I could take the next day off school and he said no. I whined a bit and played it up until he said yes.

"I want . . . I want . . . I want to tell you the secret of happiness in this life," said Dad.

"Okay," I said.

"Not. Settling. Not settling. Not ever settling for less, do you understand?"

"Yes."

"But do you really? Do you really understand what I'm talking about here?"

"Yes."

"Good. You're a good girl and I love you."

"Love you, too," I said.

"I do, you're my joy. My little . . . joy. Just . . . just . . . when you were a little girl you were . . . people! People everywhere used to stop Pops and me in the street and they would . . . they would just . . . like no one could even believe it, you know?!"

"It's okay," I said. "Everything is okay. Can you just not drive anywhere for the rest of the night?"

"Yes," said Dad and he was still making words or at least sounds when I hung up.

In all of that, the reactions were so pat: the knife, the drinking, the guilt-propelled phone call from a motel out in the avenues. Nothing about it had bothered me, mainly because I'd acted out a similar scene with my two Ken dolls in their dream house like maybe five years prior. I guess that I was a pretty theatrical kid, and I'd seen enough TV to understand the basic flow of things, the replaying of something like eight different scenarios over and over again like the simplest of dance steps. I knew what the reactions to basic things should be, is what I mean. I knew that if you told your gay husband that your previously gay self was leaving him for a woman, your gay husband would probably threaten to stab himself, and I knew that if you were a mistress, even a reluctant one, and you called your married lover and told him that you were twelve weeks pregnant (because you would have waited that long to cut down on the likelihood that you might miscarry and therefore not need to contact your married lover) he would say that baby was not his, and hang up, and block your calls until you eventually gave up and/or hauled his ass into court for a DNA test. I knew that shit, even children knew that shit. And then Harrison had the nerve to do none of it, even when I had all of my lines scripted out.

He was really happy to hear from me even before I was able to give my mournful speech—he fell and stuttered over his words in a happy way, not a drunk way, and he had so much to tell me, so many happy things, and I wasn't prepared for any of it.

"I have a cat and a dog," is what I said, eventually.

"Oh, cool, awesome, that's fabulous."

"Yes, well. I guess it's okay."

"I didn't cry when my father died, did you know that?"

"No," I said. I hadn't even known that his father had died.

"Well, I didn't. I didn't. I haven't cried since I was ten or so. I didn't have the capability. It was just gone. Then, when I woke up and you were gone, and I talked to the guy from the convenience store . . ."

"Wait, you talked to that guy?"

"Yes, of course," said Harrison, "I needed to know where you were."

"What, did you think I ran away with him?"

"No, but I figured he must've sold you a ticket."

"Yeah. What did he say?"

"Something vague in an accent. He remembered you because of the air freshener, though."

"Yeah. Damn my evidence trail of air fresheners."

"I left her," said Harrison.

"What?" I said, still on the air fresheners.

"Joan. I left her. I left the house. I live somewhere else."

"You live somewhere else?"

"Yeah, in Warwick," he said. "That's where they do *Ghost Hunters*, you know?"

"Oh," I said, and then, "Her name is Joan?"

I guess that without knowing her name things were easier than they should have been. My Godmother—a word which, in Northern California, meant a very close friend of the parents who took the kiddies on ferry rides and long weekends to Larkspur Landing or Strawberry and bought them things but imparted no religious teachings or even connotations—was named Joan. She was thin and lovely with blonde hair and classic features. Sometimes on the ferry she would see a man that she fancied and she'd tell me to go up to him and tell him that she wasn't my mom. I loved her very much.

"Yes, why?"

"I hadn't known, is all. How are the kids?"

"Getting by," said Harrison, which meant not good. I pictured them wrapped in blankets in an empty house, rocking, the little one in a filthy diaper, sucking on an empty bottle, walking around and pointing at things, getting by.

"God, what did you tell them?"

"I told Sabrina that thing about Daddy loving her and it not being her fault . . ."

"Oh, yes."

"And Joan . . . I just told Joan the truth, that I was in love with someone else."

"Oh, holy shit. Couldn't you have led with something else? Like not loving her anymore? Why did you have to drag my ass into it? I'm on the other side of the country, for Christ's sake."

"It's complicated," said Harrison, "but I wouldn't have left Joan if I hadn't met you. I'd have stayed because what would have been the point in ruining everyone else's good time? But I did meet you. And after you I knew that being married to Joan was a lie, even if you never spoke to me again."

"Well, that's . . . noble-ish."

"It's just how I feel. A few weeks ago I walked into the kitchen and I said, 'I'm in love with someone else.'"

"The kitchen? Did she pull a knife out of the drying thing and threaten to stab herself?"

"No. Jesus, who does that?"

"I don't know," I said. "Some people."

"No, nothing like that. She tried to hold it together because the kids were asleep. We talked on the phone the next day and she broke down a bit, but it all seemed pretty normal. She studied some psychology in school, so . . ."

"Oh."

"Yeah, I guess she has some skills."

"Oh."

"SO!" he said, something like an uncle's birthday bellow in his voice, some exaggerated but genuine sentiment, "to what do I owe this amazing . . ."

"I'm pregnant."

". . . honor? What?"

"Pregnant. With a baby. Almost thirteen weeks."

Harrison went quiet. According to my research, now was the time he would ask who else I'd been fucking, and in a year we'd be on the *Maury* show, explaining ourselves. This was also about ten days before I would have my first ultrasound, at which time the technician and I would be treated to the sight of not one but two fetuses hovering to and then away from each other like restless hands. The technician would squeal and I would ask a lot of questions. Were they actually twins or was one just a floating bit of something? Once I'd seen a TV movie about a man who charged infertile couples a lot of money to get them pregnant and would show them false ultrasounds. Then he would disappear with the money and a real ultrasound would reveal that there had never been any baby at all, just an X-ray of poop in the woman's colon. How devastating that was! Not a baby, but a fetus-shaped lump of poo. Could my second fetus be like that, a poo in disguise? No. No, it could not.

"Thirteen weeks!" said Harrison.

"Yeah, almost."

"I've missed so much! Have you had an ultrasound?"

"Couple of days," I said. My wallet was filled with little business cards heralding the various appointments I had coming up, reaching several months in advance. I have always been the sort to look at a date in the future and expect that the most bizarre things possible would happen in the interim. Like the apocalypse seemed really likely by June 23. I imagined calling the secretary and telling her that I couldn't make my appointment to test for Down syndrome because the apocalypse had happened, and smiled.

"I'm keeping it," I said, and I guess I expected some kind of tussle there but there was none. He made a sound in his throat like *of course you are why are you even bringing it up?*

"I'm not opposed to that sort of thing," I said, "I just do not choose to."

"Okay."

"Like, you can't make me either way."

"Why are you talking this way?"

"I don't know," I sighed, the fight stuck there in my throat like some uncooked food.

"I have a place now," said Harrison after a minute, "you can come stay with me."

This was the point where I didn't want to be shitty but I also didn't know how not to be shitty. I was a beloved TV personality on a basic cable show; I'd been featured in the following straight or hilarious-sounding magazines—*TV Guide, TV World, Science Fiction TV Digest, TV Guide's Celebrity Crosswords* (in which I was the secret celebrity), *People, People Style, Allure, Space Babes,* and *Ay-yi-yi!* I was a homeowner, albeit in a place named one of America's Worst Cities in a *Newsweek* magazine cover story, and I made good money. Three bathroom, furniture from IKEA money.

Conversely, Harrison worked as a copywriter for the Fisherman's Fishsticks company out of Warwick. He made okay money but he was supporting a wife and two kids in Providence and renting both the family home and the bachelor pad that was closer to work. And paying for a minivan and whatever the hell he was driving—some old man car like a Lincoln or a Buick from a thousand years ago. Joan had never gone back to work after the babies were born, he said; the money she'd made as a cashier at Dots, where she'd worked pre-kids was less than they'd end up paying for daycare, so it seemed a good thing all around.

I tried sighing in a very emphatic way.

"I know," said Harrison, "but what if I move and she decides that she doesn't want to move the kids?"

"I don't know."

"But, you want to be with me, right?"

"Yep," I said, and I did, even before I'd been knocked up with the Wonder Twins. There was some moral struggle there, a miniature librarian in my brain shaking her head in a slow, judging way. Sometimes it was a nun or Adrienne Barbeau. Yes, he'd left his wife, but he'd left her because of me, because of my hypnotic vagina. And yes, I was pregnant, but I was pregnant because I'd stopped taking my pill. I was not so blameless as I wanted to be, a victimized kid being led astray by a guy who wrote about crisp and crunchy coating for a living. He was a man I'd liked and then wanted and then had and then loved. I hadn't been to blame for my emotions, sure, but who'd made me suck his cock?

"I can't move to Oregon," said Harrison, to which I answered, "I can't move to Rhode Island," and the silence just sort of hung in the air like an unanswered-for fart.

"The baby," said Harrison.

"Yes."

"Can we Skype?"

"I GUESS SO," I SAID. IT WAS A THING THAT HAD ALWAYS SEEMED A BIT *Jetsons*-y. It conjured images of floating monitors and antennas surrounded with Saturn-like rings, and robot maids.

"Why did they just put that dog on the treadmill in the *Jetsons*?" I asked, "He needed to crap, not just get exercise."

"What?"

"In the *Jetsons*."

"I . . . don't know."

"Very strange," I said. My own dog and cat were doing a thing they'd started doing with some frequency, sitting side by side in front of me looking at me with bored acceptance, like two men in a hammock staring at the sky.

Harrison told me that he loved me and that he'd known that we'd be together from the moment he'd watched the YouTube of me pretending to be an evil mistress clone from space. Then he asked me if I loved him.

"Yes," I said.

"Then I guess we'll see what happens," said Harrison.

The dog and cat blinked in unison, then the dog burped discreetly and licked his chops, tasting it.

7.

WHEN THE SECOND BABY TURNED OUT NOT TO BE POOP, I CALLED Sally and told her I was pregnant.

"Fuck-a-doo," she answered. She had catch phrases and words in her arsenal that no one had ever heard of, and that made her impressive in some way, like a Willy Wonka of filth. There were also various sounds that always seemed to be occurring around her, rattling ice cubes, the rustling of cellophane, and some angry, vaguely foreign chatter, as a clairvoyant might be surrounded by the voices of unsettled spirits. She was very much the sort of woman that my Pops would call a "chippy" in a way that was half angry and half resigned.

"They can't fire me," I said, "that's fucking discrimination."

"Oh, settle down. No one's going to fire you. It's a game of camouflage—it happens all the time in this industry. Remember *Everybody Loves Raymond*? The wife on that was constantly pregnant. She hid behind counters, behind fax machines, behind shopping carts. And Uma Thurman was pregnant the entire movie of *Kill Bill* Volumes One and Two."

"I'm pretty sure she wasn't," I said.

"Well, I'm absolutely certain she was," said Sally. "The reason you think that way is because you were fooled, just like the rest of the idiot audience."

"But I'm basic cable. We don't have *Everybody Loves Raymond* money."

"Honey . . . don't be an idiot. Nerds are followers. Do you know any of the cast members of *Deep Space Nine*?"

"Personally?"

"No, I mean do you know of them?"

"I don't know."

"That means you don't. But do you know who does? The nerds. And they are loyal. If you are seventy-five in an iron lung and you show up to a convention, there will still be hundreds of nerds who will want to hear you gurgle and spit up blood, and who will pay money to do so."

"Wow," I said.

"Yes, and maybe we can sweeten the deal? Maybe we'll leak a rumor that the secret father of your babies is Worf."

"The black guy with the trilobite head?"

"Yes, can you imagine? Those babies would be like the royal family to your average nerd."

"The babies have a father," I said.

"Oh, right," said Sally, surrounded by the sounds of rolling eyeballs and jacking-off pantomime, "Harry the husband. That will be a harder sell than the pregnancy, believe me."

"Really? Why?"

"Your average nerd is very moral," said Sally. "If you pay attention you'll notice that all the things that are important to them are good vs. evil. Like The Force and all. And that thing Spiderman is always saying about responsibility. The idea of you whoring it up with a married man might not fly."

"Well, what if I appeal to them en masse, sort of like Evita, or something?"

"Worf is better."

"Yeah, no," I said, my bigger concern being weight gain. I'd gained quite a bit of weight, partially because I'd been underweight to begin with, and partially because I just desperately wanted to sit around in my underwear.

"That's not a thing," said Sally, when I told her. "You can get by with gaining like four pounds."

"Two per baby? That seems unhealthy."

"What are you, a doctor? It's fine. Kids are way too fat these days, anyway. And don't trust anyone who tells you to quit smoking;

a fetus is less traumatized by nicotine than it is by the mother's body in withdrawal."

"I already quit," I said.

"Oh, fantastic. I hope you like trauma. I hope you like traumatized babies."

I'd been shockingly straight during my first trimester; I took the vitamins and the fish oil tablets and ate nothing with preservatives or nitrates. I washed my fruits and veggies until the skin on my fingertips cracked. I banished everything with vitamin A and alpha hydroxy acids from my medicine cabinet. I purchased a state-of-the-art water purifier; I drank water. What I did eat, though, was a never-ending mound of organic crap, like spelt cupcakes with goji berry icing, and frozen bananas dipped in free-trade dark chocolate, and tofu ice cream bites, and a thing called Pirate's Booty, puffs of organic corn covered in powdered white cheddar that made the babies stir like kittens in a bag.

"I'm supposed to gain at least sixty pounds for healthy twins," I offered meekly.

"Bullshit," said Sally, "I gained fifteen pounds with my kid. Fifteen from my exact weight right this minute. Lost all of it in delivery."

"God," I said, thinking that I couldn't imagine her being a mother, a baby growing inside her and slipping from the meager flume between her nonexistent hips. I could not imagine her body conforming for a baby; in my mind the baby appeared as a fist jammed into a coffee can, each inflexible, existing together with nonchalance like a hippo and a bird.

"That's right," Sally said proudly, "a little girl. Six and a half pounds. I was in and out in twenty minutes and I was only off the phone for fifteen minutes."

"Where is she now?"

"Eh. With her dad in California. What an ass he is. You know what he does for a living? He's one of those guys who goes around to storage locker auctions and bids on them. That's his job, taking chances on smelly units filled with broken Big Wheels and moldy *Star Wars* figures out of the original packaging. I pay child support. I pay it. And every couple of years he takes me back to court to get more."

"Do you miss her?" I asked.

"Do I miss who?"

"Your daughter."

"Oh, I guess I do," said Sally, surrounded by the sound of sudden philosophy, "I miss her the way I guess a guy who'd lost a leg would miss his leg. But I get by and do what I do and pay for the leg to go to private school."

"Sad."

"Yes, there's an uncomfortable amount of poetry in life just stuck around. I think that's the worst thing, the profoundness. If things could just be shitty and miserable all the time I think I could adapt to them better."

I did that kind of phone shrug thing that happens when the conversation has gotten too weird and there's no other way to recover from it. I would go on to have several of them with Joan over the next few months, and I would never know what to say or how to end. I would blame it always on the babies, my little beating alibis, my beans on leashes in space.

AFTER POPS HAD HIS NERVOUS BREAKDOWN I WENT TO LIVE WITH DAD and Lisa at her place near the beach. It was a few months before my seventeenth birthday. I cannot lie about the awesomeness of Lisa's home, with all due respect to Pops, who would've been devastated by the fun and comfort that I experienced. You could go outside and smell salt water and the sweet coating of the Pronto Pups they sold in carts by the Cliff House restaurant. The weather was always a perfectly brisk and not too chilly sixty degrees and you could hear the seals and even kind of see them if you squinted, perched darkly way out on a rock embedded in the white swirl of the ocean. And every once in a while someone would shout that they'd spotted a great white or a humpback and its baby, and if you looked quickly enough maybe you would see it too, the foreboding peak of the dorsal fin or the breach and swallow of the whale, fleet and mysterious as veins.

Lisa wanted very badly for me to like her and not resent her, and I did like her and didn't resent her, but it didn't stop me from partaking in the various mall and car-related fruits of her generosity.

She was a real inspiration to me actually, as she never let the mediocrity of her talents or situation dictate her lifestyle. A former Miss Sacramento, she parlayed a middling modeling career into an easy, awesome job as a successful model's decoy. The unholy lovely Brazilian/German swimsuit model Jasmine Vanderbeck had just moved into the palatial, gated San Francisco neighborhood of Sea Cliff with her new husband Jack Bulley, who was the quarterback for the 49ers at the time, and Jasmine was miserable and constantly swamped with photographers. We knew her to be miserable because she told *Vogue* and *E!* and *Teen Vogue* and *Jane*. And Lisa took action. She dyed her blonde hair an exotic chocolaty brown with red highlights and spun it into a French twist. Then she put on her heels and her knockoff Chanel suit and her big sunglasses and headed down to Mitchell Bros. strip club the Sunday night after the 49ers spanked the Dallas Cowboys 38–11. Upon her entry into the champagne room, Jack Bulley jumped to his feet, the girls in his lap spilling to the ground, and exclaimed, "Jasmine! It's not what you think!"

An hour later the relieved quarterback was enjoying a friendly beer with my stepmother and closing the deal for her to become his lovely wife's decoy. He insisted that her services were essential, what with Jasmine's secret pregnancy and all, and that she would be handsomely rewarded. I need you to know that all of this, including prep, took Lisa about ninety minutes to pull off. She'd had this crazy idea—and believe me, Dad and me told her it was crazy and encouraged her to teach an aerobics class or try out to be an amazed hostess on a home juicing system infomercial instead—and after almost literally catching a pro athlete with his pants down, somehow made him think it was his own *brilliant idea*. You can't front on that, I don't care who you are. Well, Pops fronted on it a bit. He called her a human whore shield a few times, and then a few times more.

Dad, Lisa and I would get up around two every morning and wait on the stoop for the fake milk truck that would taxi us the short way to the Vanderbeck/Bulley manor in Sea Cliff. Sometimes I would get to go in and Sophia the Mexican housekeeper would make me a drink from a hard disk of chocolate and steaming hot milk and feed me imported cookies that were so fancy they were called biscuits. They were always engraved with some kind of scene, the biscuits, a sailboat or a lighthouse or a fence running the length of a field of waving wheat, and it made eating them a sort of unlawful-feeling experience, like chewing on the corner of a painting. And the kitchen was three times the size of ours, the sort of kitchen you see during demos on The Food Network, with the shiny hanging pots and all, and black and white checkered floor tiles. And then the model and the quarterback would drift in and out of the room, smiling and nodding and checking their phones as though it were an airport. Lisa and Jasmine would be chatting because they'd become girlfriends and to see them together was somehow delightful and surreal at the same time. Their faces were the same, their untamed hair, their artfully reigned in lip colors. They would talk about babies and using mud to heal blemishes and sexy topics like these little wedge pillows that you pushed under your hips during lovemaking to get more pressure on your G-spot, whatever that was. Spending time with them, watching them, was not so much an education in being a woman as it was an education in behaving like a woman. The tiny movements, the flick of the wrist while sliding chopsticks into one's bundled hair. Looking at someone with your eyes up and your chin tilted down, predatory and playful. The art and the scam of that, being known but unknowable, women as colorful maps filled with dead ends. And even if I didn't really love the implications, I paid attention. Lisa and Jasmine Vanderbeck represented what it meant to be worthy, to be a good woman. They had long, toned legs in small shorts, they laughed when unattractive men tried to make them laugh, they seemed fertile and sexual and not angry—aside from having a child, which Jasmine would eight months later, nothing could make them seem more fulfilled and uncomplicated. It scared me, the idea that people were so willing to accept what they wanted to accept, but I respected and believed in it. And I would adhere to it.

After some non-judgmental breakfast, freshly squeezed vegetable juices and egg whites and protein powders, my stepmother, in full Jasmine Vanderbeck regalia, would don her space goggle sunglasses and slide into the back of a black Bentley with a Blackberry and a Starbucks cup full of coffee with one of Jasmine's bodyguards and the driver would make his way past the gates to part the waiting rush of photographers. The paps would surround the Bentley, clicks and flashes like mad, and call Jasmine Vanderbeck's name. How did she like San Francisco?! How was her marriage going?! When would there be a baby on the way?! And the faux Jasmine Vanderbeck would cover the uncovered portions of her face as the bodyguard made a big scene of being loud and beating on the insides of the windows, as though the photographers could be shooed away like raccoons or homeless people.

So while the Bentley was basically just driving around, the real Jasmine Vanderbeck would duck into the backseat of Sophia's mid-sized sedan and Sophia would drive her around to her various appointments—hair care, hair removal, gynecological exams. When she was done for the day, Sophia would drive her back home and Jasmine would text for Lisa, still flanked by paps, to return in the decoy car. An hour or so after the gates closed, Lisa would get a ride home on the diet system deliveries truck. This occupation of my stepmother's, which took at most five hours and at least thirty minutes a day, provided us with a disgusting amount of money, to the point where Dad just gave the frame shop to Pops. (A mild slap in the face, as the shop was now something of a sore subject between my fathers. Dad and Lisa met when she came in to frame the caricature that R. Crumb himself had done of her after spotting her fine ass trucking down Mission Street. And she and Dad had got to talking about the things they both enjoyed, such as white wine spritzers, irreverent sixties comics and, shockingly enough, heterosexual sex. It took Dad half a day to decide that he would leave Pops after he met Lisa, or as he put it, "forty one years and half a day.")

All the credit or blame for my career went to my stepmother, who responded to my lackluster grades by suggesting that I "start going to things," and handing me a dog-eared copy of *Call Back* magazine. She was also the one who got me started on the eating disorders even though I doubt she ever had any idea she was doing it. It was just her life; foods were categorized as good or bad, as in "good" fasting days or "bad" binge days, and if the bad days were not bracketed by several good days it resulted in the need for colon cleanses and bottles of brown sugary ipecac. Or, sparkling laxative, which she drank from a champagne flute to be a bit festive. All of this, too, was instruction. She wasn't telling me how to be good, she was showing me.

Even her voice, smoky with us, breathy with everyone else, was a lesson: trust no one, perform always.

"If you have this power," she told me once while I was watching her peel off daddy longlegs-like strips of fake eyelashes, "you have to pretend that it's not a big thing. At least sometimes. If people don't think they can have some part of you they lose interest, at least in this country. People are lazy. Why do you think men go to strip clubs? Because they can buy acceptance. It's a business, you know? It's all a business."

I got my language from her. She said "like" and "you know" and "whatever" and I said them back to her. My mannerisms, my smoking, my giving up at school vs. my never giving up at life. All of my memories of her are in the bedroom while she sat at her vanity or in the bathroom while she was in the tub. Every morning I would climb into bed with her and we'd talk as she drank her hot water with a single lemon slice. I would go through her potions and serums and she would tell me what they were for and that was satisfying in a fairy tale detail sort of way, her pots of nymph wings and dusting powders. I liked the modern voodoo-ness of her. Her loyalty was to nature, to knowing and defying it.

"What do you see in my father?" I asked her once.

She was in front of a mirror of course. I remember her stopping and considering herself briefly.

"He gets me," she said finally, almost sadly.

It was also why she liked me; we understood each other.

The Bulley-Vanderbecks paid for Lisa and Dad's wedding in Belize. They were eloping; I was not invited. I was allowed to stay by myself but chose instead to stay with Sophia the maid in her quarters, five neat rooms that smelled like candle wax and scalp. Having worked a full day, she would feed me mac and cheese from a blue box and we'd watch the soap operas that she'd taped. American ones, although she reacted in Spanish. There were a lot of shawls involved. I just didn't want to be alone.

At times during Dad and Lisa's two week vacation I would venture to the great room of the main house and watch TV with Jasmine and the Quarterback, which was somehow comforting and sad at the same time in the same way. They watched horrible sitcoms like *According to Jim* and *Everybody Loves Raymond* and *Two and a Half Men*, and Jasmine, who'd grown up in Brazil, would constantly throw out hypothetical questions while wrapped in a light pink pashmina.

"Why does Jim have a beautiful wife? She could do better. She could do better, yes? She could do better, I think."

Or, "If Raymond and his wife hate each other so much, why don't they get a divorce? She nags so much! Always nagging! For what? For golfing? In my country we respect the mother-in-law. You respect her because she is older and she knows more!"

Even after Lisa and Dad were back and we returned to our ordinary lives at home I would hear Jasmine Vanderbeck's voice in my head whenever the television was on, any show, not just the awful ones.

Why does Andy Rooney hate everything, always? Alarm clocks, who cares? Who cares about alarm clocks? Just open the drapes and let the sun wake you like God intended!

We watched a couple of Adrienne Barbeau's movies—*Back to School* and *Escape from New York*—during that time, just Jasmine and I. I flushed with pride when Jasmine raved over Adrienne Barbeau's beauty, and wanted so badly to lean over and whisper, *that's my mother*. Jasmine and I were just alike, ordained with bones and lips and hair, with symmetry. I could never bring myself to tell her. Instead I sat beside her in a borrowed lavender pashmina, and waited for her to guess. The hardest part of Dad and Lisa together, for me, was respecting a thing and honoring it when I could truly never ever be a part of it. Maybe that's how it is for sports fans. You can buy a t-shirt but you're never going to play for the Buffalo Bills. So, I don't know. The wedding pictures were nice; I raved over them. Lisa looked beautiful and Dad looked good and they both looked very happy. I don't remember resenting anyone, really, although I did have mixed feelings about Pops losing his mind. There were no rallies or anything back then, no propositions or ballot measures. Nobody was going to give a gay man a break so far as alimony was concerned, and people's responses ran the gamut from resignation to boorishness. I once overheard Chenille, one of Lisa's "good friends," making light of the situation thusly, "well, he got it up the ass for fifteen years, isn't that good enough?" Then she went on about how her own husband would give a million dollars to be able to do it to her even once, and this was followed by a high, strange bird-like laughter punctuated by light slaps and *you're so bad's*, the unplaceable language of women who didn't really like each other but were forced to share a small space.

I did love my stepmother; she was a lot of fun and she made an effort and she cared about the things that were important to me, even if they were—and they frequently were—really stupid. Like when I was too young to vote in the presidential election and she drove me down to the Democratic Party headquarters and we spent hours calling people and reminding them to vote. And that was stupid and pointless because it was San Francisco, not Dade County, but she still did it with me, happily, and then took me to get my nails done. I guess everything was fun as long as I accepted that there were boundaries, and that those boundaries somehow cultivated this massive love between my stepmother and Dad. I understood, for instance, that if it ever came down to saving me from being hit by a train or saving Lisa from being hit by a train, Dad would regretfully bury my remains in the family plot while holding Lisa's alive hand. I didn't have a problem with it; this was hand-of-God kind of stuff. Maybe being an adopted kid had prepared me for it in some ways. You were just carried by the wind or whatever like a single little seed and you landed somewhere and were overcome by something, some growth and change, and then it was over and you had to adapt to whatever was new and green and in charge. The husk was Pops, in a bathrobe somewhere, locked up or not, sober or not. And no one acknowledging his love or marriage because he shouldn't have gone and been gay in the first place. That was the thing that maybe haunted me the worst, the idea that you could be married forever and then wake up and find the person you were married to not liking you anymore and the whole marriage to be a dream like the season opener of some terrible TV show. And then rings are just rings and not wedding rings, not really. A commitment ceremony didn't mean anything where anyone was concerned. Pops and Dad spent my entire childhood explaining to me the ways that their marriage was real, was actually real enough to become real, like a puppet or a pumpkin patch, and then nothing. It had been pretend-real, a nice story that doesn't mean anything in real life, just like any religion.

8.

THE WAY THAT HARRISON LOST HIS JOB IS DISPUTED, AND SINCE I WAS
not there at the time I can't really speak objectively about it. I
took Harrison's word because he loved me, and also Joan's because she hated me enough not to lie to me. But of course I was not
there at the time; I heard about it first by frantic text and then by
slightly less frantic phone call. I was at work, eating a jar of organic
marshmallow fluff.

The world of professionally describing fish sticks is very complex and competitive, I guess. I've heard. It's fairly cutthroat, which
for some reason I believed with only a bit of skepticism because full
skepticism required more energy and less nausea than I possessed at
that moment. And I guess Harrison had dropped the ball one too
many times. I imagined several well-dressed young businessmen in fe-
doras talking fast about fish sticks, dangling fish sticks from the corners of their mouths like cigars, throwing themselves from rooftops
after losing lucrative fish stick accounts.

There had been some signs of discontent, such as the fact that
he would text me about the babies' zodiac signs during important
meetings. Sure I knew what their sun signs would be, but did I have
any idea what their rising signs would be? Or their moon signs? And
what celebrities had birthdays that were the same as the babies' due
date? Were the celebrities assholes or good artists? Ironically, I myself
even denied some of these requests for information because I was concerned about my own piece of shit job, even though since finding out
about the twins, all anyone wanted to do around me was shake their
heads and sigh. They'd decided to make my character Lola pregnant

as well, and in the big season opener we'd reveal who the father was. That was my idea, actually, since everyone was being such a bitch to me, I just threw it out there in a really shitty, hormonal way, like, why not just do some stupid "Who shot J.R.?" parody? And all of a sudden everyone's eyeballs were dollar signs. It was going to be some robot father, I assumed, or some alien father. I made peace with the fact that I'd be spending my breastfeeding months carrying around a length of PVC pipe covered in papier-mâché and spirit gum. Harrison had no such loyalty to the fish sticks, or to the purveyor of fish sticks. He took long lunches in which he'd send me picture after picture of the same elephant mobile from different angles. He took out a charge account with Babies "R" Us. His heart was no longer in the fish stick game.

"I can't describe them anymore," he told me over the phone very soon before his career shit the bed. "I've said all I can say about them. They're long and crisp and they have parts of a fish that have been bleached and minced stuffed inside of them. They repeat on me. Do you know this is the first year in nearly five years that I haven't gotten a bonus?"

"Oof," I said, "what kind of bonuses do they give there? Like twenty, forty bucks?"

"No," said Harrison. "It's more than that."

"Sorry."

He couldn't make rent then, and he called Joan to tell her that they would have to move to Oregon. She accused him of slacking off on work on purpose, and he shrugged and said, "you know what? The fucking job is gone. It doesn't matter if I meant to get fired or didn't mean to or if I shot the place up. It's over."

Then she told him she was trying to find a lawyer, a bluff, and he called that bluff, and she cried finally and said, "what, you want me to live with my parents, is that what you want? To move me across the country so that you can have your whore and kids at the same time? You sicken me. You sicken me and you make me sick."

They sold the minivan and bought plane tickets. He came first because he couldn't wait any longer, and he ended up on my front stoop waiting for me when I strolled up with canned cinnamon rolls and white bread and cinnamon and sugar and butter for making cinnamon toast. I was on a whole cinnamon kick that week; it haunted me, I dreamed in cinnamon.

He grabbed me and kissed my belly which was honestly more fat than baby, and he told me how beautiful I looked, which was awesome and hilarious because I looked like shit. All the makeup from the show mixed with all the crazy hormonal mess had left me with a kind of cystic acne that made me look as though I'd been punched in the face by a greasy case of the mumps, and there was probably food in the corners of my mouth because I'd had the day off work and spent most of the afternoon shoving food into my mouth, an action punctuated by several small trips to the store for ever more delicious supplies.

"We will never be apart again," is the thing that he said to me, very heroic and old fashioned, and when I remembered that experience I would often picture him wearing a wide brimmed hat and holding flowers. He told me that he wanted to adopt my dog and my cat, and that he wanted to stay.

9.

THE FIRST WAY POPS STARTED GOING CRAZY WAS THAT HE GOT insanely bad dandruff; that was the sign, dry skin. He used all the usual tools first, the ion brush, the brown tar shampoo, the fish oil capsules, and nothing did anything. He went to the doctor and was actually diagnosed with cradle cap, the thing newborn babies get. It was that kind of a year for Pops; all of his dignity had tripped over its feet and split.

It just went on and on. All of this shedding, the skin came off between the teeth of a comb like stacks of morels, layers and layers flying away as though there would be something to reveal. I imagined the white yellow of his skull, half hidden like a dinosaur bone, and something like a panicked love overcame me, but it was less a panicked love than a moment of Pop's shame somehow broadcast throughout my own brain. I wanted not to be him in that moment, and not to be affiliated with him. I don't know that I ever felt hollowness at not having his blood in me, but that was the first time I'd ever felt relieved about it.

Then he started to lose his hair in random, violent patterns like a stabbed-out map, and the reason turned out to be that he was pulling it out. So he shaved his head and went around all wild-eyed, looking like some Muppet-in-chemotherapy character. And finally he wandered into a police station with a loaded gun from godknowswhere (he always told me that you could find anything in Chinatown, so maybe it was from Chinatown), and announced to the police officers that he was going to kill himself. They put him on the floor and all that; I guess it had been a slow day. Then I got a call from a lady who hardly spoke English and I kept telling her I was sixteen but she wouldn't listen, so I called Dad and he came wearing a trench coat and hat that Lisa must've bought him. I remember that being the most bizarre and surreal thing, that hat and coat. I was like, what? Are you a detective now? Did you leave us to become a detective? It was the first time I could remember being angry with him over anything, and it was all wrapped up in the wanton hubris of that hat and coat.

The week after Pops got out of the hospital he was hit by a car, an undercover DEA agent on the case; she hit my father and dragged him nearly ten feet, not realizing he was jammed beneath her vehicle. His pelvis was fractured in four places, his kneecap nearly severed, eight ribs broken, barely missing his heart. His mother, my Grandma Rose, visited for six weeks while Pops was bedridden and she shook her head a lot, her mouth puckered with the unfairness of it all. She wore a lot of flowery floppy stuff from Chico's and old lady perfume from the drug store and she was all about those purses from Vera Bradley, with those colorful vomit patterns. She was really excited, I remember, when someone got her the limited edition colorful-vomit-for-breast-cancer purse. I remember the tears from it, the disbelief. She didn't cry while caring for Pops, though. She tried to feed him even though his arms and brain were perfectly normal and uninjured, and kept attempting to make me pin the accident on my stepmother. I remember her taping some of our conversations, actually, and never saying anything about it. She would corner me in a room and start talking and then very casually press record on this old-ass tape recorder that was suddenly just there. Then she would ask me about Lisa's Mafia ties. I don't know. She was a person who I felt obligated to love but then only hated more for that obligation.

Pops was very quiet during those six weeks. With Grandma Rose there, he was allowed to stay in the house on Castro Street in a rented hospital bed instead of a convalescent home, but he still needed us to do everything for him. He couldn't walk of course, or even turn over in bed by himself because his leg with the fucked up knee had to be in this huge, bulky immobilizer. I changed a lot of bed pans, is what I mean to imply. I learned that kids shouldn't have to see their parent's shit unless a.) the kids have seen their parent's shit all their lives, or b.) the parent is like eighty and the kid is like forty. You should not be a teen and have your parent's shit thrust upon you. It is not a thing that that kid recovers from.

I had a lot of really sad conversations with him, the kind of conversations that have you staring into space for great periods of time afterward.

"How's your Dad?"

"He's great," I would answer, and then see the grimace and downgrade accordingly, "he's good. He's okay."

"And how is your father's wife?"

"Fine."

"Don't be that way. It's okay. We're all adults here."

"I'm not."

"Well. Close enough. No worries. Let's have a light."

"Where did you get those? Grandma Rose . . ."

"Fuck. Grandma Rose. Give me a light. I know you fucking smoke."

"Okay."

"Thanks. God. God. Oh that's . . . I needed that. Wait. Where are you going?"

"I don't know. To the bathroom?"

"It's a question? Do you have to go to the bathroom or not?"

"I guess I don't. I just haven't gone in a while. But I can stay."

"Good. Thanks. I want you to know that I don't hate her, okay? I just hate what she did. Do you understand that?"

"Uh-huh."

"Because it's not my place to judge them. Don't . . . what is that face?"

"Nothing. It's just that you've already judged her, right? That's how it seems."

"Well that's God's job. I'm just disappointed. I guess I'm just a disappointed person in general now."

"Okay."

Pops had taken to the Bible lately, in a hilarious way that surprised no one. Grandma Rose was Catholic, and not so secretly delighted over the breakup of her kid's longtime gay relationship. She was a staunch believer in the changing-your-sexual orientation-if-you-pray-enough method, and she was trying to get Pops on her side.

"I think about the reasons for things, you know? I like that there may be this amazing reason for the breakup, going insane, and getting hit by that car. I'm like Job, I think."

"Nothing good ever did happen to Job, Dad."

"What? Really? Nothing? He didn't get like a big thing of riches, or something?"

"No."

"How do you know?"

"I don't know. Some God movie."

"Well, I'll be damned. Maybe I'm like some other guy who had it rough. Lot?"

"Wife turned into a pillar of salt."

"Then someone. Someone else. Are there any gays in the Bible? In any of the movies?"

"No. Pretty sure no."

"Well then maybe I am Lot. Maybe all of this is because of my wickedness. That would explain a lot. Your father changed, the way you're supposed to change, and look at him, happy as happy can be."

"That's retarded."

"Don't say it like that, it's insensitive."

"Sorry."

"I can't . . . why can't I like women? I tried, I've been trying. It's just not there."

"Pops . . . Dad had magazines with naked cheerleaders in them, girl ones. In the basement. I found them."

"What? When?"

"Always. Years ago before he left."

"Well, why didn't you say anything?"

"I don't know."

"You don't know."

"I didn't know why he had them."

"Well, what did you think?"

"I tried not to think about it at all, really. It wasn't a thing I wanted to think about."

"You didn't want to think about saving your parents' marriage?"

"Jesus, really?"

"You didn't want to think about keeping me from looking like a fat, gay idiot shitting in a pan while my only love fucks Miss Sacramento?"

"I can't be here for this."

"Yes, go. Just like your father. Go. Run away into your cave of fucking lies."

And it went on like that. I was just THAT MAN, a part of THAT MAN, who was somehow both sinner and saint, a bad man who became something that people could believe in, in my cave of fucking lies. Once, when I was at Dad and Lisa's, a guy with a bad cough called asking to put Dad in a religious comic book. He wanted to make a graphic novel of his life, his life as a gay who became straight. I told him to fuck off, and he asked if I was the kid, the kid from the gay marriage and I said, *I'm sorry, did I stutter?* Then the guy coughed and said he would pray for me, which is just a religious person's way of saying fuck off back to you.

I don't know. I am not one to take sides when there is no benefit in it for me, but I could see the anguish of Pops, the way that he was like some man hearing voices, some lesser-known Shakespearean character who ends up hurling himself out of a window and then haunting everyone just because. Haunted is actually the best word I can come up with. He told me once that he dreamed of Dad every night, and until I fell in love with Harrison I don't think I really believed him. After that I knew what it was like to wake up with the memory of a person still on your breath and in your skin, and to be angry and sad and betrayed to even be alive, and to hate God and still somehow believe in God more than ever. It seemed to me that Pops' pain was catchy in some way, that I would be around it long enough and it would find a way to burrow into my bones where I would carry it always like a limp or bus money. I would be transformed by it, a veteran-by-proxy.

I have an aunt named Jane on Pops' side who is a burn doctor here in Troubadour; she relocated from Los Angeles eight or so years ago. She does grafts and face transplants and all that. She has seen so much and knows so much that outside of the hospital she can hardly function as a person. Like, try having dinner out with her. She can barely even speak to the waiter and always ends up getting some crazy shit like curried lobster and then picks at it for two hours until it's time to pick at dessert. And yet she can make a nose, you know? That is the rub—you know what you do and do what you can and after that there is curried lobster. I have always liked her. She has always been my favorite aunt.

I spent a few summers with her and her son, my cousin Avery, also adopted. He and I had nothing to say to each other in the best kind of way. When we did speak it was really polarizing. He would tell me about the patient that once stayed with them who had been in a cherry picker that touched electrical wires, the party that they threw him to celebrate his new ears. I would tell Avery about the time Carol Doda came over after a big ceremony at the Castro and explained cock rings to me. Being with Avery made me feel horrified and re-lieved. We even looked alike, not in the features but in our expres-sions. Nothing concerned us. I will always claim that as the best wrinkle prevention, feeling nothing. Avery and I lived in caves and sometimes wandered out to stare at the moon, the same moon in the same sky meaning the same thing. There was happiness in that, in ac-cepting things preemptively. We were happy kids with happy lives. We were kind and grateful kids.

Pops got a big settlement less than a year after, because the DEA did not want to go to court. Our lawyer, a terrible cliché of a lawyer who much later would go on to defend Casey Anthony, told Pops that he would have gotten more money had he been blinded or slashed across the face, something unthinkable and disfiguring. Had that happened, the lawyer explained with a sigh, Pops could've pretty much named his price.

"Yes, but he would be blind or disfigured," I said, and our horrible lawyer smiled horribly at me.

"Aren't you a pretty thing?" he said, and turned away.

At day's end, Pops walked away with nearly four hundred thousand. He used most of it to buy a flat with two bedrooms in Eureka Valley. He asked me if I wanted to live with him and I answered, "well, what do you want?"

"You're the kid, Easy," he said, and it was something of a moot point. I was barely a kid. I'd gotten Dad's permission to drop out of high school because I'd gotten a sweet gig as the number eight in a daily production at a children's theater downtown. Pops didn't know, as he was crazy and hobbled and crazier still. He limped about in some modification of a bathrobe with a four-pronged cane, looking spooky, looking like he might just suddenly grab your hand and tell you how you were going to die. I did not want to live with him. I wanted to watch *According to Jim* with a supermodel while her quarterback husband sat silently and stoically, like a pair of dogs I saw in a backyard once, one barking, one with its head buried in the dirt. I wanted to smoke backstage at children's theater and flirt with odd numbers. I wanted the life where your stepmother comes into your room wearing a bedspread and says she'll give you a hundred dollars to get lost because she wants to fuck your father in the kitchen.

But it is hard to not lie to a man in a bathrobe with a four-pronged cane. The sadness of the cane grew exponentially with the addition of the prongs; one prong meant a skiing accident, four meant the next fall would be his last.

"I'm good with whatever," I said. His new house smelled like cat-box. The previous owner had died there of AIDS, and he'd owned a cat, and I guess as the owner got sicker he sort of let the cat shit wherever it wanted to shit. I am not judging, here. I'm sure I would have felt the same way in the same situation. No one had bothered to change the curtains or carpets or anything after Pops moved in, though. There was no air-conditioning but there were sky lights you had to open or close using a long metal thing with a screw ending. And when I say you, I mean me. I mean I was constantly doing it and failing, arms weak and aching, bits of dirty window debris drifting into my face like the ashes of something. And there was no dishwasher. And there was a washer and dryer in the garage but they smelled like mold and gasoline simultaneously, and the first time I opened the washer there was an old load of underwear in there, white, black and orange with mold and at first glance I thought they were swarming with caterpillars. And instead of doing laundry I went upstairs and laid down on the new couch with the plastic still on and thought about starting a load of underwear and then dying. I did not want to live in that house. I was not fine with whatever.

"Well, maybe you should stay with your father and your father's wife. It's good for a kid to have a kind of structure, the structure of a family." Then he stuck his chin out a little, daring me. I thought of nice things to say and didn't say them. They clogged there in my chest like a wad of moldering underwear, secret and unrecognizable.

"Yeah," is what I said.

"Yeah? You have a room there? A nice girl's room with a desk and vanity?"

"I have a desk," I said, "not a vanity."

"Girls should have a vanity."

"I use the bathroom mirror, mainly."

Or I used the one in Lisa and Dad's room, which I did not mention.

"Well. Okay. Okay, then, Champ."

There was a pause because I think that even he knew how weird it was to call me champ, or slugger or kiddo or any of those nonchalant names you call a person who is younger than you. We sat there on the couch, the plastic fart-squeaking sadly beneath us.

"Well, I'm not going to force you to do anything, of course," he said, and I answered, "okay," too quickly.

"Anytime you want to hang out, it's cool," he said, and there was that awkward thing again, that slight fake swagger in the body, as though I might come over sometime and he would beat me at basketball with his bathrobe and four-pronged cane. Maybe we would sing some songs. Maybe we would start a band.

WHEN I SAW HIM AGAIN SIXTEEN MONTHS LATER HE'D GAINED TWO hundred pounds, not so fat as he would eventually become, but close and shockingly, as no one had mentioned it to me. Maybe no one knew. The house was messy but not bad, it was not a *Hoarders* situation, yet. Later I would find out that Derek, the kid who shopped for him, would often pick up and vacuum if there was nothing interesting on the television. It was early on a Monday when I showed up, so early that the buses weren't running regularly and I wound up walking all the way from downtown. He'd sent me a key to the house on a keychain with a Lucite heart with the word "hottie" embedded in it, and that was sad in a way that my own heart could not digest. It remained there, jammed into the esophagus of my heart the way that angel food cake once became lodged in my actual esophagus, the time I took another bite while still choking because I couldn't see wasting good cake. It was still dark. I remember walking down his street and knowing his place—not recalling for sure the house number—by the ghostly blue TV light washing through his living room window. All the other windows on the street were dark, encapsulating the lives of hardworking people sleeping the few hours until it was time to wake, drink coffee, exercise, and ride the subway. Pops and the TV would still be there the whole time, camouflaged by the day like a porch light. The catbox smell had been replaced by something unidentifiable, something acrid and chemical. It reminded me of the uncomfortable smell I sometimes got off of old people like Grandma Rose, the smell of ointments and general unrest, the exhaust of a fevered system exiting though the pores. I got to the top of the stairs and said, "Pops?"

There were two doors to my left, one opened and one closed. I was on my way to the closed one when I heard my name in stage whisper, guttural and pained, and I went into the television light.

There was an old mattress pulled to the middle of the room, and that's where my father lay, as though beached. He was wearing a giant Giants t-shirt and boxers. His feet were bare and pigeoned out to the sides like flippers, the heels cracked, the toenails yellow and thick and crumbling like plaster. All of the furniture I'd remembered, the plastic covered couch and the entertainment center and easy chairs, was gone, and what remained was the TV. The mattress was a new addition. Why hadn't he just gotten a TV in his bedroom? I felt oddly wounded by this setup, by the way that he lived. It hurt my feelings. He kept his eyes on the TV.

"What is this?" I said.

"It's nice to see you."

"You aren't looking at me."

"Yes, but it's still nice to be in your company."

"Where is all the furniture?"

"I sold it."

Emergency was on the TV, on one of the retro channels. An attractive doctor was working on a patient and talking and not wearing a mask. Maybe he was smoking or maybe I was just projecting because I really wanted to smoke. I dropped my backpack and Pops told me to hush and I asked why and he nudged his giant head in the direction of the closed door down the hall. He had a full beard and mustache now, really scraggly like a castaway's, like a castaway drifting away on a big mattress.

"You got a guy here?" I asked.

"So to speak." He looked at me straight for the first time since I'd walked into the room. It felt weird to be angry and even weirder that he was somehow receptive to this anger, that he seemed to have expected it. "It's just a friend. I need more help than I used to, believe it or don't. I have a friend who helps me, brings me groceries, you know. Et cetera."

"Et cetera."

"No, not like that, obviously. Just a kind stranger who helps me out." He had become, in his sadness and morbid obesity, a Tennessee Williams character.

He'd met Derek before he'd gotten really heavy, at the supermarket or something. Maybe a bar. I couldn't imagine the process of that, of meeting the person who will eventually buy your groceries when you're too fat to buy your own. Would it be easier if it were a stranger? And how did you gain that much weight anyway? Did you try? Did you look at your life one day and just feel like, *fuck it, I'm eating*?

"Are you eating yourself to death?" I asked. I was chewing gum, I think, and I think that because my jaw hurt the whole next day, so I was either angrily chewing or angrily clenching my way through that conversation. The memory of waking the next day and massaging both sides of my jaw to loosen them is so vivid, whenever someone mentions jaw pain I think of fat people and night, of standing in a room over a mattress and waiting for someone's heart to stop.

"I'm fine," said Pops. There was a cough from the other room and he dropped his voice another octave, "I'm sure this must be shocking to you."

"I wish you'd mentioned it."

"And how do you assume I could've done that? In between asking about your other father's happy new life and your school work?"

"I quit school," I said, and it hurt him more than I wanted or expected it to. He was so large, slumped there. He seemed immobile yet indestructible, like a tank on its side.

"Well, that's a shame," he said finally. "You had a lot of potential."

"I've never had any potential," I said.

"Well, you're a kid."

"So, what now? Stripping college? Burger King?"

"Beats me," said Pops, a fat man in boxer shorts disappointed in his daughter.

The next day I got some of the story from Derek, who was thin and jittery and who had green darting eyes that reminded me of marbles clacking from one hand to the other. We spoke in the small kitchen as Pops slept in front of an infomercial about an amazing wallet. Derek and I sat at a faux wood table on wheeled fabric chairs and drank instant coffee that tasted faintly of mold and salt, strange, sea-watery flavors on the tongue. He kept apologizing for the coffee and telling me that he generally got his coffee out. And did I want to go out? Get a coffee on Castro? I said *no thank you* a lot. And *it's okay.* The sink was filled with batter-covered bowls and spoons. A big school-bus-colored Bundt pan with burned-on drips of cake. Derek waved his hand in the general direction of the sink.

"Oh, Chad loves his Bundt cake. Lemon. Every night. I told him, 'buy me a dishwasher or lose me forever!' I'm not one for sweets, myself, but to each his own. I guess I could use PAM or whatever, but the chemicals make me so uncomfortable, not to mention the aerosol.

You need to think about what you're doing to the planet. Even making a Bundt cake, you know the whole butterfly thing. I'm sorry the coffee is so gray. I usually get mine out."

"Where did you meet my father?"

"Oh. God. At a bar, The Mint. The Mint because it's near the old mint."

"I've seen it."

"New Year's Eve," he said, sighing, dragging the words out. "New Year's Eve."

"When?"

"Couple of years. Before . . ." here he patted the air a few inches from his torso, sculpting himself with imaginary fat.

"Was that his resolution?"

"Ha, no. But that's interesting. Maybe I just never thought about it that way. He told me about his situation, the year he'd had. He was still limping then."

"Was this before or after the settlement?"

Derek dropped his eyes. He scratched the back of his neck a little. "Um, probably before. Maybe a little after. I'm bad with dates."

"Yeah."

"But it wasn't a factor."

"No."

Derek explained to me that he didn't want to talk about sex and I told him that I didn't really need to hear about it, either. He was sleeping in the twin bed I grew up with and staying in the guest room that should have been mine, had I ever visited. I asked him what he did for a living and he grimaced and said, "problem solver," without irony.

"I find lost things," he said. I don't think he was high as I was talking to him but he may have been coming down from something. That's how he seemed, to be sliding down a wall in slow motion and then picking up speed.

"I like your father," he said.

"Okay," I said.

"And, oh he loves you so much," said Derek, and it was so surreal, my Dad's pusher telling me this, his bringer of Twinkies, his Twix supply man. I nodded and looked away.

"It's not a bad job. I don't work a lot. It just involves a few trips to the store or whatever a day. Some special trips, like for special cravings. Donuts, KFC, whatever. One time we were watching the big hot dog eating competition on the Fourth of July, you know that one? With all the skinny Asians pushing hot dogs down their throats? Well, after that he wanted hot dogs, actually corn dogs, so I drove all the way out to the beach to get those amazing ones they sell from the cart . . ."

"Pronto Pups," I said.

"Yes! Like father like daughter, I guess."

"It's right down the street from my house."

"Isn't that funny? You may have even seen me, running by with my order. I like to be prompt. I don't like to keep him waiting."

"I didn't see you," I said.

"No. Well. It's a friendship, what he and I have, at the heart of it. A friendship. We talk; he's very deep. Sometimes he asks my input on what he should eat, like he's just out of ideas. He'll say, surprise me, Derek, and I'll bring him Indian food or Caribbean. Once it was curried goat, and he loved it and couldn't believe it. He was like, wow, all this time I could've been eating goats and I had no idea!"

"You're killing him," I said.

Derek covered his face with his hands and then dragged them back though his hair, which was blonde and gelled into hard points. He had silver rings on almost every finger, multiples. They clicked like castanets.

"No," he said. "No."

"What did he promise you?"

"Nothing. Just a place to stay, the protection of that. Can I say? Not having a roof over your head . . . it changes you. I'm a hustler, that's what I always say. Two years ago if you'd driven past the park at this time you would have seen me and two Korean boys just standing there, waiting. You hustle, you have to. Your father takes good care of me."

I could only stare at his mouth when he spoke, the sad plush animation of it, a small heart split wetly in two.

"What about when he dies?"

"He's got me, he's got me," said Derek, too quickly, and then, almost venomously, "I'm sorry, do you think someone else deserves it? Your other father? His fucking whore? You, who can't be bothered to answer a fucking email?"

In the other room Pops moaned low in sleep and it seemed to snap Derek back a bit. He tried to recover with his little gay Renfield act, his homosexual *Pretty Woman* spiel, but I'd seen him, and now I couldn't stop seeing him.

"He loves me," he said. "How often is it that you can make a person truly happy with the simplest things? Bundt cakes? French fries? Fried cheese? These things are not too much to ask. I've spent a lot of years disappointing a lot of people, and it ain't fun, let me tell you. This is fun. And it's easy. And what does he have to live for, anyway? What do any of us have to live for, anyway?"

"I don't even know what to say," I said. I stared at my gray coffee. There was a small hair in it, maybe an eyelash, spinning like a scythe.

"Can you understand the kindness in what I'm doing?" asked Derek. He looked like he wanted to touch my hand but he didn't and I was glad for it. I noticed for the first time that he was wearing Dad's old cancer walk shirt and it was very strange, a mild spark in the brain. It was like a Where's Waldo or seeing a brand name in a movie, like, a split second of *oh I recognize that*, and then it was gone.

"I'm not doing a great job at understanding anything right now," I said, and it was true. It felt like my mind was having trouble breathing. I wanted a cold drink and a nap.

Derek got up and stood at the sink and began fiddling with the dirty dishes. He picked at the dry drips of batter on the Bundt cake with his fingernails; his rings clanged hard off the metal, like warning shots.

"What you said about a New Year's resolution was probably pretty apt," he said, his back to me. He was the first person I ever saw wearing Tripp pants, those huge long comical black things with all the silver chains on them, weighing them down even more.

"That's why I said it," I said.

"Yeah. I don't know. Even when I met him, before all of the

weight there was a kind of fatalism to him. He just seemed like a person who didn't have anything to lose. It was weeks before he mentioned you. I asked if he had kids the night we met, you know, because
a lot of the older guys do, and I wasn't really in that place, to be running around with all these little kids. I'm a kid myself; I'm too selfish.
And he said no, he didn't have any and he didn't want any, and I was
like, oh, okay, hello, soul mate. Then after the first hundred pounds
or so he was like, yes, I have a daughter.

"But I found out you were older and lived with your other father and I was okay."

"Okay."

"It was around the time that I was starting to ask about the
weight gain. I was being tactful, of course. I'm not one to judge people
by the way that they look. Well, maybe at first, but not later. And he
asked if I could move his mattress into the living room. And he didn't
want the other furniture. He didn't want it. He wanted the room to
move and grow so I sold it and he let me keep the money."

"Move and grow," I repeated weakly. I imagined Pops as a
giant sea turtle and Derek his curator, working hard to create a bigger
habitat with the adequate plant life and everything. I could see Pops
submerged in his holding tank, watching, his fat lifting him to the sur-
face like a glob of dirty foam. It made my throat hitch, as though I
might cry or spit but I did neither. I coughed, to cover, and then
coughed again.

"Maybe you can appreciate it as a project or a life's work?"
asked Derek, he turned to me, his butt pushed back against the sink,
and threw a hand towel over his shoulder in a pleading way, looking
to see what would make me bite.

"I don't know," I said.

"Because it makes sense to me on some level, like a spiritual
level."

"How old are you?" I asked.

"How old are *you*?" Derek asked back, and we sat there for
a minute thinking less of each other, a sad stalemate, a Mexican
hate-off.

It was an awkward end to an awkward exchange; the whole

thing petered out like orgasmless love, sweaty and accepting. He showed me his/my old room. It smelled like pot and sandalwood, like any boy's. On closer inspection, he had a baggie of pot next to a huge Ziploc bag filled with brownish-colored powder, on the outside written in Sharpie: Henna Mix 6/09–DO NOT EAT. His computer was on to a screen saver of Robert Plant bare-chested and in mid scream. The pile of scrap paper next to the printer was a copy of Pop's deposition from the car accident, which I'd never seen. On the top page he was talking a lot about Dr. Seuss, about how he was a communist. Then Derek showed me the thing he was most proud of, a white college-sized mini-fridge filled with sugar-free Red Bulls and Diet Pepsi and bottled water. He offered me something and I took a water. He knelt and patted the fridge kindly, like it was an old and faithful horse.

"It was a gift," he said too mysteriously, as though maybe I wouldn't guess who had given it to him.

I SAW POPS FOR SOMETHING LIKE SIX MINUTES BEFORE I WENT BACK TO Dad and Lisa's; I crouched beside him. His breath was cabbage-y, compost-y.

"Well," he said. "I'm not going to ask you to take care of yourself, because you won't. I guess that I'll say that I'll see you when I see you."

"Yes," I said. We did not hug or even touch. I shook Derek's hand because he was standing in my way, because shaking his hand was the only way out.

10.

Harrison and I lay around a lot more than I would have imagined. I'd never lived with a man, at least not in that way, so I had nothing to compare it with. I assumed it would be more sexual, I guess. It was appropriately sexual. We would shower (not together), brush our teeth (together), and settle into the darkness of our bedroom, where lovemaking would begin with all the trappings of an electrical fire, pops, sparks, flames. Then a nice amount of snuggling and a mutual roll over, turned from each other, connected at the backs like butterfly wings.

But during the day we hung out and listened to music. We got a record player from the thrift store, an actual record player that played actual records, and albums bought in a thick stack that we did not examine before buying. We spent our off hours laid out on the modest tan shag of the rug and listened to the records in their entirety, no matter how awful they might be. I guess you could say we were lucky for the most part, as many of the albums were well-known and had obviously been well-loved by their previous owners. There was the soundtrack to the movie *Hair*, and the soundtrack to the movie *Grease*, the cover of which opened like a yearbook filled with production stills. *The Graduate* was in there, too, right next to *Graceland*, and Jackie Wilson singing standards. But also Alvin and the Chipmunks singing the songs of Frank Sinatra, and an audio tie-in of Disney's *The Jungle Book*. Those were hard listening, as was the offering from '80s girl rap supergroup J.J. Fad, but we settled in with an obscure collection of R&B covers—Stevie Wonder singing "Blowin' in the Wind" and, best of all, the Four Tops singing "Walk Away Renée," which began and ended with surrealism in which you could drown. The beauty of men wearing matching velour suits who did little dance steps and generally went around calling people sugarpie and honeybun singing mournfully about the empty sidewalks of their block not being the same never failed to make me cry, first in a controllable way and then in an ugly, snot-filled way. *And when I see the sign that's marked one-way*: That's how it started. That's how the fucking song started.

Harrison would sing along, to me and not to me, and stroke my hair as the patch of sunlight on the rug gradually moved from one side of the living room to the other, the dog following it.

He would say things like, "You're so beautiful pregnant," when he'd only seen me not pregnant in person a handful of times, and it made me wonder what he was actually seeing. A roundish face and big boobs? A baby gut spilling precariously over low riders? We held hands everywhere, in the grocery store and in the farmer's market, and old people smiled at us a lot more often than old people didn't smile at us.

Suddenly, there were new regulations about farting on the couch during *House*. Or any regulations, really, as the dog and cat had no qualms on the subject, too busy watching the pint of ice cream in my hand as though it were a bomb strapped to my chest that they must somehow defuse by stealing and devouring it and leaving its chewed up cardboard carcass moldering beneath my bed.

It was a strange beauty.

TV and TV commercials. Terrible episodes of family-friendly entertainment. It was hard to comment on the possible wrongness of the affliction—a kind of shared not-experience broadcast inelegantly into our frontal lobes with its giant destructive pitchers of Kool-Aid, and rootin'-tootin' wheels of cheese in cowboy hats—when we were so enthralled with the idea that we'd seen the same things. Arnold's best friend on the show *Diff'rent Strokes* WAS nearly molested by a bike shop owner played by the same guy who played the station owner on *WKRP in Cincinnati*. Natalie and Edith WERE almost raped on *The Facts of Life* and *All in the Family*, respectively. These WTF moments had not happened strictly in the perverted brains of our youthful counterpoints.

At first Harrison and I had nothing to say to each other that didn't involve music, sex, or television. Or crossword puzzles on the internet. Our relationship came out of the electrical ruins of that, in a sweet, astonishing way, until TV was no longer necessary for us to be happy together, until we were able to accept the everyday dumbassness of us and enjoy it. Harrison was a lot of fun.

We would race through O'Bannon's to the frozen section to be the first to find the box of Clams Casino, to hold it aloft and yell "CLAMS CASINO!" much to the horror of anyone else in the aisle.

We would walk a huge bag of dirty clothes to Suds Laundromat—also in Troubadour Center—even though we had a state-of-the-art washer and dryer at home in our own laundry room. No one else was ever there on a Sunday, say, and we'd pull up plastic chairs and admire the graceful ebb and flow of our socks and jeans while eating the vile snackage found in the ancient vending machines: stale Cheetos and Sun Chips and Chuckles jellied candies like a life sentence for the jaw. The radio always turned to the Spanish station, with the male singers gargling painfully about things too horrific to be translated. What could be so mournful, so irrevocable, we wondered, to have to sound like that? Were they even words?

"If everything ended right now," said Harrison once in the laundromat with the overhead lights out, a summer storm taking speed outside, "I would still be so happy."

I CALLED SALLY A LOT TO TALK ABOUT THEFT. I THOUGHT ABOUT TRYING to contact Sybil, but after the showdown at Señor Squawk's, when having sex with Harrison had only been hypothetical, it hadn't seemed the best option. I guess I wanted Sally to make me feel better. I wanted to know if she thought that a person could steal another person.

"Oh, God," she said. She always said oh, God. She always asked me what I wanted her to tell me. Did I want her to let me off the hook, or something? Is that what I wanted? I just wanted to know if she thought it was possible for one person to steal another person away from yet another person. I was just me, one woman. I did not have any magical spells or what have you. I owned a home but I owned it in Troubadour.

"I don't know if I'm the one to help you," said Sally.

"You've been with married men. Women have . . . been with your husbands. I guess you have as much insight as anyone."

"You just start to hate everyone," said Sally. "And then you just stop caring."

"Still, though," I said, "you'd never expect any woman to, like, pledge allegiance to you, right? Just because you're both women?"

"You know that I never expect anything from anyone."

"Because it's on your husband, right, or your boyfriend? He's the one cheating. He's the one who took vows."

"Well, fine, Grasshopper, whatever. But you'd have to look at the other side of that. What's stopping Golden Boy from sniffing skirts in your neck of the woods? You have to look at what people are capable of."

I don't know what I said then, probably nothing. I probably said nothing for a good, long while.

"Or else I could just tell you that you're a good person and that everyone still loves you," said Sally. "I guess that would be no skin off my ass, either, right?"

WE TALKED ABOUT BABY NAMES. I WAS VERY CAUGHT BETWEEN SOMETHING traditional and something that would really inform a kid's personality, like LOLA. Or CANDY. There was some part of me that believed you could set a child's life in motion by bestowing them with a particular name, and I couldn't deny the intriguing aspects of that.

"Well, naming a kid Adolf or Destiny is all shits and giggles if you want to raise a Nazi or a stripper," said Harrison. "You have to come to terms with whether or not you're giving a kid a proper name or if you just want to give a big fuck-you to society."

"I can do both," I said.

"So, is it about you or the child?"

"If it comes out of my vagina, I think I deserve to have it be about me to some extent, honestly."

"I'm sorry, but that can't be your answer to everything," said Harrison.

He asked me if I wanted to name one of the babies after anyone in my family, and I laughed about that for a while.

"Well, I know you don't have much of a relationship with your father," said Harrison. "But maybe some aunt. Some great cousin?"

Most of my fathers' extended families had shunned them for their sinful "lifestyle" many years before I'd been adopted, so, honestly, there was really nothing there. I had many "aunts and uncles," some wearing leather vests, some not, who would come over and hang out after my bedtime. I was always allowed to make a *Sound of Music*-like entrance and say farewell in my little *Care Bears* or *Strawberry Shortcake* nightgown, and whatever visitor would comment positively on how I'd grown. So, there was really nothing there, either.

Harrison, conversely, had already blown his wad on his existing kids. Sabrina had been his maternal grandmother; James his late father. He mentioned that he and Joan had agreed that she would get to name all future children.

"Maybe it would be fair to have her name the twins, then," I said, too shittily, and even Harrison flinched a little.

Maybe we would have to wait and see the babies' faces before we could give them their rightful names, I reasoned, suddenly diplomatic, suddenly very good indeed.

"Who named you?" asked Harrison. "And why?"

"Well, I'm not . . . you know, my name isn't really Easy. My folks weren't that out there."

"No? God, how exciting. Is your real name hilarious, or something?"

"I guess? It's Esme."

"Oh," said Harrison. "That's not hilarious at all."

"No, it's just a cumbersome name, really. It's like too fancy, too winsome. It's like walking around for your whole life constantly wearing an ascot."

"Now, there's an idea. How did you get your nickname?"

"I don't know," I said. "The usual way. Some abbreviation of the name gone rogue. One of them started calling me E or Ease, and then it just . . . evolved, I guess."

"Well, that's disappointing," said Harrison. "With a nickname like Easy, I was hoping you'd have a ton of stories about being a really popular girl in college. Lots of crazy, nameless sex with boys and girls and various school mascots."

"Gross!" I said, shuddering. "I'd never go to college."

We went to bed that night determined to call the baby Oprah, regardless of its gender.

HE TALKED TO THE KIDS TWICE A DAY, FOR FIFTEEN MINUTES OR SO, which made him very happy, and then once a day to Joan for about an hour, which made him very sad. Sometimes he would set the phone down and do something else for a while—smoke on the porch, use the bathroom, make a sandwich—and then pick it up again when he was finished. He was never called on this. She never suspected she was talking to herself at all.

Of course I asked what sort of things she talked about, and he would make this face as though I couldn't even imagine. These were topics that he referred to as "married shit."

"When you've been married for a million years, the whole thing just breaks into like five or six fights. There are other fights, like peripheral fights, but they're just, like, little inlets that lead back to one of the five or six major fights."

"That sounds awful," I said, and I meant it. A geography based on, fueled by, fights? I could not imagine such a life.

"Oh, fuck yes. You never relax, ever. So, most of what she says is based on those fights. Sometimes she's just really angry about them, sometimes she wants me to know that she knew this would happen all along, and sometimes she wants to try and apologize for her part in it, or what she thinks her part was."

"Really? She apologizes?"

"Guh. I guess. They are apologies of sorts. It's generally like, 'oh, I should have known that you were very weak,' or, 'I shouldn't have gotten fat.'"

And of course I broke in with, "Wait, she's fat?" because it was still a time when I was in some way looking out for my future interests. If fatness was a deal breaker, I needed to know about it.

"She's not fat," said Harrison, "She's fatter, I guess, than when we met, but who isn't? I'm fatter. You wouldn't see her and say she was fat or skinny. If you had to say anything, you would say that she was, like, pear shaped?"

I recoiled at the term.

"That's bad?" asked Harrison, "I don't know. It happened very gradually. There was this one day when she came home and she was dressed in clothes that her mother would wear. Like, woman-of-a-certain-age clothes, you know?"

I shook my head.

"Like, when women stop dressing to look nice and start dressing to be comfortable. Long, un-tucked button-down shirts and those jeans that make their asses look like diapered asses. Elastic waist-bands. T-shirts with cats on them."

"Jesus," I said. This stuff, these excuses were like gold to me, like gold pieces to a puzzle, a mystery that I would figure out and offer up as evidence to Joan and to the rest of the world. I am not a bad person because . . . look. Look at what I've found! There was no way out of this ever. Look. Look and see.

"Yeah, I'm not saying it's fair," said Harrison, "and I'm sure she and every wife in the world could come back and give a thousand reasons why their husbands don't give a shit anymore. But I was the one who had a problem with these things, not her. And I'm the one who didn't think enough to talk about it. And I'm the one who stopped giving a shit."

He explained that he and Joan actually had attended marriage counseling in recent years, but that they'd never been back for a second appointment. He'd asked the therapist where all her degrees were, an uncomfortable moment. But he could not help himself.

"Mostly she wants to know when I stopped loving her, what she could have done, and why do I love you."

"Well, that last one seems pretty obvious," I said.

"Yes, but not to her. I think most wives would be like, 'oh, blonde, relatively young, has money.'"

"Oh, thanks for adding that 'relatively,' ass," I said, pushing knuckles into his ribs, and he laughed.

"God, you know what I mean. I mean you're not a kid, but you're still ten years younger than Joan."

The "not a kid" part was hard to hear—as "like a kid" was genuinely how I felt probably more often than I ever felt anything—but I shrugged and nodded anyway.

"But she wouldn't see things that way," said Harrison, "because she thinks all that stuff would eventually be trumped by the fact that we'd been together so long and had kids."

"Eventually," I said.

"Yes, well. She didn't deny the fact that she wouldn't expect a man to pass up a good time. But, you know, you don't really hear about men leaving their wives and kids for good, and I'm sure lots of people had her ear, saying things like, 'oh, girl, he'll come around.' and, 'oh, girl, he'll figure out what's important,' and, 'oh, girl, he'll come crawling back and then you'll fucking OWN him for the rest of his life.'"

"Wow," I said, "I had no idea."

"Yeah, marriage isn't for pussies. It's tactical. From the beginning, you're plotting your territory, you've got your little game book. You know what to hide of yourself and how to hurt this person, and you know your limitations."

"Yeah, they don't really talk about that shit in the bride magazines. It's mostly how to have great skin on your wedding day and is it tacky to still pass off a pile of cupcakes as a wedding cake."

"People who have been married for like fifty, sixty years, I would say that most of them have died to an extent. Either the wives or the husbands, one of them has given up. They don't fight because there is no reason to fight, and someone just gives in before anything goes down. Then, I don't know, hopefully they get dementia and forget all the fights and game plans and then you have those picturesque little old couples on park benches and walking down the street holding hands. I think the brain has to collapse a little for those things to happen."

"Jesus," I said.

"Yeah." said Harrison, "It's funny."

11.

WHEN JOAN FINALLY SHOWED UP AT MY FRONT DOOR I THOUGHT she was selling something, honestly, Tupperware or religion or a subscription to something. She just had that look about her, the look of someone whose pay is based on her trustworthiness. She looked robust, not fat, but hearty and at least generally prone to cheerfulness; she had good skin and hair. She'd settled into her forties maybe even before she had to—she had a shining bob and an untucked button-down shirt and some kind of sensible shoe, the same genial red/brown as her hair. My first impulse was not to hurt her.

"Are you Easy?" she said, and then I knew and was scared. I knew the way that things worked. Perhaps her shirt was untucked for a reason. Perhaps she was concealing a weapon. She wanted to come in.

"I don't think that that's a really good idea," I said.

"YOU don't THINK it's a good idea," said Joan.

"No, not at all."

"Is my husband here?"

"Not at the moment, no."

"But he is staying here?"

"I really am uncomfortable having this conversation at this moment."

"Oh, I'm sorry," said Joan, "I'm really sorry that you're uncomfortable. Would you like to hear about the super awesome day I've had?"

"I don't know. Kind of." Maybe by phone, I thought. There had to be a better way than this.

"Well, I got to my parents' house and the first thing my father says is, 'you brought this on yourself,' then he wanted to know how much weight I gained with my son. My son who spent the whole morning screaming in the car. And then my mom, my mom, the kind one, is talking to me about hair dye, as though that would make a difference in anything. She's telling me that if I took more time to myself my husband would come back to me, because men respect women who have their own interests. And she takes me into my old room and it's just like when I left, the bed, the shit on the walls, and I break down, I just lose it. And she asks me when's the last time my husband and I were intimate. Intimate. She wants to know when we fucked last and was I attentive to his needs."

"Maybe you should come in," I said.

She looked around really hard, dashing about and sticking her head in all the rooms like maybe she would find a meth lab or something, and it would explain everything, every bad thing in her life. It almost made me wish I had something scandalous in one of my rooms, or at least exciting, like a tank of helium and some balloons. I'd even cleaned. All the beds were made, all the floors were vacuumed. It must've been a disappointing scene for a suspicious wife.

Then the dog jumped on her and the cat ran from her; they generally took turns doing this to guests, just to throw them off guard. Joan was fine about it—she said so; I apologized for Noah's behavior and she said it was fine.

"We've had dogs. We had a dog like this one once."

We. The we was like a katana, slipped from obscurity and then right into the belly. I would regain control, but not for a while.

"Oh! Oh, Jesus," said Joan and she crumpled to the floor the way singers do in music videos after their boyfriends played by Tyson Beckford have died in motorcycle accidents. Was it a stroke? Was this how strokes happened? Then I realized she was looking at me, at my belly filled with babies.

"Oh, god," she said. "He didn't . . . is it . . . I didn't."

"Hang on a minute," I said, and then, stupidly, "don't move."

I went into the kitchen and poured her a glass of cold water from the Brita pitcher, and when I returned to the living room I found that she had moved, somehow, from the floor to the couch. Her face was in her hands. I set the water on the coffee table in front of her. There was a four pack of white toilet paper on the end table for some reason that generally had to do with the fact that I'd been too lazy or distracted by the television to bring it all the way from the grocery bag into the bathroom, so I dug my fingers into the plastic and extracted a roll and underhanded it to her in a way that I'd hoped was jaunty, but ended up being horrible, of course. She startled and then nodded, and sat there for a moment with the roll of toilet paper in her lap, awkwardly trying to find the end. I sat across from her in the too-plush recliner I'd impulse-bought along with the rest of the impractical shit in my house. It was the color of a wine stain. The cat had taken to sleeping in it. I knew that when I stood my ass would be shellacked with patches of hair in impossible-to-decipher patterns like a child's art project. Joan managed to pry a wad of paper from the roll and was now dabbing it beneath her eyes and nose. She said something that was mostly muffled by the side of one hand. The ending sounded a lot like "so stupid."

"I didn't know you didn't know," I said.

"No, I didn't know," said Joan, "and even now I'm sitting here hoping that you're a tramp and the baby belongs to someone else."

"It's twins," I said, and later I would wonder if it was retaliation for the tramp comment. Almost certainly. Almost certainly it was retaliation.

"Twins. Wonderful. I always wanted twins but they don't run in either side of our families."

"They probably run in mine . . ." I said. Adrienne Barbeau was the mother of twins; that was not lost on me.

"Wonderful. How far along are you?"

"Twenty-three weeks? I think twenty-three weeks."

"How are you feeling?"

"Okay," I said. It didn't strike me as odd that she'd asked. Having babies, I'd found, was a woman's truest link to other women, a secret society of vomiting and saltines. I would never disregard women again in the way that I had. I would never again not ask an obviously pregnant woman how she was feeling.

"I guess this calls off the cage match," I offered.

"Your face isn't pregnant," said Joan, and then, sniffling, "sorry, that was awful."

"Forget about it," I said. I still did not like the way she kept referring to Harrison and herself as "we," and things in general as "our" and "ours." I did not like the way that she was clever, and not obese. I'd been hoping she would be obese, probably much in the way she'd been hoping that my babies were fathered by some homeless teen who hung out beneath the bus station breezeway.

She was staring into her water so hard I almost wanted to ask her if there was something wrong with it. Maybe a dog hair; it would have been fair, as dog hair was everywhere. Instead she said, "You shouldn't be handling a cat-box while you're pregnant."

"He's an outside cat."

"Even being around him. It's dangerous for pregnant women to be around cats. Cats scratch. They have feces under their nails."

"Gross."

"Yes, and dangerous. Very dangerous," she set her water down and leaned forward, her elbows on her knees, contemplating me. "Were you in Monterey? What was that? Did you sleep with my husband in Monterey?"

"Yes, I was there," I said, and she nodded, waiting. It seemed an odd time to feel so modest. I said, "that is where the babies were conceived."

"Yes. So you were trapping him? You've never heard of birth control? Condoms?"

"I had some reactions to the pill," I said, blindsided. In most of the situations of my life, and this would be no different, I'd found that the questions that are the bluntest and put you on the spot the most could've best been answered thusly: FUCK THE FUCK OFF. Instead, I finished with, "He said condoms feel like nothing."

Joan did that tiny swallow that people do when they are about to spit or throw up.

"Monterey," she said, "he almost cried. He wanted to go so badly, I'd never seen him that way. And I said, 'Tell me why. Tell me why this is so important to you.' And he said it was the shark, that great white shark. It meant something to him. He had to see that shark."

"We did end up going to see the shark, honestly," I said, "and it was amazing. It's an amazing aquarium. Just beautiful. If you're ever in the area . . . it's not to be missed." Being nervous had made me a Monterey travel adviser for some reason.

"I always figured we would take the kids one day," said Joan.

"Oh," I said. At the moment Harrison was out pounding the pavement for a job, which seemed sweet and impractical. He would take anything, he'd told me. I had images of walking past a restaurant downtown and seeing him in the window tossing pizza dough into the air. Men in love, sigh. Like an epidemic. Like a zombie epidemic.

"Did you know," said Joan, "that there is such a thing as a sea otter serial killer?"

"No."

"In the wild, yes. One unbalanced sea otter has been going into a community of sea otters and he just starts killing them. Drowning them, holding their little heads underwater."

"Jesus."

"They say . . . well, they hope that he's doing it out of love."

"Like Dr. Kevorkian?"

"No, but that's funny," she said, not laughing. "No, the guys, the scientists, they think that maybe the crazy sea otter will hug the victims to death, and that the drowning is sort of a by-product of that. Like the otter doesn't mean it. Like he's a little furry Lennie Small. He just needs someone to put him out of his misery. . ."

"Well, he shouldn't have been messing with Curley's wife," I said.

Joan looked at me hard, "I guess I hadn't expected you to get that reference," she said. "This would be easier on me if you were stupider. And not pregnant. And didn't have a beautiful home."

"I own it," I said.

"It's lovely," she said, and then, to herself, "I'm sitting in the home of my husband's mistress complimenting her, and talking about otters. This isn't going the way I'd planned."

I nodded. I thought about telling her the whole story about

the John Steinbeck Wax Museum and how racist it was but I didn't, ultimately, as it had led to me fucking her husband.

"How did you plan it would be?" I asked, because honestly, it didn't seem like a confrontation that anyone could have foreseen. It was strange but tensions were not particularly high. Even Noah, as keen a barometer of energy as that great white, had flopped down asleep on the floor between us like a side of beef.

"Um, I guessed that I would appeal to you. And talk about the kids. And maybe I would show you some pictures of Harry with the kids and you would be overcome, and then this whole thing would be over." She pinched the skin between her eyebrows like a woman in a pain reliever ad, "And then Harry would get his job back magically and we'd move back to Providence and this would all be some terrible dream. Maybe I'd wake in a barn, having hit my head, and the beautiful marriage I never had would just start happening. But then you were pregnant. Are pregnant. So, I can't really play the good father card with you."

"I guess not."

"Well, what I had meant to do, what I've rehearsed for the last few nights while the kids were sleeping, was to ask you very professionally what you knew and when you knew it. Very coolly, like that woman on *Law and Order*, the brunette whose mom was Jayne Mansfield. It's a shame because I really had the disgusted, disinterested voice down. May I try it on you, just for the hell of it? I'm pretty good. In high school I played one of Anita's friends in *West Side Story*, and more than one person told me how natural I was."

"Okay," I said, trying not to sound weary. Pregnancy had made me weary as a second nature and I found that it insulted people at times. Like the checkout kid at O'Bannon's. Some people took it really personally. It bothered me to some extent playing straight man to the wife of my babies' father, but somehow the threat of seeming impolite was greater than that irritation. I don't know. A lot of aging drag queens stayed with us when I was a kid and they were always up in the very early or late hours speaking musically of bygone days. This experience was not unlike that.

"What did you know," asked Joan, disgustedly and disinterestedly, "and when did you know it?"

"Harrison came to my . . . convention thingy, and admitted he was married. Then like a month later he invited me to Monterey to see the shark . . ."

"Wait, what convention thingy? Here? In Oregon? Was that when he was fixing the deck for my parents over the border?"

I nodded and then she looked pretty interested but still disgusted.

"I hate finding out shit like this, man," she said, and the usage of the word man gave her a weird youth and credibility, like one of the Li'l Rascals or Lou Reed. "It's like everything in the last twenty years, now I have to second-guess it. Maybe that time he went out for a walk five years ago he was really banging some bitch behind a Dumpster. How's that for security? There is no security. Safety is a fucking lie we tell ourselves so we can get some sleep at night, but it's not real. Not really."

"I didn't know about the kids until after . . . things had gone down in Monterey. And I left. And I didn't talk to him until I was almost out of my first trimester."

"So, I guess you're above reproach then?" asked Joan, still on the Dumpster. "I guess you want some kind of I'm Not a Homewrecker badge? You know, whether your generation believes it or not, women owe something to other women. Something, some benefit of the doubt, some . . . I'm sorry, Jesus. This is just a lot of information that I don't know what to do with. It just keeps coming. It's like *I Love Lucy* and the chocolates and the conveyor belt. There's only so much I can stuff into my mouth and bra, you know?"

"Yeah," I said.

"I'm starving," said Joan. "I haven't eaten in three days. The divorce diet, what do you think? Maybe that's my ticket out. I bet in this case wives either lose or gain a ton of weight. Somebody pays, whether it's the husband or the wife. Someone is always paying, am I right?"

I don't know, she was losing her mind a little. It was part resignation, part *Live at the Improv*. The babies responded to the quickening of my heart by kicking and punching each other rapidly, a thing that would continue several years out of the womb whenever they sensed unease. Combined with the discomfort of that, I had shaved intimately the night before with great awkwardness and Harrison's mentholated Gillette foam and now my vagina felt like a cough drop on fire. I had attempted it, I guess, for overtly sexual reasons, assuming that Harrison would find it sensual, but once the hair was gone my precious lady had seemed oddly bereft, like a toothless old woman. And shaving was not the most efficient way to remove all the hairs, I found. There were short, sharp little stragglers a bit further toward the back like the beard on a mussel, and it felt like sitting on several of the plastic threads from which thrift store price tags often hang. It was a difficult conversation, at a difficult time, filled with residual difficulties.

"So, the kids and I will live in Weed with my mom and dad," said Joan conversationally, as though I'd asked. "And that will suck. My dad and I don't get along, hence the whole 'I brought the divorce on myself thing.' And my mom. She's no help. She'll tell me to try harder and take some college courses, because that's her answer to everything. I hate that the kids have to see that. You know, sitcoms have lied to us. Moving back in with your parents as an adult is not a hilarious, growing experience, it's basically the truest way to ascertain that you've failed at life. It's an affront to nature. You don't see birds going back to the nest with their own baby birds. Birds have the decency to be eaten or killed. They would spare themselves the embarrassment! But say what you will, that miserable old couple stayed together. A triumph of settling! Are your parents still married?"

"No," I said, after the moment it took to realize she'd been speaking directly to me. She'd gone from monologue to one-woman show and there seemed no stopping her. I was surprised to be included in the act, to be plucked from the audience that way, probably for the purpose of mocking.

"That's the way of the world," Joan said, in a mock-editorial, *Springer* kind of way. "Divorce. Babies having babies. Widespread panic. Can I tell you the way that my husband proposed?"

"No," I said.

"We were living together. It was late. I'd just worked two jobs and came home and cooked dinner. He was being a jerk, a selfish jerk. I'd caught him in a lie. He didn't work—he'd told me he was out that day looking for work but then I met the girlfriend of his scumbag buddy at the pharmacy and she told me that Harrison and her boyfriend had been at the strip club all afternoon. Right? In the fucking afternoon. I said, 'You're trash, I deserve better,' and he said, 'Then leave or let's get married, it's all the same to me.'"

"Ew," I said.

"I know," said Joan, "and then we married and it went on for twenty years. Two years of dating plus eighteen years of marriage and two children based on the fact that he didn't give a shit. And this. And I can't even hate him, even though I want to hate him so much. But I can't, I just can't."

And then she started crying again, harder this time. Big, full-bodied sobs that doubled her down over herself. Noah looked up with concern, one of his ears folded back like a change purse. I let her cry for a while—wondering how and if I could somehow sneak out of the house and drive the fuck away—and then asked her a few times what I could do to help.

"Nothing," she said.

And then, "be a bad dream."

And then, "I'm starving, do you have anything I can put in my stomach? I feel like a piñata filled with bile."

I thought about that; every minute of this conversation had been a bizarro version of what it was supposed to be. I almost wished she had punched me in the face. It would have been quicker and less awkward.

"I have bread and tuna and some noodles, ziti. I have cheddar cheese. I have some English muffins . . ."

"What about soup?"

"Soup?"

"Yes, soup. Like a can of soup."

"Tomato," I said. It was always there in my cabinet, perhaps for artistic purposes.

"Tomato," repeated Joan, tasting the word, "yes."

She was asleep when I returned to the living room with a bowl of tomato soup and some goldfish crackers artfully arranged on my super post-ironic Tom Selleck TV tray. She was curled up on her side with her legs up and Noah, who would nap with Charles Manson himself, was snoozing beside her. I thought about saying something dumb like, "soup's on!" so that she would wake up and eat and leave, but I didn't. I left the tray on the coffee table and waited in the kitchen until Harrison came home.

"Oh, Jesus," he whispered.

"Yes," I said, "this was my day."

She woke an hour or so later and sat up shivering, seeming discombobulated. Her soup had grown a skin. She thanked me for having her and searched around for her coat in an almost panicked way. Harrison hid in the bedroom until her car was out of the driveway.

"What did you guys even talk about?" he asked when it was safe to come out.

"*Law and Order*, serial-killing otters, *Of Mice and Men*, cats and pregnancy, the way you proposed marriage," I said. "And other stuff. Tons of other stuff."

"Well, that's Joan," said Harrison, sighing.

12.

WHEN WE FOUND OUT THAT JOAN HAD HERSELF COMMITTED WE were at the gynecologist, where I was getting an ultrasound. It was also the day when we found out the sex of the twins, a boy and a girl. The girl was smaller but she moved a lot more, like a woman in an office who is constantly shaking her knee up and down to burn calories. I knew that they whaled on each other a lot, the babies, but it was interesting to see them doing it. They reminded me of the brothers from the band Oasis, just constantly staggering around and falling into each other and punching blindly in any direction. They were growing well and they had all their stuff, the technician told us. Their little hearts blinked on the screen like cursors.

Somewhere in there, Harrison's phone rang, and he squinted at the number and excused himself to a darker corner of the room. The girl baby fell asleep and still she punched her brother; he was good at blocking, for a fetus. I could hear Harrison trying to be quiet and doing a fine job at first but then letting it get away from him.

"Oh, Jesus," he was saying a lot of things like that. Then he asked the technician for a pen and a scrap of paper and we both started watching Harrison more than we were watching the babies cramped into my body. It was a wonder to me that twins could ever be alone after being born, that they didn't have to keep wearing another person constantly like a fur coat.

"Is everything okay?" I asked, and he shrugged and shook his head at the same time.

To the technician he asked, "Do you know this area? How would you get to Two North Hospital from here?"

"Kill a guy, I guess," said the technician, whose front tooth was broken on the diagonal in a very cute and jaunty way, as though she'd intended it that way. She reminded me of Pippi Longstocking with that tooth. "No, seriously," she said, "just get on the highway."

I GUESS SHE COMMITTED HERSELF ON THE RECORD, BUT APPARENTLY THERE had been some really strong suggestions from her parents, especially her dad. I don't know, maybe she'd been telling him about the otter serial killers.

I asked if I could wait; I sat in a pleather chair while Harrison got patted down and I read a magazine, a *Jane*, which had been out of print for some time. And it was raining, which was awesome. I always seem to remember days like that as raining anyway, so that was a nice little bonus. The whole thing took maybe ten minutes, and Harrison came out with that look he got sometimes when he was tired or pissed off, the look that's really no look, when he's so filled up he just has to switch it off completely for a while, and on the car ride home he was quiet for a long while, helped along by the fact that I was not asking.

"How many people get to say that they genuinely drove another person crazy?" he said, "and have proof?"

"It may have been a pre-existing condition," I said.

"Well. Fingers crossed."

"How did she look?"

"Oh, the way they look. Pale. Dark circles. Very tired."

"What did she say?"

"She was going on about how it wasn't like *Cuckoo's Nest*, and how she'd wanted it to be like *Cuckoo's Nest*. And she made some jokes about Indians and drinking fountains. And she asked me not to tell Sab."

"Ouch."

"But I can't imagine Sab doesn't know. Her grandfather is not the most tactful."

"No."

"No. And let's just say that he doesn't have an inside voice.

So that must've been interesting. Oh, yeah, and there was a knife involved."

"A knife?"

"It was a Swiss Army knife for fuck's sake. I guess she was going to give herself a tracheotomy with it."

I shivered a little but he didn't notice, or if he noticed then he didn't call me on it.

"She didn't hurt anybody, or herself, but Jamie was in the room, his grandmother was holding him."

"Oh, shit. Was he freaking out?"

"No, he was just watching. At least that's what she says. God. Perfect."

"It'll be okay," I said, a thing to say.

"At least we get them."

"Who?"

"The kids. At least we get them. I was afraid that she would want her folks to have them, and we'd have to go to court. Easy?"

"Oh, I just didn't know," I said. I had met them for maybe a half hour. Harrison and I hadn't touched the entire time. We went to Tastee Freeze and all three of them sat on one side of the booth. Sabrina stared at my belly and told me about the books she was reading. Later, Harrison told me that she asked about the babies' father on the car ride back to Weed, and that he'd changed the subject.

"But you're fine with it?"

"I don't think that I have a choice."

"I GUESS I SHOULD HAVE SAID SOMETHING," SAID HARRISON. HE WAS hurt; no one ever got hurt like Harrison, ever. He hurt at a twelfth grade level. If he hurt your feelings and you told him about it, it hurt his feelings. It defied logic, even gravity. It was his own language. It was his own solar system. You couldn't go up against something like that, you let it wash over you, dissolving you like a lozenge.

"It's okay. I just have some concerns."

"You knew I was a father when we got together."

"Yeah, I actually didn't, but that's beside the point, anyway."

I put most of Sabrina's room together by myself. There was some bookcase that was giving me issues so I got some help with construction from the guy who'd been going through my recycling bin in exchange for beer (I couldn't drink it, so whatever) and ten bucks. I chose the bean bag chairs in deep colors like royal purple and red and emerald green, colors from Prince's closet circa 1984, because I disliked the idea of pink, as it seemed pandering to a teenager. There was a carpet so lush it enveloped you to the ankles when you walked on it, and a desk and computer and a floor lamp and a queen-sized bed with a trundle pull-out in case she wanted to have more than one friend over, a shocking but intriguing notion to a woman such as myself, who'd only ever had one person sleep over at her house when she was a kid, a male cousin who was sequestered at our place until the bed bugs were gone from his bedroom.

I bought a bunch of random books online, anything that seemed interesting. *Winemaking for Dummies*, that sort of thing. The Stephen King library. I arranged all of these books in her hobo-assembled bookcase in a fun, random sort of way like colorfully tilting buildings or teeth. And all the linens and shit were choice. Major thread counts, dust ruffles.

The baby had a room, too, decorated with alternate Thomas the Tank Engine and Bob the Builder motifs. He had a toddler racecar bed, which I assumed would take the sting out of the whole divorce thing.

"So, yeah," said Harrison, still hurt, "her dad is dropping them off tomorrow."

"That's really soon," I said. "Like, super soon."

"You know, if you aren't okay with this . . . I just AS-SUMED . . ."

"I am okay with it," I said. I did not ask him to think about what everyone always says about the word ASSUME. I did not do that at all.

"We have a boy and a girl," he said, softening, and I nodded.

"And a boy and a girl."

"I'm going to go home and write in my diary that Joan was committed today and that it was my fault."

"It wasn't your fault."

"I didn't cry when my father died, did I tell you?"

"You started to. Did you drive his ass crazy, too?"

Thank Christ he laughed.

"No. Colon cancer took care of that."

"Damn."

"It was not pretty. They sew your asshole up, did you know?"

"Who sews my asshole up?"

"The doctors, when you have colon cancer. You shit in a bag. You have no reason for an asshole anymore so they sew it up."

"No," I said. "No, I did not know that."

"Yes. They do that. It seems barbaric in a way, but it's just logic, closing an unneeded hole. It's crazy the shit in this day and age that seems so strange and unexamined. Like seeing-eye dogs, that seems as though it could be updated."

"I've never thought about it in that way," I said.

"No one has. That's the point. So, yes, I didn't cry. I spent some time with his dead body and I didn't cry. But when you left me, I flew back to Providence and walked into the garage and sat down and just started bawling. Just huge sobs. For about a half hour. I'd told Joan not long after we met that I had no emotions, and she believed me."

"That's awful, sweetie, I'm so sorry," I rubbed his arm up and down briskly, as though for warmth.

"But I don't want you to believe it, is the thing. I don't want you to believe that I have no emotions. This thing, you and me and the babies and the kids, this is what matters to me, and it's the only thing that ever mattered to me, and even though that's probably what drove Joan crazy, it's still true. It still happened and is happening and it's important to me."

"I know."

"Well, I don't think you know everything there is to know."

"What, do you have another wife, or something?"

"I just don't think you know what it's like to be in a relationship for so long and just not give a fuck, and I hope you never do. It's bad. It's oppressive in the way that heat is oppressive. You can't breathe but you get used to not breathing. I'm not this guy who just abandoned his family. I'm not this statistic . . ."

"No one thinks you're a statistic."

"Everyone thinks I'm a statistic. Men are pigs, men are dogs, men will look at anything, men will fuck anything . . ."

"That was actually *my* thesis."

There was that screech, that overdone movie screech, of tires as Harrison pulled over to the side of the road and the babies kicked and punched in unison to the 'what is happening, what is happening' playing in my brain. Also, the 'is this how it ends? Is this how it ends?' I half expected to look down and see a Swiss Army knife sticking out of my chest, but then Harrison's tongue was in my mouth and his hands were on my boobs.

"I need you to know that nothing meant anything before," he said when his tongue was securely back in his own mouth, his head so close to mine that his eyes were only visible as a wet glint in the darkness, "and I can't help Joan, even though I feel bad. I am not what I do, at least not right now. I'm yours. I'm your husband, all of that."

And when I was able to answer, I said, "Okay."

I thought about telling him about my own father being carted away to the nuthatch, and I even know why I was going to tell him, which is probably why I didn't end up telling him. Maybe you would never stop talking if you constantly said what was comparable to what. You would just be talking and talking until everyone in your life had died or walked away and then died, and you were this broken old corpse person, mouth still moving ever so slightly like a little bird wanting to be fed.

13.

JOAN'S DAD DROVE AN OLD MAN CAR, A BROWN CAR. IT MADE ME wonder when I'd last seen a brown car and I couldn't remember, just like I can never remember the last time I ate an orange. The kids looked very small in the back seat. Later Sabrina would tell me that her grandfather made her sit in the back to tend to Jamie, even though Jamie ended up sleeping the entire trip.

I'd wanted to stay inside the house until Joan's dad was gone, but Harrison wouldn't hear of it. He was big into defending my honor. He may have even just wanted the bastard to say something about me so he could spit in his face. Harrison told me I couldn't hide, and I tried to explain to him that sitting in the house with the AC on watching television was technically not hiding, it was watching television with the AC on. No dice. I was standing there when the car pulled up, holding Harrison's hand.

Joan's dad got out of the car so quickly I flinched, but then he shook my hand with three big pumping shakes, and told me he was Bill Hutt and I must be Easy and asked me how the hell I was. He was wearing one of those types of hats that only old men and kids on Halloween can get away with, a Panama, I think, with a big tropical print band. I don't know what it is about old people and the tropics, I never have. Maybe it's just to rub the retirement thing in even further; maybe if you work long enough you never want a single person to forget the fact that you could be in Barbados at a moment's notice. And then you'd get to talk about the economy for four hours, so win-win for you, old person.

It was another one of those times when the surrealness of the moment just brought up so many shameful feelings. There were many things that happened during that period that I took a pass on, morality-wise, but even I was pretty sure that the father of the woman whose husband I'd made babies with shouldn't be standing there giving my belly luck-rubs. I stood there mourning a bit for Joan and her traitor pirate of a dad with his tropical ways and obsolete car. It should not have been that way. Anger would have been something I could have understood, even welcomed. Sabby got out of the car more slowly, with Jamie on her hip. She was wearing a tank top and cut-offs and she was taller than her grandfather was. I watched her watching him interact with me. She sniffed a little editorially, and looked away.

"Sab," said Harrison, waving her over. He kissed her cheek and the baby grabbed for him, and the easy transfer from Sabrina's arms to his made me part misty, part envious. The envy was something that I acknowledged but tried to ignore, as it seemed ugly, an ugly, selfish thing, the sorry feelings of a girl irritated about not getting to plant a flag somewhere first, of someone for whom love alone would never be enough. In unison, the babies tumbled inside me. It made me think about the song where the old lady swallows a bunch of animals to kill a fly she swallowed in the first place. The babies had grown so quickly from spiders to birds to cats, their uprisings were so sudden, so adamant.

Bill Hutt wanted me to know that I had such a glow. It was hot out there, standing in the driveway. That was where the glow was coming from, if there was a glow at all, but I kept my mouth shut the way one does when they want a conversation to end. He seemed like a guy who had a 'great story' about whatever topic came up, from the weather to bear hunting. I did not like being the excuse for an old man to talk, so all I said was thank you but then he wanted me to know about his sister, who was pregnant with twins for forty-eight weeks. That was when I noticed that the baby was looking at me in a fairly hateful way. He was also really congested for some reason, so his glaring was broken apart by short huffs making him sound and look not unlike a cross baby boar. In a cute way, I mean. Cute, but not kidding.

Before he drove off, Joan's dad wanted me to know that I could call if I needed anything. It dawned on me in a vague way that he had not addressed Harrison or the kids at all in this conversation, nor had he mentioned his institutionalized daughter, even in passing. I blurted out some question about whether or not he was going to visit Joan while he was in Troubadour. I may have been possessed, I'm not sure. That's certainly the way that most everyone there reacted to me.

Bill Hutt shook his head low and looked like he wanted to spit sorrowfully, but he did not take his hat off.

"Naw," he said, just like that. He said, "Easy, I learned a long time ago that there's only so much you can help a person that don't want to be helped. In the end, you have to know that the good Lord will provide. You can raise your kiddies the right way, the way you see fit, but He knows all and He sees all. You don't get to know more than Him. You have to trust that He don't make mistakes."

I nodded. It was weird in the way it's always weird when a basically malevolent person starts talking about religion to you, the way you expect their shadows to show horns and a triangle-y tail. Like that movie *Night of the Hunter* where Robert Mitchum's evil reverend quotes Bible verses to his stepkids when what he really wants is to slit their little throats. We had a copy of the *Night of the Hunter* book, an old paperback with yellowed pages and an original price tag of thirty cents, in our bookcase back in the old house on Castro street when my dads were still together. I opened it once and flipped through the stiff, bad-smelling pages and found two small pictures cut down into squares from larger pictures. One was of a woman's round ass as she bent over, the other of a woman's massive breasts. These were from actual photos, not a magazine. In the ass-shot I recognized our living room sofa as the sofa the woman was bending over. It was this weird, corduroy but not quite corduroy material, gold-colored with white and brown swirling flowers—we'd had it for years. I remember thinking maybe whoever owned the sofa before us had also owned the book, and that's when you know your denial is pretty bad, when there's a part of your brain that thinks the other parts of your brain are idiots.

Bill Hutt offered me the flat of cans of soup in his trunk, the idea of which made my stomach turn. Old man soup, possibly navy bean, in the trunk of a blazing hot old man car for maybe *hundreds* of years. The cats inside me revolted.

"No, thanks," I said, waving, and when he was far enough down the road, I looked at Harrison and the kids and said, "what the eff was that?"

"He talked about offering you that soup the whole ride down," said Sabrina, almost sadly. "The. Whole. Damn. Ride."

That was around the time when I figured out that she and I would be friends.

JOAN STAYED IN THE HATCH FOR TWO WEEKS, AND THEN SHE WAS OUT FOR about twenty minutes and went back in for two weeks. In that time I drove Sabrina to see her three times, and was the one that picked her up when she was discharged for twenty minutes. I signed for her, got her outside and into the car, and before my belt was buckled she was asking for water. I went back into the hospital to fill a plastic cup at the bubbler and when I turned around she was right there, clutching her handbag.

"I think they didn't leave me in long enough," she said, like she was a pan of brownies or something, still unset in the middle.

THE TIMES I BROUGHT SABBY TO SEE HER MOTHER WERE THE HARDEST, because she didn't want to go and I'd have to sweeten the deal in some way. Starbucks and Hot Topic, all the sorts of places we had to leave Troubadour to visit. Bright, paint-colored tight pants cut close to the leg with hanging silver chains. And of course a phone, cutting edge to the point of being instantly obsolete. We met in the middle when it came to food, me being a woman pregnant with twins and she being a teenager. We ate things of all manner, sloppily anointed with cheese. Melty, highly questionable foods. Crispy things that stained their wrappers with spots of clarity.

"Mom says I'll never get rid of my muffin top this way," she said once, with equal parts self-deprecation and irritation.

"You don't have a fucking muffin top," I said.

"That's not how she sees it. Muffin top is her favorite thing to say, that and baby-fat. I was like, 'mom this is how girls get eating disorders,' and she was like, 'oh, ha-ha, el-oh-el! You know I love you!'"

"Well, she does love you," I said, because it felt like I was supposed to say it. It was pretty awkward, still, like when your mail carrier tries to talk to you about anything other than mail.

"Well, yeah, obviously, I guess." I admired that about her, her ability to get several thoughts into one breath. It seemed super time-effective. She was a teen; she didn't have a moment to spare.

Generally, the number of gifts or places we'd go was in direct correlation with how much time Sabrina would agree to spend with her mother. And I'm no fancy big-time lawyer, but I believe that's what is known as bribery. At first it seemed uncouth to mention, but finally I said, "Yeah, so, you're angry with your mom, or whatever," and her face and hands and shoulders did a million things before she finally answered.

"I'm not . . . mad. It's just the whole drama of it that I can't deal with. It's just . . . okay, there's nothing fun about being a kid, there is so little that is fun when you are a kid, and I can't even have that. The goofing off. The laying around and hanging out with my friends and whatever. There's never any time where I can just do nothing. I love Jamie . . . I love him so much, don't get me wrong, but if I wanted a kid when I was fifteen, I would have just gone out and gotten pregnant." Then she pulled down the visor mirror and smudged the liner under her eyes with her finger.

"I should probably say some stuff about how hard it's been for your mother over the past few months." Actually, this was a thing that her father should have been saying to her. I understood that, Sab understood that, Sally understood that. Everyone understood it but Harrison, who could not be around Joan for more than two minutes without going off on some tangent. It was better this way, he explained, for me to take the lead. He explained that it was better for everyone.

"Right, of course," said Sabrina. "But even before that. Just disarray. Just everyone else is the victim."

"Well, it's hard for her."

"You don't have to do this," she said. "I don't blame you. I'm not mad at you."

"Well, that's . . . good to know," I said.

"I like you, you're cool. You don't get in my face."

"I do try to not get in people's faces. I really make an effort."

"It's good; you're a good stepmom. I could tell you stories that would curl your hair about stepmoms."

"Jesus, really?"

"Oh my god. Just . . . evilness."

"Wicked."

"YES. Yes, exactly."

I would wait in the car for Sabby when she visited her mom if it wasn't too hot, and when it did get too hot I would wait in the waiting room with the sad people who couldn't understand why this was happening to them. The sad people would try to have conversations with me, and when that would happen I would wish that I'd stayed in the car even if the car had been fucking on fire. They glommed onto me I guess because I was so obviously pregnant and that meant that I was either angelic or pitiful. The people there tended to decide for me. Actually, I was just really hot, or I had to go to the bathroom.

"That's a lovely dress," a woman in the waiting room once commented. The hair she had left was dyed a brown blood color and combed across her scalp hard, clinging like fantastic plants from under the sea.

"Oh, thank you," I said. "It's from Old Navy."

"My brother was in the navy."

"No, the store," I said, and the woman's eyes became shocked and small, as though I'd spoken against the navy in some way.

"He died in '99."

"Oh, I'm sorry."

"That's what this place does to you. The nurses steal, everyone steals. They wanted to know why I cried on Halloween when the chocolate was gone from my bed. They said they would give me more but I said, 'that's not the point.' The point is that if someone says that chocolate will be waiting for you on your bed at a certain time and it's not, that person has LIED to you. Even if it was stolen. A person has their WORD, and that's all that they have."

"Yes," I said, terrified. There was an anger in her that seemed really ready to explode into something bigger, something hard to contain. Ever since my father was hit by a car, I've expected huge, violent, sudden acts—like, one minute you're crossing the street and one minute you're under a car suddenly. I don't know what that is, some evolutionary offshoot maybe, some healthy fear left over by some caveman relative who assumed the moon was a big, evil fireball bent on destruction. Which is not too much to ask, honestly. Fucking fish know where and how to swim to their place of birth to spawn and die, and humans won't get out of an elevator filled with ax murderers because they're afraid of hurting the ax murderers' feelings. The babies had made me more willing to kill people, that was for damn sure. I'd have taken that crazy old bald woman down, if I'd had to. Luckily for both of us it didn't come to that.

"You just wait to die," said the woman, and in my hypersensitive state I looked at this woman's remaining hair and thought, *dye?!*

"There's no difference between this and an old folks home!" she said, and I didn't really know who she was striking out against worse, old folks homes or mental institutions.

"Well, I hope it works out better for you this time," I said, too cheerfully, and Sab came stomping sullenly out into the waiting room. She was still pissed that she couldn't bring her phone into her mother's room (Cell? Quarters?) but I was secretly glad that her contraband had been confiscated by The Man. I had this awful, shuddering image of her texting calmly as her mother wept and wept in her blue crazy pajamas. Sabrina stopped dead in front of me, her eyes tearless and angry.

"She asked me if I thought you were prettier than her," she said. "I said, 'what do you think?'"

The almost bald woman and I looked back at her, aghast.

"What?" said Sabrina. "Was that bad?"

I left her at the house when I went to pick Joan up the second time; Sabrina and I were both happy with this decision, and Joan didn't question it. I signed the same papers I'd signed the first time; they checked my purse the same way. The same woman complimented me for the second time about the same silver-dollar-sized compact from Estée Lauder. But this time Joan seemed calmer. She squinted in the sunlight like a woman off death row.

"Nice day," she said.

Weed is something like a hundred-thirty miles from Troubadour; it was a hot, long, pee-break-filled drive to the coast. Joan ate fried fish strips from Long John Silver's and kept commenting that she hadn't worn a belt in a really long time. She seemed thinner and quieter, and she kept saying things suddenly but acting as though we'd already been talking about them.

"It's just such an *unsafe* world for children. You can't get used to it, especially after you have kids. I think the strangest thing for me was going to work at a dentist's office sometime after 9/11 and realizing that the World Trade Center was just like a big office park. Just dentists and lawyers and people like me, with families, trying to sell magazine subscriptions to pay the rent. Before that I thought it was like the Pentagon. Just government or army people. People who were trained in battle. Isn't that crazy?"

"Yeah," I said. When I watched the first tower collapsing, I assumed that every person who'd been in the building had already been escorted safely from the building through a fire escape, in a neat, single file line. I assumed there was a person whose job it was to lead them. Then I called Victoria's Secret and ordered two holiday-themed Miracle Bras, one in Poinsettia and the other in Gold.

"Where is my husband this fine afternoon? I didn't really think he'd show up with flowers, and yet . . . making you do his dirty work seems pretty cowardly."

"He's home," I said, too abruptly. I was wondering which was worse: hearing him called *coward* or *husband*. "And, I'm not doing anyone's dirty work. This is fine, this is normal. You and I have a good rapport, or, we are starting to. It's a good thing to work on—our rapport."

"Ha," said Joan, just the word *ha*, like that. "You need to work on your improv. By chance, I caught an episode of your . . . program the other night. It was on in the TV room but then someone turned it off because of what you were wearing."

"Which episode was it?"

"I don't know, something about strippers who were also vampires."

"Oh, Vampire Strippers, sure. I didn't wear a hell of a lot in that one."

"No. It made the patients uncomfortable. We watched *Growing Pains*, instead."

"Did Alan Thicke keep his clothes on?"

"For the most part," said Joan.

She asked me if I wanted to hear how she and Harrison met. I am able to make a sound like a shudder without actually really shuddering. I would make an excellent TV dad, I think, with that sound I can make.

"It's non-sexual," said Joan, and I made the sound again.

"I didn't really think it would be," I said. What sort of meeting is sexual, other than the ones that are?

"We were in college. I liked him; he was very cool to me. I was not his type, but I knew his type—I was friends with a girl he liked. So I convinced him to go out with me to make her jealous, knowing that she already had a boyfriend who was in the army. It was a big scam. I thought myself so clever. But then what I got out of it was a thing of convenience, nothing passionate or real."

"He didn't have to fuck you," I said, and it was shocking, a shocking thing to say, even to me.

"What can you say about nineteen-year-old boys? They like to fuck. My vagina just got in the way between his cock and some other vagina."

She made me stop at a gas station then and she got corn nuts, the BBQ kind. She came back to the car with the corn nuts and a gigantic blue slush for me.

"There's no caffeine in it," she said, and I thanked her. The cup was roughly the size of two stomachs. My cup holder could not handle its girth at any point so I held it awkwardly between my legs like a frozen radar gun or vibrator.

"You need liquids," said Joan. "You need a lot of liquids."

N

I WANTED TO EXPLAIN TO JOAN HOW EVERY MOMENT OF MY LIFE IS
being Wilford Brimley in *The Thing*, in the part where he knows that
all human life will be wiped out by the Thing but he doesn't tell the
others because they couldn't handle it. I am all about everyone else
adhering to the status quo, honestly. Why torture people with reality?
Just let them talk on their phones and buy new phones and be happy,
is what I think. I could tell her anything, so I told her about the children's book that my manager Sally Balls had written and published a
few years prior; the name of it was *Stealie: The Ghost That Steals*.
She'd gotten the idea from moving into her new house in Portland;
every time she had work done on the place her prescription shit went
missing from the medicine cabinet. This also happened whenever her
daughter spent the night. Ghosts.

"God, did you call her on it?" asked Joan.

"It was like performance art," I said, "so I didn't want to ruin
the flow."

Some people, I think, are in your life to be weird. They are
the nutty sitcom neighbors, rushing in to borrow peanut butter and
tell you about the two Swedish exchange students they banged the
night before. The Great Gatsbys of the universe, Tad Allagash-ing
around to give your existence some difference, like paprika.

"Once she got super-high and thought she wrote this amazing
country music and it turned out to be all Kid Rock songs," I said.

"She sounds like a real character," said Joan, and it occurred
to me that I really didn't have another word to describe Sally, and I
was both sad and grateful for that at the same time.

I noticed that as we got closer to Weed, Joan seemed to get
more fidgety. She picked her teeth in the visor mirror a lot and said
"oh" and "well" a lot, but not together. I asked her if she was okay.
I had more Sally Balls stories. I had nothing but Sally Balls stories.

"Do you have a good relationship with your father?" she
asked.

"Which one?"

"Your father."

"I have two." I said, and then to cut off the whole *your actual father not your stepfather/I have two fathers/how does that work/they are gay/you don't have a mother?/she may be Adrienne Barbeau* conversation. "I was adopted by two gay men when I was a baby."

"Oh. Wow."

"Yeah, sorry to just stick that in there when it brings up a whole other topic than the one you wanted to talk about, I just didn't know any other way."

"Oh, that's fine. Don't be sorry."

"I have fine relationships with both of them."

"Well! It really says something to those in-defense-of-marriage people to have a gay couple raise a child and be together for so long," said Joan.

"They divorced when I was a teenager," I said. "One of them accepted he wasn't gay and married a woman; the other one ate himself to death a few years ago."

She was quiet for a long while and when I looked at her she was obviously stuck between being horrified and not knowing what to say. I have that effect on people. I always forget that the crazy shit of my life is still crazy to people who aren't already bored of it.

"I don't have a great relationship with my father," she said finally, trying again.

"He seems like an acquired taste."

"I'm just so used to disappointing him. I feel like he would be disappointed if I stopped disappointing him."

"He tried to give us soup."

"Oh, sure. He's a giver. To everyone else. It's like *The Jazz Singer*, only I'm not good at anything."

"That's rough."

"A girl needs a good relationship with her father."

"That's what they say."

"Maybe if I'd been good enough for that soup-giving bastard just once I wouldn't have had to trick some dirty bastard into dating me," said Joan, and the tears and snot just sort of exploded out of her, a flash flood of weeps.

"There sure are a lot of Carl's Jr.'s on this road," I said.

"I make you uncomfortable," said Joan, when she was able. Her nose was running a lot; I half expected her to hone her Kleenex into a point and just jam it up one of her nostrils the way you do when you have a nosebleed.

"You don't make me anything," I said. By then I had accepted her blurts as sort of a preemptive strike against meanness, sort of like the fat girl from my high school who was always telling the story of shitting her pants during the school-wide fun run for cancer. There was a weak power in that, a power with too much milk and not enough salt, in telling everyone your worst thing before they could make fun of you. But my understanding of that didn't make it any easier to think of things to say to Joan. And there really were a lot of Carl's Jr.'s on that road.

"Well, I wouldn't blame you for being uncomfortable, if you were uncomfortable. That was a whole other thing. They put me on some pills and there was this whole conversation about taking them and them causing certain birth defects and I just hadn't come to terms with the fact that there would be no more children with Harrison. That there will be no more children with him. Even now. Even now part of me wants to not take the pills, because Harrison could climb through my window at night and make love to me and get me pregnant. It could happen tonight. And then maybe our baby would have some kind of birth defect."

"I would probably still take them," I said, "just for the hell of it."

"I know that. But I don't know it in *here*."

"Well, that's valid. It's a pretty bizarre time for all of us."

"Yes," said Joan, "I often wonder if I will hate your babies."

"Oh, God."

"I do. I wonder if I will see them and hate them, or if I will love them because they are part of my own children. It's not true hate, of course, it's jealousy and hurt feelings. But it's so soon. If this were three or five years down the line I feel like I would be more generous. Or maybe not. Maybe I'll be dead in three or five years. I have no idea, but I'm of no threat. I wouldn't hurt anyone. I wouldn't hurt a baby, ever."

"I'm a little uncomfortable right now," I said.

HER MOM AND DAD LIVED IN A CUTE, CALIFORNIA-Y HOUSE, NOT UNLIKE my own. The front steps were covered by a ramp, though, and that ramp and the rest of the porch were covered in the greenest of green AstroTurf. The whole scene was that of someone or some ones who started a lot of things and then forgot about them, a weary mixture of Christmas and Halloween decorations and American flags. The side yard was littered with the corn carcasses of many moons past, bent and decaying like some hellish jungle gym. It was how my brain felt, that house, lumped together and condemned.

"That was my room," said Joan, still in the car, pointing at a small front window. "Is my room."

We'd been sitting there for a while that felt like a very long while. I had to pee. I had to pee in the way that felt as though all of my body were a water balloon that was constantly being injected with more water. Before I got pregnant I don't think I understood having to pee, the way religious people don't understand pure love until they know God, or whatever it is that they say. Being pregnant was a crash course in urination.

"Do you know that they still have the same shower curtain from when I left for college?"

"That seems unsanitary."

"No, she takes it down every week and sterilizes it in bleach. My mom. It used to be clear with a big Mickey Mouse in the center. Now it's just clear."

I thought to say something about how twenty years of bleach and rags probably evened out with buying a shower curtain every year, but I didn't, nor did I say the thing about her mother's technique only being successful if a person's time was worth nothing to them. I had a lot of valid points to make about shower curtains but I didn't want to make the conversation go any longer than it had to.

"She wiped that mouse away," said Joan.

Her dad came out then and stood on the porch looking at us, leaning on a pillar like he should be smoking or looking off into the distance or both. He did a little half wave. His shirt was off; he had an upside down triangle superhero emblem of chest hair and flappy little breasts.

"Well?" I said, and Joan nodded. We opened our car doors at the same time like private eyes.

I PEED AND EXPERIENCED THE UN-MICKEY SHOWER CURTAIN, AND THEN Joan showed me her room. There was still a portable crib there and a sleeping bag rolled and leaning against the closet door. Joan's sheets had Winnie the Pooh on them. Then her dad stuck his head into the room and asked me if I wanted to sit down. He'd asked me like twelve times already. Joan's mom stayed in the living room, where she sat with her hands folded in her lap. She was very quiet and no-eye-contact-y, like the Vera in the movie *Alice Doesn't Live Here Anymore*, not like the Vera in the show *Alice*, who tap danced and married a police officer. Joan apologized for her mother, which was when I started to figure out that she was only acting like retarded Vera because she disapproved of me, not because of nature. After that Joan wanted to show me the rest of the house and I apologized and said I had to get back for work, which was a lie. All my work shit had been over the phone as of late, as viewers were having a hard time masturbating to a woman who was pregnant with twins. (In my defense, though, the ones who could masturbate to it, masturbated HARD to it.) Anyway, the writers ditched the *who impregnated Lola?* storyline and instead just had characters calling Lola, and my voice would appear over a picture of me from when I was hot and un-pregnant. I had no ethical problems with this, seeing as I was paid exactly the same salary for sitting on my ass and eating a tub of organic frosting. It was similar to the situation Suzanne Somers had with *Three's Company* during her contract negations. Then she got too expensive and was replaced by some other random blonde.

But Joan just didn't want me to leave her alone with her parents. Being locked up in the hatch was easier, she said.

"I just don't know how long I can last here," she said.

"Just don't take any shit off them," I said.

"Yes. Says the woman with a loving relationship and one dead parent and another parent in another state."

"I'm getting pretty uncomfortable again."

"Yes. That was unkind. I am not meaning to be unkind, but sometimes it just sort of rears up inside of me like a wave. It's just there suddenly, ruining everyone's sand castles."

There was a mirror on the back of her bedroom door, scrawled with eyeliner and lipstick. Just all kinds of doodles, like the margin of a teenager's address book. I guess a teen from the thirties, maybe. I haven't seen a kid with an actual address book for a while, if ever. Big wide eyes with fat teardrops. Fat lips. Houses with little curls of smoke coming from the chimney. Seeing it all at once, seeing everything all at once, made me feel as though my eyeballs were about to collapse.

On my way out, Joan's mom and dad had a weird fight over the obvious fact that Joan's mom did not want to say goodbye to me. It was this bustling, gruff fight, a Beetle Bailey sort of fight where it's just this great big spinning dust ball with fists and swear symbols coming out of it.

"I miss the kids," said Joan, her first and last mention of them during the whole of our road trip. "And Harrison."

"They're all good, and they're all around. You can call anytime, or visit."

"Really?"

"Yes, it's fine."

"You're a generally very kind person," she said, "but I know that none of them really wants to see me, not even the baby. Babies sense crazy. It makes them very uncomfortable."

"Well, it's not okay to just fucking check out," I said. "When those kids are old enough they'll figure that they should have done something to save you, and they'll torture themselves over it."

"Maybe they *should* be doing something," said Joan, and it was one of those times when some awesome line like *you make me want to vomit* would have been so apropos. But in the end I just said goodbye to her, and drove away.

14.

I AM A PERSON WHO GETS CALLS IN THE DEAD OF NIGHT. I AM ALWAYS beneath covers hearing some terrible news. I am never knowing where I am, who I'm with, how old I am as someone blurts out their loud, terrible truth. I have come to accept that I am a last resort for people in most cases, and that's comforting and discomfiting, concurrently. I am a person for whom people reach from their darkest depths, but there are a hell of a lot of idiots in front of me who had to say no first.

Joan made a call like this. Her still-husband answered and she asked for me, which was fine because Harrison didn't recognize her voice. She was not at her parents' house, she said. She was calling from a phone at a diner. Not a phone booth. She went off on a small side-rant about how there aren't any phone booths left in America and how that was affecting the popular culture. Sometimes you just had to be in a phone booth wearing a long overcoat and having a life-changing phone call as the rain outside beat against the glass, she said. The lady behind the counter had taken pity on her and let her use the phone. I was not surprised by that. Joan was at a point in her life where it was impossible not to take pity on her. She was like a lost puppy in a phone booth in the rain. In London.

"I can't stay here any longer," she said. "I'm losing my mind here."

"Well, they probably won't let you," I said, assuming, in my half-sleeping state, that she was saying that the kind diner lady who'd offered her the phone would not let her stay. Names of things washed up and drew back. The babies kicked and fought.

"What?" said Joan. "No, they don't care. They want me here so they can break my brain. They are old, they have no other hobbies. They can't control me. They can't . . . I'm forty-three, okay? They can't put that whole 'my roof, my rules' on me. I'm a mother. How are they? How are the babies?"

"Moving around a lot."

"What? They're still up?"

"No, no. I thought you meant the babies inside of me."

"Oh. No."

"What the EFF?" said Harrison. He'd stopped saying fuck since the kiddies arrived. It was a small contribution that he seemed super proud of.

"They're great," I said.

"Oh," said Joan, but more sadly. It made me wish that I'd said okay or fine or good, some mild, less offensive downgrade.

"Jesus, who is it?" said Harrison. He flicked on the bedside lamp and we both hissed and squinted like bats. I mouthed JOAN and he said "JOAN?!" aloud. I nodded while trying to also shush him, hands fluttering to and away from my mouth frantically, attracted and repulsed, like a bug to a light bulb.

"Don't put him on," said Joan, "I can't talk to him."

"I don't think that will be a problem," I said. Harrison poked me in the upper arm and said, "WHAT. DOES. SHE. WANT?" in the loudest and slowest of failed stage whispers. I in turn popped my eyes at him and shook my head and shrugged while still trying to shush him. It was like bad mime school in that bed. We might as well have just screamed in one another's faces.

"I don't want ANYTHING," said Joan, as though she were speaking directly to Harrison, then, to me, "Tell him I don't want ANYTHING."

But, she did want something, and Harrison and I both knew it, no matter how artfully we would try to wriggle out of it. She didn't want for me to call her parents and try to reason with them. She didn't want to go back to the hospital. She didn't want an all-expense-paid trip to the Florida Everglades with a Jet Ski and a vibrating chair filled with cash and prizes. She wanted to stay with us. And the kids. In our house. For as long as it took for her to not want that anymore.

"I wasn't always like this," said Joan, and her voice was getting that certain sound to it—aging Broadway star reflects on life, all powder and crow's feet and tipped back dangerously in a director's chair. "I was young and strong, I ran around braless. That was a reality to me: the sun in my face, and me so wild and unfettered."

I looked at Harrison, who was now playing *Tetris* on his phone, and covered the receiver with my hand, "She's doing this whole thing about being young and braless."

"Is she drunk?"

"I don't think so," I said. I had these images of her perched on a stool at the long, lit counter of the diner—maybe the diner from *Nighthawks*—going on and on as the waitress gave her the side-eye. The waitress would be chewing gum, maybe drying a glass.

"I don't know if there's really a way out of this," I said.

"Fuck her."

"She's the mother of your kids."

"She has a perfectly good place to go, it's just not ideal. So t.s. She can get a job and find a place of her own and keep a garden and then go be crazy in that garden."

"She's sick."

"So am I. And my wife is pregnant with twins."

We stopped for a minute and stared at each other. In my ear, Joan had turned the topic to pineapple soda and how she hated it and how her mom kept buying it specifically because she hated it.

"I'm talking to your wife," I said.

"Yes, well, that's a temporary thing," said Harrison. "I won't be married to her forever. We'll divorce eventually. I guess when she's not crazy anymore."

"And then?"

"What is this? And then I don't know. You and me will still be together. I mean, I want to be together with you. In that way."

I looked at him some more. Joan was still on the soda.

"It's not a proposal," said Harrison. "It's not. I can't even say that I'm brave enough to propose to you right now. What if you said no?"

"I don't know. I'm pretty sure I wouldn't say no."

"Well," said Harrison. He put his phone down but he didn't do anything else. I'll admit I was surprised that he put his phone down. He really liked *Tetris*.

"So you are asking?"

"I . . . yes. I would like to marry you after I'm done being married to crazy Joan. But I will admit that I have no idea how you even divorce a crazy person. And I feel weird proposing to someone else while I'm still married to a crazy person. The whole thing is pretty discouraging, actually. But I feel like you and I are married, in all of the ways that people cherish marriage. Not the awful, resentment-filled ways. But yes, if you're asking if I'm asking, I'm asking."

"Yes," I said. It was a moment before I realized that the other end of the phone had gone still.

"Jesus," said Joan.

And after that I think a lot of the decision was based on obligation, not so much from Harrison but from me. The wife of the man I was dating had heard his half-assed marriage proposal to me while he was still very technically married to her. What happens after that? Chainsaw enema? Of course sitting there in my bed with my belly doing gymnastics, next to the man who put the tumbling babies there in the first place, talking to a forty-three-year-old woman who couldn't reconcile her relationship with her mother's pineapple soda, I could see the cautionary tale of being married to Harrison. It was hard to forget his trespasses, not to mention my own, with her shuttling back and forth into our lives like the ghosts of Christmas past and future combined. It was hard to not see myself in her, in her oh-in-a-hundred-years-no-one-will-give-a-fuck attitude and her sudden, heartfelt testimonials. Perhaps if something that I thought would last forever ended I would end up the same way, telling people at the bus stop, at any bus stop, that I'd once pretended to be a giant space princess in a tube top, and now I couldn't remember the words to any songs. Taking Joan in was like tipping karma at the door, I guess. It meant I could be a whore but a good person, and after a while maybe the whore part would fade, fade the way my angel wing tramp stamp might fade, and I would just be a nice wife in a nice house, being nice.

15.

I SPENT MY EIGHTH MONTH OF PREGNANCY, QUITE THE SIZE OF AN RV, on occasional bed rest. The babies, whose size and subsequent lack of space made them lackadaisical as sea lions, had nothing better to do than find uncomfortable places to wedge themselves. They fought like fat tabbies in a heat wave, unfocused slaps and pokes that transformed seamlessly into sleep. I spent my upright hours waddling back and forth to the grocery store, eager to upholster my nest with items that the babies really had no use for, like paper towels. We had a closet just for toilet paper, stacked up neatly and painstakingly like a wall constructed by the Three Pigs' hoarding, incontinent older sister.

"You're like that anorexic from that movie, the one who kept chickens under her bed and then died," Sabby had told me weeks prior on a run to Costco for Comet.

"What movie?" I asked, and then, "she died from the chickens under the bed?"

"No, she died because Angelina Jolie talked her into killing herself. *Girl, Interrupted*. That was the movie."

"I don't see the connection."

"Oh," said Sabby, "just crazy people not being able to live without things."

"You think I'm crazy because we need paper towels?"

"No. I don't care that much, honestly, I was just making conversation."

Joan had been a hoarder. I knew this because of the time Harrison and I were watching the show *Hoarders*, and he'd said, "yeah, Joan was a hoarder."

It was a small thing that, at the time, made me feel pretty good about myself. I asked him to explain in detail but he kind of shrugged it off once it was out. She's kept it under wraps, he said. I liked the image of Joan, whom at that point I had yet to meet, as some obese, flabby-armed woman sitting in a ketchup-stained recliner surrounded by the wrappers of old Whoppers and the randomest of shit, like old fan blades and shopping bags filled with Diet Coke bottle caps. He said it hadn't been like that. It was just that once a thing had been useful, like a stroller or a pair of shoes, she couldn't part with them. It wasn't what I'd hoped for, but it was better than nothing in the sad way that most things are better than nothing.

In any event, it pleased me that Sabby was more likely to associate me with a crazy movie character than her crazy mother. I, too, liberally enjoyed the resentment she had for her mother, even after meeting Joan in person, although I recognized it as a really shitty, self-serving addiction, and also an unavoidable one. It would have been lying to myself to say that Sabby seeing me as a younger, cooler alternative to her mother didn't also make me feel young and cool. It was like that time in the MoMA when I could see the reflection of myself sitting on the toilet in the aluminum stall door and I accepted staring at myself, because I looked really good. It has always been hard for me to turn down a compliment from the universe, even a backhanded one.

Telling Sabrina that her mom was coming to live with us was the first time I'd ever seen her mad, at least mad at me. She kept asking me why I had to go and ruin a perfectly excellent situation, innately understanding that her father was just along for the ride on this one. I tried on a kind stepmom voice and told her that she would understand someday. I actually said this a couple of times and would have gone for more had she not called me on it. Then I caved and admitted that I was covering my ass to the universe to some extent. Sabby did that thing that really small kids do when they puff out their lower lips and blow their bangs up like a skirt.

"You're better than that," she said.

"Yeah, I'm not sure that I am."

"Look, if this is some shit about you being a homewrecker,

I don't care. Jamie doesn't care. Dad doesn't care. This is like, you trying to convince the rest of the women in the world that you're still okay."

"I really don't know what it's about," I said, thinking that what it was about was probably the thing she'd just said it was, offhanded as blowing her bangs, "I just know that the mother of my fiancé's kids deserves a little respect."

"Oh, fuck that. I was planning on calling you mom when school started in this year, anyway."

"Oh?"

"Of course. No one here knows me. And it's okay to feel good about it, so you don't have to tell me that it's unfair to my actual mom."

"Is it okay for me to be in some way delighted?" I asked.

"I just want you to be ready for when she comes here. It won't be like you think it will, with love and understanding and all that. It will be awful awkward days and awkward, awful nights. You just have no idea."

I guess I felt challenged by this. At that time I had a real *Extreme Makeover: Home Edition* outlook on things—I couldn't understand what terrible situation would not be bettered in some significant way by a little drywall and a big reveal, or whatever the therapy-based equivalent to that was. Walls would be broken down; people would fall into one another's arms. I knew this to be true because I had seen it with my own eyes. A failed marriage was not cancer, it was not a brain tumor, it was not dealing with the loss of a child in Afghanistan. Easy-peasy, for most people.

WE WENT SHOPPING TOGETHER, SAB AND I, TO GET STUFF FOR JOAN'S room. I guess I'd thought that it would be a good way for her to bond with her mother even though her mother was not there. Maybe she'd remain a real teenaged badass until she saw a snow globe, or something, and then all her childhood dreams of having a magical relationship with her birth mother would come flooding in and she'd break down and run into her mother's arms as soon as we got home.

I don't know why that seemed like an important thing. I guess TV had effed me to the point where I had some basic understanding that a girl couldn't be happy without being able to enroll in a book club or a salsa dance class with her mother, much in the same way that a boy couldn't be happy unless he and his father were constantly throwing a ball back and forth. They would throw that ball for hours on end, until the skin of their hands chapped and bled, until their fingers cramped into painful claws of carpal tunnel, just so long as they were together. In the end, though, Sabby had no desire to light upon a snow globe and feel real feelings.

At Charles Caraway's she pointed to things impatiently, and made crazy faces when I questioned her choices—such as maybe her mother didn't really want bunk beds, or Oregon Ducks sheets. She wanted to go hang out in the skin care and makeup aisles, and so did I, but that seemed somewhat unsaintly. I always bought her a ton of shit because we had a ton of money and because I knew that I owed it to her on some level. She called me on it sometimes. She would say things like, "look, if you never buy me another thing, I'd still like you, so you can relax, okay?" And I would laugh and not believe her. The buying helped us both in some way; she liked getting stuff and I liked feeling not guilty.

"I smoke now," said Sabby, pointing to a pink lamp, the base of which was crossed ballet shoes.

"I don't think so," I said, and then, "really?"

"I don't know which thing you're referring to with which comment."

"*I don't think so* was about the lamp. Unless your mom is into that."

"She's not into anything. She's into ruining holidays and blaming."

"Huh. Then I guess we're in the wrong aisle."

"You don't care that I smoke now?"

"Um . . . well, it doesn't shock me. How old are you? Fifteen?"

"Yeah."

"Yeah, so, no, I guess that I don't care. I don't know how your father might feel about that," I added, wondering if one might have stronger feelings had they contributed in the making of the smoker's lungs. I thought for a moment how I would feel if the babies smoked and I couldn't get too upset about it. It didn't help that I pictured them smoking as infants, wearing little suits and sitting at a bus stop.

"I'd prefer you didn't smoke around me right now, or, like, blow it in the babies' faces when they're born, just as a favor to me."

"Who does that?" asked Sabby, and I shrugged. "No offense, but you are so paranoid about being fucking pregnant."

"I know. I can't help it. It's a lot of pressure, especially on the bladder."

"Gross. People have babies all the time, in third world countries, during wars. You smelling some smoke isn't going to make those kids retarded, or anything."

"Jesus. Can I just have this for the next couple of months? Then you can put your fucking butts out on my face if you want."

"Yes," said Sabby, and laughed.

We found a good bed, a queen-sized one with a mattress that was so expensive it made me do a genuine double-take at the price tag.

"That was awesome," said Sabrina. "The fact that it was a dangling price tag really took it to another level."

"That's right," I said, "A lot of people wouldn't have understood why that was funny, just that it was funny."

Sabrina flushed and shrugged.

We bought the bed and a few pieces that matched the headboard, a set of drawers and two night tables, and some pillows and some blankets in neutral colors that implied nothing, like white walls. Sabby picked out the sheets, finally—sheets in a t-shirt fabric, light blue with white clouds.

"So her crazy ass can just float away," she said, a bit wistfully.

"It'll be okay," I said once we were safely rooted in cosmetics. "Nothing bad is happening."

"I just don't want her to come and take us back to her parents, or come and get better and get a place and try to make us live there."

"If she got better, maybe that wouldn't be such a bad thing, though."

"She will only ever get better enough to fool other people. Her insides will still be what they are. She'll still be angry, and she'll still hate her father and dad and all men and me," said Sabrina. "Can I have this?"

She held up a big jar of apricot scrub.

"Of course," I said.

"Thanks. And, besides, Jamie and I are good where we are, with you guys. We love you guys."

"And we love you."

"Is this color too trashy?" asked Sabby, pointing to a lipstick that was a shade somewhere between black and Joan Crawford's blood.

"Yep."

"Can I have it?"

"Only if you get the nail polish, too," I said, "and throw in some pore strips for me."

"Gross," said Sabrina.

"Oh, honey," I said, "you have no idea."

I HAD TERRIBLE DREAMS, DREAMS IN WHICH I WOULD WAKE AND KNOW that someone was in the house, and that this person knew where I was. Sometimes I would dream that there was a sort of scheduled break-in, and then in my dream I would sleep through it and then I would hear the window creaking open and I still couldn't wake up. In all of these dreams I was by myself; Sab and Jamie were gone. Harrison was gone. I was huge and pregnant and defenseless in these dreams, and someone strange was in my house at night, and coming to find me.

16.

I PICKED JOAN UP FROM HER FOLKS' PLACE. IT WAS LATE AND I'D rented a U-Haul and that was late too, but it was not the time in my life where I cared about paying fees on late U-Hauls. I could've bought it. I repeated that to myself a few times aloud during the drive up, "I could afford to buy this U-Haul. I could own this U-Haul." It represented some echelon of accomplishment to me. How many people had I known in my life, honestly, who could afford a U-Haul?

All Joan's stuff was lined up in front of the house when I drove up, and she was out there too, sitting on a trunk like *Annie* or something. It was very strange. It made me feel as though something were lodged in my brain and it wouldn't swallow down so it stayed there, uncomfortable and dangerous, like it could go at anytime. That was the first minute that I'd felt like everything was too much, and I was sorry that we'd invited her to stay with us.

THERE IS SOMETHING VERY COMFORTING, LET ME SAY, ABOUT NOT HAVING a mother. When you have no mother, suddenly the world is your mother—every hot-ass on the street, every congresswoman, all the ballerinas of the universe. You have this feeling as though someone great gave you up so that you too could be great, because, certainly, things have to mean things. Certainly, your true mother could not be a struggling college student who sold her eggs to avoid stripping. I am not sure what that is called, the phenomenon that makes people automatically assume that they're more special than everyone else, but I do personally blame the movie *The Matrix*. Not everyone can be THE

ONE, but everyone can think they are. Pure escapism. And I myself am not above this.

I used the can at Joan's folks' place again; the only soap this time was a melted down old soap crayon, a pale green-brown the shade of lightly moldering things, tiles or tennis shoes or fresh corpses. I didn't dry my hands because there was a stain of some sort on the available hand towel, a reddish stain. It appeared to be more of the spaghetti sauce variety and not so much blood, but it felt like an un-wise choice. Perhaps the color of one's blood changed based on age or health. I knew that being pregnant had caused the volume of my own blood to increase by fifty percent. Blood was mysterious. I did not feel comfortable underestimating its abilities to camouflage itself as marinara sauce.

Joan's mother was not around this time. Joan made up some mild, lie-sounding excuse about her mother not feeling well and going to bed early, even though it was around three in the afternoon. There was middling furniture involved, even though I'd told her on the phone that we'd picked out new things.

"It's hard for me to be without my things," Joan explained, and then she made a face that was half-joking and half-shame, "I'm sure that you've heard about that to some extent. It gets worse when I feel worse, if that makes any sense. There are times when I just need my shit around me all the time, like when a kid will make a big fort in the living room out of blankets and chairs and they get in there and think that no one can see them. I mean sometimes, like when Harry was around, I could really be reined in; it didn't seem like that big of a deal. But now—well, not right now, but right after he left, it got to a point where I could not bring myself to throw away an ice cream sandwich wrapper. Sab had eaten an ice cream sandwich, and she went to toss it—and she couldn't because the garbage was so over flowing that it had tipped over onto the kitchen floor and mixed with actual non-garbage things that just happened to be on the floor. And I guess I freaked a little. Not proud of that. It happens, but I'm work-ing on it. I have a little book, the little book they give alcoholics. *One Day at a Time.* Because it's all an addiction. We're all on the same crooked path, it's just some of our paths are crooked-er."

The whole time she was speaking, she was lugging shit into the U-Haul, more stuff than furniture, Hefty bags filled and poking out dangerously and big printer paper boxes with signs taped on them. I saw BARBIES and BARBIE SHOES and X-FILES TAPES. I kept almost asking if I could help because I didn't know what to do with myself. I'd found that being pregnant was usually pretty good for that because you could always just rub your belly and people generally did not expect you to do anything else, but Joan had a hell of a lot more nervous fucking energy than most people. You couldn't just rub your belly and feel good about it. She made you feel like you should be rubbing your belly and cooking a roast and painting with watercolors, too. Like you needed to make a big nervous energy sponge with your body to sop some of her up.

"I don't know why I reacted that way. I mean, I guess I do logically, but that helps nothing. You're still crazy. Understanding what you're doing doesn't help unless you can get yourself to stop doing it. Just, in that moment, I was overcome by the uses of that ice cream sandwich wrapper. Like art projects, the way that some outsider artists will use non-traditional materials. Or, maybe it could be recycled in some way. Or, maybe that it would just be lonely where it was, in the garbage, eventually in the dump. That maybe incinerating it would hurt it. Do you know what that is like? To have guilt over ice cream sandwich wrappers? You can't live. I dare anyone to live that life. It's not a life for anyone."

"Can I have a glass of water?" I asked, and Joan moved too fast, as though I'd asked for a blood transfusion. She brought me a brown-hued glass filled with vaguely cloudy water, and I looked into it hard.

"It's just from the tap," she said, I guess because I was looking like I assumed it had come from the toilet, and I thanked her.

She started getting things into the U-Haul more quickly then, and even though I went round to the driver's seat and sat down with great sounds of pregnancy and exhaustion, she continued to make conversation with me, or, really, have a conversation with herself that was loud enough for me to overhear. The babies began leg-wrestling, a thing they enjoyed while in a car, perhaps spurred on by rumbling engines.

"When I was a kid?" said Joan, "a really small kid? I disliked flushing toilet paper down the toilet, even after I'd used it. So I must've been really young, just almost newly potty trained. I had it in my mind that flushing used toilet paper was cruel—it wasn't its fault it was used. I would hide it behind the toilet or in the clothes hamper, behind the bath powder and things on the shelf, the toiletries. And of course my mother finally called me on it and I was able to explain myself. Her reaction was fine, I guess, she didn't shame me. She told me that to keep these things around was dangerous because there were viruses, and these viruses could make the family very sick. So, I stopped eventually. After a while. But she probably should have taken me to the doctor because I was obviously developing human associations with objects, you know? There's such a thing as being too caring. It's too much when you can't sleep at night thinking about what happens to used toilet paper after you flush it. Of course we didn't know about these things back then, the signs of them. It would be immature of me to blame her. Even if she is obviously to blame on some level."

"Yeah," I said.

"What did you say?" asked Joan, "I didn't hear that."

"I said, 'yeah,'" I said, and tilted my forehead down to the steering wheel. I heard the back hatch of the U-Haul slam down vaguely, moments passed, and Joan was beside me.

Her dad came out at the last minute, just before we pulled out. He had that hat on. He was waving a big mayor's wave. He came to Joan's window and spoke past her to me.

"Getting big!" he said.

"Yes," I said.

"Twins!"

"Yep. Yessir."

"Double trouble! Be sure to send your address along so me and the Missus can send something along!"

"That's not really necessary, but very sweet, thank you."

"Oh, none of that. Harrison makes quality children. They'll be an asset to the great state of Oregon."

"Jesus Christ," said Joan.

"Okay," I said, "thanks."

"Take care of yourselves!" he called. He knocked on the roof of the U-Haul twice just like a taxicab, and off we went, just like a taxicab.

When Joan came to live with us she went around smelling things for a long while, and when Harrison appeared from the bedroom, she said, "well, look who we have here!" too loudly, like an uncle at a wedding reception.

She hugged the kids too hard, too, as though trying to resuscitate them. Jamie whined a bit and looked back and forth from his father to me, unable to translate our grimacing nods, and Joan's attempt (I guess) at levity with Sab ("Well, I was wondering where all the eye makeup in the world went! It's on your face!") was met with cool disdain.

We got into this pattern where I would drive Joan to the O'Bannon's in the Troubadour Center like two or three times a day; I didn't always have to go in, sometimes I was able to wait in the car, but these times were few and far between. She explained a scenario that really scared her, in which she found herself in a crowded place like a supermarket or a movie theater and she just started screaming the word "nigger" at the top of her lungs. This had apparently never happened, but was enough of a concern to keep her out of public places alone. She wanted me to guess the last movie she'd seen in the theater. I said that I didn't know and she asked me to guess.

"*Battlefield Earth*?" I asked.

"No," said Joan. "What is that?"

"Some sci-fi thing. John Travolta."

"Nope."

"I don't know . . . *Speed*?"

"No, *Castaway*. We saw *Castaway* in the theater."

"Oh," I said.

"Wasn't that so long ago? I've never even been to a movie with the kids."

"Well . . . DVDs and that, videos. It doesn't really sound that bad. Who even goes to movies other than teenagers?"

"People in love."

"I guess," I said. Harrison and I had seen a few movies in the theater. *Land of the Dead*, the second *Resident Evil* and *There Will Be Blood*, the last of which resulted in terrible Daniel Plainview impressions that lasted more than a week and, like recurring fevers, came on at the oddest and least opportune times.

"You should go to lots in the next few months," said Joan sadly, "after the twins come you just won't have the time."

"I don't really have the time now," I said. It was true. Uncomfortable with Joan constantly in the house, Harrison had gotten himself a job washing dishes at an organic restaurant in Ashland. Excellent dish washing was his passion, he explained, and it really helped to release the stress of having to share a bathroom with his future ex-wife. I was supportive to this dream of sorts, and he assured me that it was a happy environment and a really easy job, I guess because vegans do not really leave a lot on their plates, at least not in Ashland. The really awful job, he said, was cleaning the bathroom. I didn't want to hear a lot more than that, but I did because by then it was like whatever. It takes the body a while to adjust to bean paste and the like, I guess. I guess that is a thing that they do not tell you in the various vegan brochures.

Anyway, Joan's doctor, Dr. Chew, made it really clear that our going to the store many times a day was a good thing if we could afford the gas. Of course she knew that we could afford the gas, she watched my show and asked me to sign an *It Came From Beyond!* mouse pad, what she was really asking was whether or not I could stand to do it. And I could. As long as we were always relatively close to a bathroom and a chair, it wasn't really that bad of a deal. Chew knew about the fucking around that had happened between Harrison and me, of course, but somehow this never came up. She did take me aside a bunch of times to express her admiration of me, which I would "aw" and "man" my way out of, generally. The doctor seemed delighted that Joan had agreed to have me be part of her therapy. She insisted it would help our family blend, which sounded a bit too much like blade, which reminded me a bit too much of knives. For the most part, I remained unconvinced.

Leaving the house was key for Joan, so far as Dr. Chew was concerned. The worst thing that could happen would be for Joan to not ever leave the house and just surround herself with her shit and rot there. I didn't really agree that that was the exact worst thing that could happen to a person, but I didn't say anything about it, since Chew had a degree and all.

I would wake up in the morning and feed the kids, get Harrison off to work, check in with Sally and then Joan would drag ass out of bed with a primary store list. Like grape juice and nutmeg. And we would go get the stuff. Sab stayed with Jamie; it was just me and Joan, and Joan going on about how she'd known 9/11 was going to happen.

Then we'd come home, Joan would take her shit back to her room, I'd do some work and two hours or so later there would be another list. Wax paper, *People* magazine, Noxema. We would walk the long, cool aisles silently, almost reverently. It was only ever uncomfortable when people would try to talk to us, like the time a bag girl asked Joan if I was her daughter. That was pretty bad. The drive home, which was short, thank fuck, consisted of Joan clutching her plastic bag of groceries and talking about how she never looked in the mirror and how her body was just this useless bag of skin that she dragged around like Marley's chains.

So, that was hard, I guess: the feeling of getting away with something that you have no business getting away with. Everything that I did or said was somehow horrible to her on some deeply personal level. I told her that the babies were due on Halloween, and she immediately returned with "they were conceived on Valentine's Day," very coldly, as though I were putting it in her face, a thing I hadn't even realized. Then she explained to me that Harrison had never missed a Valentine's Day in all the time that they'd been together other than that one, the one where he put two babies inside of me with his penis. It was as though the whole of my mouth and throat were lined with pleasant things to say that were actually terrible things. They popped out in tapioca clusters like frogs' eggs; there was no stopping me, the *faux pas* landmine of me, and all I could do was apologize, which of course to Joan meant nothing.

God, she hated my town. What was the point of it? Why were there so many losers? I didn't know how to answer these questions of course. I fit in. The losers made me feel as though I were a queen, as though I were their queen, jagged Diet Coke can crown and all.

"Forfeit Valley, indeed," she said once, beside me in the car as we rode past free clinic after free clinic. "You can't even visit this place without feeling like you've lost a bet you never made."

"You probably just feel that way because you were committed here, twice." I had found that the longer I was pregnant the more likely I was to say things I'd have been better off just thinking. Maybe I even liked it a little. It probably had something to do with the very low likelihood that someone would punch me, at least in the stomach.

SHE NEEDED TO BE REINTRODUCED TO HER CHILDREN, IN THE WAY THAT that one great white had to be reintroduced to the ocean after six months in captivity. There was a process to such things. I imagined Joan supine in a long tank, a technician caressing her back, a rush of clean water over her gills.

I kept asking whether the process was aimed to protect the patient or the children and no one could really tell me even though they all seemed to cut their eyes like saboteurs in a movie, like they knew but weren't telling. Everyone wanted to talk about anger and especially unresolved anger and they kept acting as though there was a difference between the two. But wasn't resolved anger not really anger, didn't it become something else, acceptance maybe, or a kind of mourning? Was it all unresolved anger and the people who said they had resolved their anger were lying? Eyes were cut. I made a little game of seeing who had a diploma and who didn't, and I judged the therapists without diplomas with unconcealed snark. It was a preemptive strike. I would not be pegged by a fortune-teller. If someone intended to shame me they better had damn well gone to school for it.

Dr. Chew had several diplomas, and she appeared to be younger than me as well. On one of her many shining oak bookcases sat a gold framed picture of her and Mario Batali smiling off the back of a boat and hoisting a large fish between them. I wanted to spit a little, but with admiration. Her skirts were very brief, footnotes, really. It reminded me of playing Barbie Color Forms as a child and dressing Barbie in a bikini top with a bottom made out of a dog's dish, which I'd chosen for its color and brevity. Following that experience I never failed to refer to sporting a tiny skirt as "wearing the dog's dish." Dr. Chew was wearing the dog's dish, and from where I was sitting, that dog appeared to have been on a diet.

Also she had very small glasses that sat on the edge of her nose so far down they didn't seem possible. Cartoons wore glasses like that because they were drawn on, and it was not a practice that translated well to real life.

"Do they have to sit together?" asked Joan, her ass frozen an inch above her own chair. "It's hard for me to see that. Could they just push their seats a little farther away from each other? Put a little space in there?"

Dr. Chew looked at us encouragingly, as though we knew what to do. When we countered by doing nothing, she cleared her throat and said, "Hey, do you mind? I don't want to start things off from a tough spot."

I could tell that she wanted very badly for this to go without a hitch, a testament to her youth. If this meeting with the adults was a success then Sab would come to sit and listen to all the reasons why she should not blame herself. The baby was either too far gone or not nearly far gone enough for therapy. Dr. Chew instructed that we keep an eye on him over the next few years and if he developed any anxiety over making stools she would start him on play therapy, a thing that involved a sandbox and dolls to represent every member of the extended family. This suggestion of treatment was at the same time so grotesque and hopeful that it left me momentarily at a loss for words. It seemed determined to cure one random thing with another random thing, such as toenail fungus with a fried potato, or acne with a trip to Brazil. I felt so concurrently in awe of and suspicious of therapy.

Where was the point, I wondered, where you just started throwing everything to the wall to see what stuck?

I said, "I'm pregnant," which of course was synonymous with *I'm not moving.*

Harrison half-stood and angrily scooted his chair a few inches from mine. Then he looked at Dr. Chew like a rebellious circus performer, a cranky monkey, and sat down again.

It was clear that Dr. Chew was an indulgent parent to Joan, that she listened to Joan's insignificant problems and made them seem significant. Joan would not have pulled such maneuvers with us, in our house, but here she was still damaged, and her damage won her a little sulking time.

Dr. Chew did not ask us how we felt. Rather, Joan talked and Harrison and I were judged, roasted nearly, on our reactions. If the facial expression seemed incorrect somehow, perhaps with knit brows or the rolling eyes of a mad horse, the face maker was singled out bluntly like a kid in geometry class. Neither Harrison nor I was in any mood to apologize. Especially Harrison. I might've been moved to apologize had I, say, spilled coffee onto Joan's lap. Harrison, in the same situation, would have asked if it was "hot enough for her."

Joan proceeded to tell the story of when Harrison "left the marriage." It was a good yarn. I knew what happened and I still felt on the edge of my seat somehow. There was tea involved, green tea. She made a point to mention that when Harrison left the marriage she was enjoying a cup of green tea. Surreal moments like that have always killed me. Like the day we learned the preposition "but" in kindergarten and my teacher, Mrs. Haas, who Pops once referred to as "a little Jew in ugly shoes," said the word "but" multiple times in multiple ways. Sitting there in our little floor circle, I craned my head around wildly to see who else understood that we were witnessing comedy gold. BUT. BUT LIKE BUTT, LIKE WHAT YOU SIT ON. LIKE ASS. DOES NO ONE ELSE . . . ? IS THIS JUST ME GETTING THIS? I felt constantly held back by the level of jokes around me when I was a child; I suffocated in the bland, Popsicle-stick pun-y-ness of them.

"Someone comes downstairs to talk to you," said Joan, "and

you look up and suddenly you're listening to the fact that they are in love with someone else. That seems wrong in a way. I'd like to get some sort of mandate, like, there should be a limit to what you can come downstairs and say to your wife. I would like to be on the board of that committee, because I've been there, my God I have been there."

"Oh, Jesus Christ, now a comedy routine, Joan? What about asking directions? What about men leaving the seat up? Why not save the doctor and us a bunch of time and write your musings out for the world to enjoy? Send them to Erma Bombeck, why don't you?"

"Erma Bombeck is DEAD," Joan hissed, as though Harrison might have been somehow involved in this death.

"I know where she is, Joan, that's the joke."

"Well, it's pretty inconsiderate and not funny. You know that my aunt died of kidney disease."

"Actually I didn't. Actually, I didn't even know that Erma Bombeck died of kidney disease. But how awesome of you to make yourself the victim, yet again. You're such a trooper. No one can insult Erma Bombeck or your dead aunt without really meaning to fuck with you a little, right? It's all so clear now!"

"Where did you meet Mario Batali?" I asked Dr. Chew. Her small glasses appeared a bit sweaty, like the windows of a dry cleaner's. She was shaking her head a lot, to the point where it seemed less a comment on her surroundings and more of an unfortunate tic, vaguely equine. She also seemed to temporarily forget Joan and Harrison's names; she stumbled around with some J's and S's until finally resorting to "Guys! Guys!" like a scoutmaster in over her head.

"I'm not going to sit here for two hours and take the blame for every bad thing that ever happened in her life," said Harrison. He wouldn't look at Joan, who watched him with the sad, hypnotizing serenity of a big-eyed ballerina painting.

"We're here for Joan, though," insisted Dr. Chew, "to support Joan."

"Really? And why is Joan here? For the free Danish?"

"I understand that sometimes the cruelty we inflict can make us feel good momentarily . . ."

"No, I don't think you understand anything about it. It's like *Harvey*, the movie *Harvey* with Jimmy Stewart and the giant invisible rabbit that only he can see. That's what the craziness is, but no one can see Harvey but me. And because I'm the only one who can see him, the problem must be my problem. Well, even after she was committed, no one can see Harvey. Just for once I'd like someone to acknowledge what a crazy, conniving, selfish bitch she is. Just once."

Joan stared calmly at her hands throughout this, the thumbnail of her left hand cleaning under the index fingernail of her right.

"That is very strong language," said Dr. Chew. "And you're making a lot—A LOT—of insinuations."

"He doesn't really think that she's a giant invisible rabbit," I said, and Chew sort of spun on me in her chair and told me that I wasn't helping, even though we were there to help, ideally. It reminded me of the time I was five or so and a friend of my dads took me to the circus. The woman got into some kind of argument with her own child, also along for the trip, and when I asked what they were fighting about she told me chillingly that it was "none of my beeswax." It was a hell of a thing to be thirty and still have things that were none of your beeswax, and I felt nearly the same indignation I'd felt as a child. Don't invite me to your fucking circus or therapy session if you only plan on insulting me—I'd assumed that this went without saying.

I excused myself and walked down the hall to use the bathroom. This entailed many things in my late-second trimester, hoisting and balancing and lowering, listening to make sure that the stream of my urine was where it was supposed to be, much in the way a blind woman might strike a batter-filled spoon loudly against a cookie sheet to help her get her bearing. My own vagina had become a distant star to me, what with the babies' sloping real estate. I had the discomfort of knowing that my pubes were growing into a sharp triangle shaped by my inner thighs, like the wiry beard of a wise old karate master. I'd been half tempted to ask Harrison to do some pruning, but then the light hit the angles of his sweetly old fashioned New England-y face and I'd chickened out at the last minute. I remained curious about the goings-on of down-there, but in a rather Zen way, as though I'd accepted that this was nature's way of telling me I didn't have to worry about it for a while.

I washed my hands with thick pink liquid soap and waddled back into Dr. Chew's office, where at least two people asked how I was doing. The larger I got, the more people seemed to fear me. Perhaps I seemed liable to explode and douse everything within a five-mile radius with fifty percent more blood, water, and tissue; perhaps people assumed I would fall on their properties and sue. Exploding and litigious, that was me. Joan and Harrison sat grimly and silently, their knees pointed away from each other. Dr. Chew asked if they wanted to do a little role playing and I could tell by the slightly hysterical timbre of her voice that it was not the first time that she'd made that suggestion to them.

"Are you sure?" she asked, looking back and forth between them. It was very Regis Philbin, very *Who Wants to Be a Millionaire?* Obviously very much was riding on them doing a little role playing. Obviously, it needed to happen YESTERDAY.

"I think what I really want to know is why you met Mario Batali and not where," I said, sitting, "I think that would be the better story."

Dr. Chew frowned at me, then in an instant seemed to give up.

"It was for a charity auction," she said. "My brother bid on it for me for my birthday."

"Wow. I'll bet he knows a lot about fish."

"My brother or Mario Batali?"

"Mario Batali."

"I don't know," said Dr. Chew, suddenly more irritated with the memory than she was with me. "It turned out not to be a one-on-one trip; there were like six other people and he didn't really talk to any of us. He didn't come on the fishing trip. We all got a picture and then we ate at his restaurant later that night, but it wasn't him cooking. He had to catch a flight right after the pictures."

"Oh, that sounds like bullshit."

"I know. That's what four thousand dollars buys you."

"Four thousand dollars? I hope he kissed you first."

"What I mean to say is that it's hard to be around the two

of you," said Joan. "I am very grateful for your kindness but, in some ways, I can't help but feel like I was just hit by a bus and then I have to be thankful because that same bus is giving me a ride to the hospital."

"It's not my kindness," said Harrison. "If it weren't for Easy and the kids you'd still be schlepping it back at your dad's house with my alleged well wishes. Nothing good can come of this. You think you're going to learn something? You think you're going to come to terms with something? That'll be the fucking day. You'll still be in your little poor-me corner wondering why everything bad happens to you."

"I don't see why you have to be so EVIL to me!" Joan wailed, her fists at both sides of her face like James Dean's you're-tearing-me-apart freak-out in *Rebel Without a Cause*. "You MARRIED me! I had your BABIES!"

I looked sadly back at the framed picture of Dr. Chew on the boat with Mario Batali and the big fish and sighed. Knowing the true story behind it was a sad comment on things, on fun, fanciful things, and on charity auctions. I actually wanted to ask Dr. Chew what charity it had been, but I didn't because I knew that, in my current state, I couldn't handle the disappointment of it being for, say, some school or park or statue. I couldn't even abide some endangered animal, really. It needed to be kids, sick kids who were cured specifically with the four thousand dollars that Dr. Chew's brother had blown on her. Any alternative was completely unacceptable.

"Fucking things fall apart," I muttered. I assumed it had been a quiet muttering, and yet everyone glanced up at me as though my pre-maternal state had left me prone to the odd profundity. How naive they were. I couldn't even keep track of my own vagina.

Dr. Chew tried to follow me with some jive shit about the seasons, about fall and winter being deaths and the spring always coming just in time with its squirrels and darling buds and so on and so forth. I did not have the heart to tell her that the squirrels from the previous year had not even bothered to hibernate, the winter was so mild. They raced through the yards and along porch railways, poking their little faces against frosted windowpanes as though to say, "yeah? what of it?" Troubadour was not a town on which to base one's metaphors; it could only end in humiliation, in heartache.

"I'm hoping we can do this again very soon," she said. "And that we can work up to Sabrina. The goal of all of this, of this pre-healing, is so we can be strong for Jamie and Sabrina."

A mild shrugging guilt passed through the room.

"What I want most out of this is for my kids to look back and see that I fought for them," said Joan as everyone was collecting their coats. It was loud and stilted and seemingly directed at no one. It was as though she'd lost her place in the play and chose to simply wander to the center of the stage and say anything.

Dr. Chew and I turned immediately to Harrison, waiting to hear the mean, funny thing he would say, but this time he didn't even shake his head. He took my arm and led me quickly out to the car, Joan lagging behind to talk and explain herself to the doctor.

"Can you believe that thing about Mario Batali?" I said, when we had been waiting for some time.

Harrison laughed and said that he couldn't.

17.

I FOUND OUT THAT POPS WAS DEAD THROUGH THIS ASIAN KID NAMED
Kien. I was still living with Richard and Sybil; I'd just gotten my
job with *It Came from Beyond!* It was a quiet, good time. I wasn't
thinking about either of my fathers, or anything. I was pretty happy,
and pretty stupid, and happy being stupid.

The kid called the house and asked for me. The first two times
I missed his call, and then one time I didn't call back. The fourth time
he called I was home by myself.

"I have information about your father," he said. He had a
slight accent. It made what he was saying sound humorous, in a
Peter Sellers kind of way. He introduced himself as a good friend of
my father's.

Which father, I asked, and he told me which one. I asked if he
needed anything.

"Not now," said Kien. I'd walked right into that one, I guess.

I had expected him to die but I figured there would be some
big scene first, some deathbed apology, an Oscar-winning moment. I
would forgive him, or maybe he would forgive me, and there would
be tears from someone, probably both of us.

"How did he die?" I asked stupidly, like the time a guy told
me about the death of his hundred-year-old grandmother and I asked
how she died.

"Something with the heart. Brought on by the weight. He had
diabetes, did you know?"

"Did he die of the diabetes?"

"No, a heart attack."

Then why did I need to know about the diabetes, I wondered a little meanly. It seemed like piling on. Man goes to the doctor and the doctor says, "you're fat." the man says he wants a second opinion. The doctor says, "you're ugly, too." How is that okay? A brain can only stand so much before it breaks like a giant dinosaur egg, I think. I did not want to know about fallen arches or diabetes or toenail fungus. The man was dead and gone, and his previous shits and bitches were no requiem. I asked about the body.

"In a vase," said Kien, and that was a perfectly fine answer that I didn't understand at all.

"He was cremated. It was his wish."

"How did they get him out of the house?"

"Through the garage."

"He's in a vase, then."

"Yes."

"Is it a big vase?"

"It is . . . sizable."

"Sizable," I repeated. I imagined the guys at the morgue having to hack my dad into chunks to get him in the oven, him all just pieced out like a bucket of chicken, like a mixed fucking grill.

"God. Well," I said. It was all I could manage. I didn't know if something was being asked of me, or what. One of those situations.

"I regret to inform that he did not leave you."

"He did not leave me," I repeated.

"Anything. He did not leave you anything. I imagine that he wanted to, but his last few years were unprofitable."

That made me laugh a little, but so quickly that I didn't have a chance to wonder if laughing was mean or not. It was. There was a lot of mean in my gullet, I guess.

"No," I said, "people aren't paying guys to eat themselves to death anymore? Fuck this economy."

Kien stalled a little, and I could tell he was trying to catch up, language-wise. It made me feel as though I should repeat myself, or maybe fax my reply.

"He was kind," he said.

"Sure," I said. I tried my best to remember him at his kindest. Once we came across a blind man at the supermarket who'd gotten turned around and didn't know where he was, and Pops put him in a taxi and paid for the taxi. I don't know how old I was then, maybe twelve, maybe thirteen. I guess that I was proud. It seemed to go above and beyond. Certainly, it was a kind thing to do. I asked Kien if I had to go to a thing.

"A thing?"

"A memorial or whatever. Does my other father know?"

"No, I am calling partly because I am hoping that you will tell him. He should know. It is right for him to know."

"They've been apart for a while," I said. "There's nothing there. Is there a funeral, or whatever?"

"No, everything is done. We planted tree."

That last bit, *we planted tree*, made one hysterical part of my brain sort of secede from the rest of my brain. It floated off, braying to itself. We planted tree! We planted tree! There is nothing left to say! We planted tree!

I asked, "what happened to Derek?" and Kien did not know who I was talking about, so I said, "he's a guy Pops paid for food and sex and whatever. He was a little guy with lots of rings. He made Bundt cakes."

"Just tell your father," said Kien, now more of a low demand than anything. "He deserves it."

"He sleeps with a lady now. They have kids. Other kids. Even if he wanted to know, I'm not sure that he exactly deserves to know."

"No! You dead father! You dead father deserves it! You child, you have no sense of things. Everything a joke. I have to leave now, goodbye."

Dial tone.

That whole thing was weird and comical and sad, like in a movie when a sexy Latina gets mad and forgets her English and starts screaming Spanish in a hot way. There was nothing sexy about this, of course. I was making it a joke because everything was a joke. I called Dad without even thinking, a little shamed. My stepmother answered. She was happy to hear from me; she was up with my baby brother, Henry, who had a fever. They were "camping out" on the futon in the living room watching the Sprout Channel. Henry couldn't keep anything down so she'd had to resort to suppositories, those slick little bullets of medicine, to make him feel better. I told her I was sorry to hear he wasn't well, and she thanked me and went quiet, waiting for me to explain why I was calling in the first place.

"Oh, my father is dead," I said, trying for a conversational tone. "The other one. Not the one you're married to, of course."

"Oh, Jesus. Oh, Jesus, I'm sorry. Dad is asleep. Do you want to talk to him? Of course you want to talk to him, please let me get him." In the background, Henry coughed in a painful, mucus-y way, and then started to cry, a serious cry, the kind where there are several moments between each sob in which the baby tries to catch his or her breath. I could hear Lisa fretting without words, caught between comforting the baby and comforting me. She wanted to get Dad.

"No, no," I said. "Don't get him. Let him sleep. It's not . . ." *a big deal*, I somehow kept myself from saying, "an emergency. He's dead. He's not going anywhere."

The baby had fizzed down to a manageable fuss.

"Are you sure?" asked Lisa. She suffered from the same stepmotherly guilt that I eventually would. She expected my sudden, terrible anger. She braced for it.

"Yes. I don't even know why I called. It was all a lifetime ago." *When Dad was gay*, I nearly added, but didn't because I was afraid it might sound bitter. I wasn't bitter; I wasn't anything.

"It wasn't for you. It was your lifetime. They cared enough about each other to raise you together."

I didn't know why that didn't register. I wanted it to; I wanted to be the perfect Kübler-Ross model, but all I ever felt was acceptance. I was a kid and I was healthy. I had a job. Experiencing grief was not really on my agenda. I said a few things about the brevity of life, about the Berenstain Bears, and insisted that Lisa get back to Henry. I asked her to email me some new pictures of him and of the new baby, and to let me know when he was feeling better.

"I'll have your father call you in the morning?" Lisa offered.

"It's not really a priority," I said. And it wasn't, to anyone. No one ever called me back; no one ever really said another word about it.

SAB STARTED SCHOOL ABOUT A MONTH AFTER JOAN CAME TO LIVE WITH us, and although I missed her it was really something of a relief to not have to watch the two of them and their sad ballet of disinterest and despair, of trying too hard and not trying at all, of melancholy and simmering anger. It made suppertime very complex, to say the least.

Sab had befriended a sullen, red-haired girl named Nicolette from down the street, and the two of them had become quite preoc-cupied with spirits and the occult. Suddenly, candles and incense be-came a thing in our house. Suddenly, the moods Harrison and I would fall in and out of were no longer moods, but unsettled spirits attaching themselves to us, and feeding off our energies. She could see them there on us like backpacks, she said, extracting energy from us with their undulating proboscises.

And there were ghosts in our house; Sab and Nicolette in-sisted upon it with such passion that one couldn't help but believe them on some level. Maybe it was "mommy brain" or "oatmeal brain" or whatever it was people called the process of babies feed-ing off the various enzymes responsible for memory and clear thought, but this spiritual awakening of Sab's came during a time in which I was constantly losing, forgetting or misplacing things. Of course, she was quick to let me know that it was not the babies, but the ghosts. Joan brought them with her, she said. There were three of them, and Sabrina could see them. They trailed sadly be-hind Joan with dipped heads and slumped shoulders, and they had naked, sexless bodies like aliens or the Grinch. Their faces were just gaping black openings, one for the mouth, two small ones for the nose, and two big ones for the eyes. They checked up on me a lot, these ghosts, I guess. Joan sent them out subconsciously; they were the badness that had come loose and now clanged around like screws inside of a thing, the fuselage of her.

I said, "Sometimes a person can just be unpleasant without the supernatural being involved. Sometimes a person can just dislike another person and that can actually be the end of it."

"You don't have to believe me," said Sabby. She'd taken to wearing a silver ankh around her neck that Nicolette was said to have "done something to" to make it into protection from negative spirits. This had involved blood, I guess. When I heard that I'd gone on and on about how dangerous cutting oneself could be, and Sab had shrugged and said that it wasn't a big deal because Nic had had an existing scab, so it hadn't been cutting so much as it had been picking.

"It's not that I don't believe you," I said, "I just want you to understand that sometimes there are really basic explanations for things that don't have to do with the Mayan calendar or whatever. I was sixteen before, too. Your mom has a lot of strikes against her to begin with, is what I'm saying, so we don't really have to add ghosts to that. She's ill and pissed off and hurt, and most of the reasons she's hurt and pissed off are living with her. So."

Sab looked at me strangely, not sadly, not angrily, but more as though she pitied me. She asked me what my spirit animal was. I didn't know. A dog? A serial killer otter. Maybe a bear? She asked me if I would wear a certain token for protection if she promised that she would not cut herself.

"There's not really any protection against anything," I said. I don't think that I meant to say it, a thing I believed with the fervor of any child. "I think that we tend to distract ourselves with stuff, with rituals and things, and then we don't think about everyday horribleness. I mean, there is beauty, of course there is beauty, but some people need to say a thousand Hail Marys before they can allow themselves to see that beauty."

"I worry about you," said Sabrina, a girl who worried very little. She worried about Nicolette running away, and having her mp3 player run out of batteries during a long road trip through a vast land with no Radio Shacks, and she worried about me, great with children, believing, really, in nothing.

JOAN AND I WOULD COME ACROSS EACH OTHER AT VARIOUS TIMES DURING the day and startle. Generally we would both apologize for nothing, for being seen, for the awkwardness of sharing the same space. I tried my best to waddle to the set at least once a day, and stay and chat about my swollen ankles and the other disgusting oddities of my pregnancy until someone took notice of me and shooed my round liability of an ass away. I would take Jamie to the park and call encouragingly from a bench as he managed not to eat sandbox sand. People looked from him to me and had me pegged as a breeder, or Catholic, or both. Old people seemed to take great joy in this, young hipsters, not so much. More than one bowling shirt wandered away muttering about carbon footprints, Holden Caulfield-ing its way to the co-op. We'd visit Harrison at work, a young mother and child aglow with all the things there were to be aglow about, a magazine ad for bronzer or baby powder or even Amway, the selling of all things to be sold.

Then we'd return, the baby and I, and find Joan at the computer or in front of the TV or lecturing the dog, and we would sink into the weird ooze of it. Even Jamie understood the discomfort of the situation. He squirmed in my arms like a tiny Rodney Dangerfield, all popped eyes and tugged collars. And Joan would ask us where we'd been in a dreadful sing-songy way which implied that no answer could be correct. The park? Oh, it's a shame that Jamie has such allergies. To see Daddy? Well, looks like he missed his nap because of it. That's a nasty scrape . . . what do you have? That? Well, I guess that's fine if you don't mind infection.

She would reach for him and he'd look back at me in an inscrutably wise way, as though to ask, "you really think this is such a good idea?"

I called him James, after Harrison's father, his father who was dead. Harrison's father James had not eaten himself to death, of course, he'd taken the slightly more dignified route of colon cancer, and left Harrison with nothing other than a warning to have colono-scopies once every three years after the age of forty. At the very least I had a good story, a lovelorn fatty who went in through the front door and came out for good through the garage. He could never accept the things, or specific thing, that happened to him, and so he remained the rest of his life in a kind of belief limbo like a song lyric playing over and over. I sometimes found myself aching for Pops, for his weapon of choice being food and not booze, not pills or gambling or sex. To me he shared the same imagined breath as the San Francisco man who somehow caught fire in the porno booth; there was no dignity in their appetites. Jokes, muffled laughter would always adhere themselves to these men because what else? What else was there? If you couldn't laugh at a man in a flaming porno booth, if you couldn't then excuse yourself and make mention of your own deafening badness, how would you even know you were alive at all? It was the kind of death that made it okay to laugh a little at all deaths, actual or metaphorical, it was standing on one leg screaming *Airplane!* quotes into an open grave, wrong and satisfying as Russian roulette.

JOAN WOULD WATCH ME AND SAB VERY CAREFULLY, THE TAG-TEAM LUCY and Ethel of us, the way neither of us laughed after we said something funny, even if it was really funny. We out-dried each other. We pushed and pushed at comedy bits until they hung gracelessly in the air like boneless skin sacks, mined of their comedy gold. Our commitment was legendary, legendary in the making, and that in itself was a kind of love, a kind of love affair, which I understood was unmistakable.

"I'm not crazy about your relationship with my daughter," Joan said finally, in a long-ish commercial break between acts of *Frasier*. I was not surprised, but I was shocked. It was like a death that everyone had already come to terms with and you didn't expect your heart to flutter but there it was in your chest, fluttering.

"Oh?" I said. There was some guilt, I guess. Some chagrin, some knowledge that I'd been caught, even though I had just a vague idea of what I'd been caught doing.

"It seems counterintuitive."

"To what?"

"To being a child."

"I don't follow," I said, following, certainly, more than I was letting on. I was sitting in my emerald green recliner, my pregnancy chair, with the cat stretched out across one thigh, still as a stole.

"She should have friends. She should be with those friends. She should join groups. The choir, or something. She was in the choir when she was eight and she really enjoyed it. She was a very theatrical child. She played Cindy Lou Who in a Grinch play in a children's theater in Providence. It doesn't seem normal for her to spend all her free time here with you, a woman in her thirties."

Inside of me, the smallest of rearings, something bitchy and hungry. A hunger brought on by bitchiness, a bitchiness brought on by hunger. I muted the television.

"I'd be interested to hear the things that you think you know about Sabrina," I said with a kindness thick and false as Oleo. "I wonder if you know her favorite band?"

"Fall Out Boy."

"She wears that hoodie ironically," I said, spacing out the word i-ron-ic-ally like Guinevere explaining humility to Lancelot in *Camelot*, in great Redgrave-ian syllables. "Her favorite band right now is Gorillaz."

I did not add the "duh" but it was implied.

"Well, I was in an institution; I can't be faulted for not knowing my kid's favorite band," said Joan, but she'd lost some steam already; I understood her desire to not go up against me in my royal pregnancy, in my home that I owned, and in which I frequently fucked her husband, and I admired it. It meant that she was paying attention.

"I want you to understand the difficulty of this," said Joan, wetting her lips, her eyes trained to muted *Frasier* having a comically muted argument with his father, also muted. "You have my husband. I'm still . . . I don't think you realize how easily things come to you."

That made me think of watching *The Way We Were* with

Pops on the little white TV/VCR we kept on the kitchen counter, the first line in the brilliant story written by brilliant Hubbell: In a way he was like the country he lived in, everything came too easily to him. But at least he knew it. I grasped for struggles I'd endured— my fat, gay father had DIED—and came up lacking, but at least I knew it.

"Look," I said, "I'm not Sab's mother; I'm not trying to take her from you."

"You don't have to try, it presents itself to you and then you can't resist. It's a fan club, I understand that it's a fan club, and I understand that you can't help yourself. But that doesn't make it any easier on the rest of us."

"I don't hear anyone else complaining," I said stupidly, angrily. My hormones would not be ignored; they would push to the top of my throat, all of them, as though tussling for a microphone.

"I just want you to put yourself in my position for a minute, or for a while. Those babies in there . . . you don't want someone else raising them."

"Don't tell me what I don't want. Take them right now. One of them has their foot wedged into my bladder."

Joan laughed a little sadly at that, and I was very tempted to take that as a sign of "all good" and unmute the television, but then she started talking again.

"You know, it's cliché to assume that the craziest person in the room is also the most profound . . ."

"Yes, it is. I myself would never make that mistake."

Joan looked up sharply. We stared at each other until at last she looked away. I would come to look back on this moment as a missed opportunity of sorts, a question that, if phrased differently, I might have been able to answer. I would've liked to have fanned the meager flames of their mother/daughter-hood, behind a tree quietly feeding Joan Gorillaz lyrics to woo Sabby at her balcony. I could've done that, certainly, had only my massive ego been fueled in advance. Was that the tight fit all along, not the twins but my outsized sense of self-satisfaction? I would look back at this version of myself and shudder, in the way that all people looked back at school pictures of themselves and shuddered. The acne of the soul, the too-bright lipstick, the ugly silk shirt, one half black, the other half black dots on mustard. At the time it felt normal, a fitting payment for room and board and access to one's own glum children. I unmuted *Frasier*, just in time for the closing credits.

"These are difficult days," said Joan, still looking away.

18.

THEY CAME ON HALLOWEEN, LIKE EVERYONE SAID THEY WOULD.
I'd worked out in the easy, chick-lit and -flick part of my brain how I would have to go into labor. No one would be available to help me other than Joan. Perhaps Harrison would be stuck at work, perhaps washing dishes meant for some king or Prime Minister. Perhaps he would be stuck in an elevator. Sab would be at school. Sally would be in the air on her way to some photo shoot or book signing, or she would be personally firing someone in China or Italy. And, really, what help would she be to me anyway. She understood, and more importantly I understood, that she was the sad and occasionally profitable comic relief of my life, my wandering, editorial laugh-track, omnipotent and somehow unjudging. The laugh track remained whether Edith was the victim of attempted rape or not; it remained to save me from the horrible silence of it all, and for that I was grateful.

Joan would not be crazy in this scenario; perhaps the gravity of the situation would jar her from her craziness and she would become efficient and deadly serious, the way that people can become when you really need them to not be crazy. Like old ladies who can lift cars off of children or perform tracheotomies on people in the backs of moving cars. Never mind that both of those examples were things I'd seen on TV or in a movie, or heard about from a less than credible source. I believed that crazy was open to adapting to situations.

The labor would just be upon me, and I wouldn't have a moment to spare. I would be panting and waddling and my water would break comically. I would be a mess but somehow Joan would be in control. There would be some superhuman truck-lifting unfolding inside of her and suddenly she would have these feelings of maternity toward me, me a kid without a real mom having babies of her own. We would get through it together; she would hold my hand through labor and I would be making those TV labor sounds even though I'd never been to one breathing class. She'd tell me to push and I would push because I trusted her and then there would be these two babies, goop-free and cooing in our arms.

I believed so strongly in this scenario that more than once I tried to sabotage situations in order to make the whole thing more likely. After vigorous lovemaking I would suggest to Harrison that he call into work and ask if they needed help with any shifts, and since I'd heard that taking stairs sometimes brought on labor, I would schlep up and down again and again the three stone steps that lead to the front porch. If there was a Chinese tea that was rumored to cause labor, then I owned a case of it. Sneezing, orgasms, spicy foods. The babies wrestled each other throughout all of it, ignoring me in the loudest, most obvious of ways.

And nothing came of anything until I was roughly forty-four weeks and the size of a Volkswagen. And everything by the book. I woke up thinking I had to use the bathroom and sat shivering in my giant nightshirt for a while assuming that I was constipated, and then wiping myself and finding blood. Then I sat up in the living room for a while watching an infomercial about a juice maker and scribbling out the time between my contractions in the margins of an *Allure* with Fergie on the cover. Or maybe it was Amy Adams. Some attractive woman with red hair and white skin. And eventually Harrison woke up and took me to the hospital and after I was examined for a minute or so a woman in scrubs printed with little fairies told me that I was in labor.

It hurt for a while. Sab showed up with pizza for Harrison and herself and the three of us sat and watched *It's Me or the Dog* and waited for my epidural. It was the one where that crazy dog stares at the cupcakes and I laughed a lot, even though laughing was pretty painful. I took some amount of pride in the fact that great discomfort could not stop me from laughing at a dog that stares at cupcakes. It was a thing that I wanted to believe about myself that actually turned out to be true.

The breaking of my water was not comical but rather horrifying. I felt it burst, the way one might sense an organ bursting; I let out a breath and there was this terrible sense of a membrane thinning and breaking, and there was this gush of fluid, blood and water and . . . stuff, and it just kept coming.

"Gross," said Sabrina, almost admiringly, as though I'd just burped the alphabet in its entirety.

What followed was a normal procession of pushing, heated oils and vagina snipping. Then, one baby. Then, another. Wrapped in their pink or blue blankets they stared up at us distractedly, then looked to the lights above, where their eyes settled. Now this is interesting, they seemed to be saying. Now this I can get into. They rested upon the great, empty stretched-out piñata of me. There was no end to the metaphors for the ruin of my body. Beanless bean bag chair. Unblown-up blow-up doll, still seeping all manner of wetness. There was such beauty and also a fair share of not-beauty, and I lay there with the babies, accepting that.

EVEN BEFORE THE BABIES WERE BORN I HAD BEEN CONDUCTING LITTLE experiments on myself, trying to gauge my goodness in relation to my badness. Sometime before Harrison came to live with me I'd bought a copy of *Fit Pregnancy* from the supermarket and enjoyed it, reasonably. It was glossy and filled with hysteria. Don't eat this! Don't stand too close to THAT. And the pictures of the massively pregnant women with glowing skin doing their yoga at sunset in the presence of gauzy scarves and large fans really appealed to me. I'd be sitting there in the living room reasonably enjoying my magazine and one of many 3 x 5 subscription cards would come tumbling out, suggesting that I partake on a regular basis. I was not above this. Of course I'd never been one to keep a stringent eye on either my stamps or my personal checks, so I simply filled out the card and left it in the mailbox with my outgoing bills. Ten or so days later I received a magazine, actually another copy of the same issue I'd bought a month ago. That seemed cheap of them; I was more than a little offended by it. I was in no hurry to send my check, wherever my checks might be, heated and dusty atop the fridge or stuck in a side pocket of the Corgi purse I wore sometimes to offset guilt for never carrying a purse. It always made me feel like a girl playing at grown-up, very much the way I was at three or so teetering around on a pair of my father's wedge thong sandals, swinging an enema bag as though it was a Birkin. I would forever leave purses on the bus or at work or in other people's homes; they were all enema bags to me. Lovely, expensive, beautifully crafted enema bags.

I received another copy of *Fit Pregnancy*, enjoyed it moderately, and again forgot to send the check. This is when the letters, gradually stern, began to arrive. Their envelopes, in muted fall colors, heralded my doom in an exaggerated type font. Had I forgotten something? The publishers of *Fit Pregnancy* certainly had not forgotten. I did not get a third copy of the magazine, and the script on the envelopes seemed graver and graver still, as though it were concerned for my health. Perhaps I had died and that is why I was unable to pay the perfectly reasonable fifteen dollars that I owed Condé Nast. Condé Nast, at least for the time being, seemed willing to give me the benefit of the doubt.

After three months, the letters from Condé Nast became increasingly urgent. They'd lulled me into a false sense of complacency to a point where I'd been able to forget the entire nasty business surrounding the fifteen dollars in question; I'd crawled out from whatever denial I was in, no longer peeking out at the mail on the coffee table with a kind of glee-filled terror. Now they wanted me to understand that they knew I hadn't forgotten. They wanted me to know that they'd given me ample time to sort this mess, and it really wasn't okay with them, not by a long shot.

It was around that time that I began to wonder how far I could really push it. No one knew my real name; the subscription was made out in the name of E. Hardwick. Just the smallest and most innocuous of vowels. Not my full name, not even my nickname. Not my social security number. A vowel, my last name and the address of the house I'd just moved into. They had nothing on me. I knew, heart in my stomach and stomach in my heart, that I could not be implicated.

The letters kept coming, sometimes duplicates, sometimes several of them mixed in with that day's mail like thin, stiff fish, resigned even in death. The phone started to ring at times of the day when things were at their most still, and when I'd answer no one would be there. Maybe a metal scrape, the start of a recorder that could never quite manage more than a stutter. Then the hollow refrain of my own voice, "hello? hello?" as though I were calling down deep into a hole. If they couldn't hurt me, not really, they seemed determined to make me think that they could.

What was fifteen dollars? What was twenty? What was anything, really, when you thought about it?

Is this how one loses one's mind? Would I look up one day and be flanked by Joan and two large representatives from Condé Nast shaking their heads kindly but sternly and one of them reaching out to grip my arm and take me away? Was this madness at last, the act of paying too close attention to one thing for a long enough time? I felt so bound to my badness, to the things that I'd done and the things I didn't stop, and in that moment I wished that I'd been born a man, in another country with no Internet access. I wished that I'd been expected to tend goats and that I'd tended them without incident, happily, for the whole of my life.

For a period in my early twenties when I was living with Sybil and Richard I kept a dishpan beneath my bed so that I didn't have to keep getting up and going to the bathroom at night. I drank a lot of water and tea, all the clear beverages, and it was cold in that house besides. Sometimes Richard would be up late on the computer with all the other lights off and he would not look up when I padded down the hall. This made for many uncomfortable silences during the day. Oh, I saw you up last night, you may have been masturbating . . . I wasn't sure if I should say hi, or not. Much better to pee in one's room and pour out the sloshy contents in the morning when no one was about. The correlation of all this being that there was never a time in all of my dishpan peeing that I was for a moment not afraid that I would be found out and mocked. It was, in fact, probably my greatest fear, a thing that I now find odd. What was the big deal? I emptied it every morning and washed out the dishpan in the bathtub to some extent before sliding it back under my bed. I never did in it public, say. I never urinated in front of a child. And yet this secret haunted me day and night. Being a homewrecker was that experience times ten, and it never ended, unlike the dishpan experience that ended when Sybil and I were moving out and I just stashed the rinsed-out pan behind a pile of car parts in the garage. Maybe Richard found it and actually used it for something— good for him! Maybe he actually washed dishes with it, or scrubbed out the tub or whatever people do with those things when they're not peeing in them. It really didn't matter what he did with the dishpan, I'd kicked the habit, the shit was over. I could never leave being a homewrecker behind car parts in my friend's husband's garage; it was sewed on tight like Peter Pan's shadow. Someone was always finding out, and for that person my badness was fresh and new, my adulterous, twin-making sex was happening again and again, like a haunting.

19.

SAB GOT A BOYFRIEND FOR ABOUT A MINUTE; I DID NOT LIKE HIM. He came by the house at a time when Harrison was at work and Joan had decided not to come out of her room for a while. Her door stayed closed for days at a time, emitting the vaguest smells of urine or vomit, or perhaps a complex mélange of both, and would open just a crack at last, allowing for a single bloodshot eye.

The boy's name was Brendan.

Boy. Well.

Although Sab had read me his stats very carefully—tall, polite, English major, seventeen, dark hair—but he was not in my living room five minutes before excitedly blurting his real age, nearly twenty-two. And English major, my fat ass. He'd lost his driver's license drag-racing; his last job was the December before, tying Christmas trees on the tops of family cars in Troubadour Center.

"Well, I'm no elitist," I said, "but there may not be a future in that."

He had one of those too-short penis head haircuts. When he sat, his knee bounced and when he stood he was like a bad actor who didn't know what to do with his arms.

He didn't live anywhere. He crashed places. Although I had given birth, I was still swollen as a tick then; I took things very literally. I imagined him as a small plane with a douchebag haircut spiraling into homes and breaking apart against sleeper sofas and futons. He made lots of jokes about Mexicans. Sab sat beside him with her choppy hair a newly-dyed splatter of teal and black and smiled adoringly. It was one of those moments in which I was both inside and out of myself; I could think clearly and carry on a conversation with this person and still be waiting for the joke to end, for Bob Saget or Howie Mandel to creep from behind my drapes with a live studio audience, to give me a large basket of fruit, to shake my hand and tell me that I was a good sport.

I had a talk with him on the porch, in the cold. He smoked. Sab peered out from her bedroom window, her breath catching wild on the glass like a bull's. I talked about appropriateness; he seemed to understand but then he showed up the next day to give Sab a kimono and a series of drawings he'd done of naked fairies. I talked about police officers.

Later in Sabrina's room, as she huffed silently, a stick of lavender incense smoldering on the nightstand beside her, I tried to explain twenty-one-year-old men who dated fifteen-year-old girls to her. I tried to tell her that it was like when rappers like DMX or Ja Rule got the opportunity to work with terrible actors like Steven Seagal and were really excited about it because at least they were in an actual movie.

Sabrina didn't understand this analogy.

It is not that you aren't so beautiful, I reasoned. It is not that you are not the most beautiful girl in the world.

It's just that teenaged girls are like Ja Rule and DMX; they are just so glad to be in a movie that they don't care that the movie stars Steven Seagal. Teenaged girls don't care that twenty-two-year-old men don't drive, or that they live like homeless people, or that all the money they get from their Christmas tree tying jobs goes to pot and acid or whatever. Teenaged boys are like that, so what? So why make waves when you are dating a boy who can buy you cigarettes? What I wanted her to know was that that was not the real story.

When you are twenty-two, I said, you will want more. You will expect more out of life, and out of people.

"Will I want things that don't even belong to me?" she asked in a really shitty way and I could tell from her eyes that she'd been sorry from the moment she'd thought to say it.

"Maybe," I said.

"Well, I don't understand why people get to decide what is so wrong and what is so right based on nothing, on age. I don't see how that's fair."

"It's not fair," I said. "You can date that kid when it's legal. It's not a moral issue."

"I disagree. You just don't like him. This has nothing to do with age."

"You're right," I said. "I just don't like him. The fact that his wanting to fuck you is illegal is just a bonus."

"Oh," said Sabrina, sighing, and then, "well, thanks for telling the truth."

"It's all that I can do."

"I didn't really expect it."

"That's also a bonus."

"Sorry about the stealing part. That was fucked up. I just really need a cigarette."

"Don't worry about it," I said. "It's such a confusing thing, what's okay and what isn't okay and what's accepted and who's a whore. It's a furious balance."

I felt as though I should lean forward and stroke her hair but in the end I could not make it seem organic enough; there was not enough of a save for me if she were to pull back and away from my hand, if she were to shudder.

I RETURNED TO WORK ON *IT CAME FROM BEYOND!* THE DAY BEFORE Thanksgiving, having cleansed myself in every way possible, from juices to enzymes to brightly-colored drugstore colonics.

People wanted to talk about the babies, to see pictures of them, and I gave in meekly, as though I had no choice in the matter. In truth, the almost month since their birth had been a terrifyingly cocooned period of time, a time in which day ran into night, a time in which the television was always screaming some advice at me. Advice about babies, mainly. And all this really scary information about the many things that could be wrong with my babies. What had they been exposed to? What had they been exposed to while still inside of me?

I gave so much money to St. Jude's and to Shriners that month, all of which felt like preventative medicine.

Their names were Wanda and Abel, names from nowhere that had belonged to no one. They were very small; the weight of some great uncle or second cousin seemed too great a burden for them to bear. They shared the same middle name: Freeman. I had given that name to them while I was still pretty loopy from the epidural, because of Morgan Freeman. At the time I couldn't think of anyone more dignified or worthy than Morgan Freeman, and I felt that the babies could benefit from sharing his name. Harrison had, for some reason, agreed completely.

JOAN DIDN'T COME OUT OF HER ROOM FOR A VERY LONG TIME AFTER we brought the twins home. She even timed her bathroom breaks. I can't even say how long this went on, maybe a week. After a while it just became so natural. Then, one afternoon I was watching Montel and I flinched, sensing her standing there in the doorway. She was wearing her nightshirt over cargo pants and pink fluffy slippers. She shuffled forward and stood in front of the babies in their matching bouncy seats. She looked at them.

"This one's Wanda," I said. "That's Abel."

"Beautiful children," she said. There was something off about her voice, a gurgliness, as though she were speaking around a mouthful of something.

She said, "They look like Harrison."

"I know." It was pretty unfair, but in a funny way. In a way that made me feel proud.

"I can't remember them ever being this small," she said, and it took me a second to realize that she was talking about Sab and Jamie. "It was so long ago."

She was taking on her grand dame monologue face, a thing she'd been falling into more and more often during the past month. Everything was a tragic story that had to be told with great reverence and sweeping hand gestures, everything was a terrible thing that had happened only to her.

I opened my mouth to ask her if she wanted to hold one of the babies, but something stopped me, a whiff of something in the air. She was unsteady on her feet; she knelt before the babies.

She said, "You always think that you have more time." There were all manner of stains down the front of that nightshirt, browns, reds, green-white dabs of toothpaste. I asked her if she was all right.

Joan startled at that, at me asking if she was all right, then she appeared to be thinking about it. She looked at me, then to the babies. She stood and shuffled back to her room.

SALLY MET ME IN MY DRESSING ROOM ON MY FIRST DAY BACK AND TOLD me I looked fat and sloppy. She looked very thin and red, like a strip of bell pepper in a stir-fry. A bad chemical peel, I guessed, but then she took her sunglasses off and there was a blindingly white sunglasses imprint left behind. Over-tanning; I imagined her screaming at some kid who'd forgotten to set the timer on her bed, or whatever. I just didn't mention it; even though she'd mentioned my fat sloppiness. Being a mother had not made me more tolerant, but it had certainly made me a better liar.

She had my script. The movie was Harvest Slaughter, one of those knock off *Halloween* deals from the seventies, all masked killers and big knives and sexy babysitters. I would be a sexy babysitter, something that gave me great pause, even after a month of cleansing.

"Maybe they can just film you from the waist up," suggested Sally. "You certainly have the cans for this role; it's just that the rest of you looks like a truck."

"I just had twins," I said.

"Yes, yes, Wanda and Apple."

"Abel."

"Right, Abel, whatever. Did you bring your autograph book? You excited to meet Adrienne?"

"Adrienne who?"

"Barbeau, the guest star this week."

"Adrienne Barbeau?"

"Yes, you know her? Now there's a great set of cans. You know, without all the excess . . . bloat you have going on."

"She's playing my mother?"

"Right. No, idiot, she's reprising her role in *The Fog* . . . you know, the sexy radio DJ. It'll be funny. What the hell is wrong with you? Are you knocked up again?"

"Is there coffee?"

"In the green room, yes, but it ain't fresh. And I have my eye on that last cruller, so. Be smart about it."

The hallway was bright and very still and it was one of those times when a person is very aware of the loudness of their own shoes and breath. The only way I can explain that walk to the green room was exactly the way it felt, in hysterical, easy images. Like, I don't know, the birth canal. Or that same white light that all jerks talk about when they almost die, the one more competently explained as a whiting out caused by lack of oxygen to the brain. And I could hear a voice suddenly, her voice, deep and exhausted and talking about coupons.

"Well, did you use the ones that were in the glove compartment? The glove compartment? Yes. Well, they're there. No, I'm not mad. I'm not mad, it's just that I can't understand why anyone would be so determined to pay full price for nicotine patches. Five bucks is five bucks. Okay. Well, I sincerely hope that I never become so jaded that I just start throwing cash out the window. It's a problem. It's a real problem."

It struck me that this was the voice that should've screamed at me for leaving my wet towel on the bathroom floor for eighteen years and with that came a feeling of such epic loss that I could barely breathe. I stopped in the doorway of the green room and there she was, all Adrienne Barbeau, sitting on the sofa in a white blouse and black cigarette pants looking like the hot-ass biological mother of my dreams. She'd finished with her phone call but she was still reacting to it, irritated at whomever for not seeing the value in a valid coupon for five dollars. As she was looking away I stared hard at her face looking for myself. Maybe the eyes? Dark, disappointed eyes with those two vertical lines between that look like elevens. Good skin. Really good skin. Her hands, one still holding her phone, the other resting on her knee, were skinny but nicely shaped with no crazy old person veins. They could be my hands, I thought. She looked up and shook her head.

"Oh, Jesus, I'll bet that was loud, right?"

Something happened to my body in response. Some shudder or shrug, and somehow it was acceptable.

"Well, you're sweet," she said, "but I shouldn't get so carried away in public. The next thing you know, all the blogs are calling me a bitch and I can't get arrested in this town. In any town."

"I'm Adrienne," she said when I couldn't say anything, "and you're Easy, I know."

"You know?"

"Of course. The show is great. A real throwback. It's about time, if you ask me. How long ago was Joe Bob Briggs? Do you even know who Joe Bob Briggs is?"

"Yes."

"I can't tell how old you are, forgive me. I can't tell how old anyone is these days. Would you like to sit?"

I sat. She was really pretty, pretty in a way that made me want to blurt out stupidly how pretty she was, and she had that excellent older woman smell, that smell like a fifty-dollar candle, a beautifully improbable mixture of scents. Tangerine and ginger. Anise and black pepper. Pomegranate and anything. She looked like she drank a lot of water, one of those people who say "lots of water" when you ask them what their beauty secret is.

"Well," she said. "You look wonderful. Didn't you just have a baby?"

"Twins," I said, "Just like you."

"Are they here?"

"No, home with Dad."

"Oh, that's tricky," she said. "That feels so . . ."

"Hollowing," I said, because there was no other word to describe it, really. I could not tell if having babies had given me something to die for or had just made me give up a little. I was cored; I could feel the extremities but not my heart and guts. It was like those little

Christmas ornaments you make out of clothespins, Santas and angels and reindeer with little faces and long legs and nothing in between.

"Yes," she said, nodding, "That's exactly it. But my twins aren't babies anymore. They're damn near grownups. And I was much older than you, I assume, it took me a much longer time to bounce back. You look young and strong. Still, I know that it's hard to be away from them."

"I pump every two hours," I said. This was one of the basic humiliations of my life, sitting on a bathroom floor with my udders hooked up to a milking machine.

And understanding me with her perfect maternal instincts she nodded and said, "It's remarkable how dehumanizing that can feel, isn't it? Even a thing that should be so natural—the pump sort of makes you feel like livestock."

Her own age seemed impossible to know. There were so few lines on her face, and yet she lacked that pulled lizard face that a lot of the older actresses have. Maybe she'd had a lift? Maybe she'd done something to her neck? I kept seeing her in her thirties, in labor with me, doing all the huffs and puffs in her white johnny with the blue snowflakes, only in my mind I leap out fully formed, fully dressed, like Athena from Zeus's skull. It was a moment of bloodless triumph, my birth, the start of a bond so powerful that no amount of time or distance could dilute it. There was kindness there in her face, and I knew it was the truth at last, that this woman was my mother and that I was her kid.

"Jim Nabors always spoke really highly of you," I said.

"Oh?"

"Yes. Always."

"And how did you know Jim?" Something seemed to be playing out on her face, some awareness. Jim Nabors, sure. Jim Nabors was the key.

"He was a friend of my fathers," I said, "Of my two fathers. Of my two gay fathers."

"I see," said Adrienne. She stood abruptly; for a moment I thought she was leaving, then she turned slightly to the coffee machine and came back to the sofa with the last cruller on a napkin. She rested

SHE CAME FROM BEYOND! 213

the napkin on her knee and began to eat the donut delicately, ripped into small pieces. It was the way you would want to have your mother eat a donut, if you had some choice in the matter.

"Are your dads in the business?" she asked. Her mouth was full but it wasn't boorish or uncomfortable in any way. It made me wonder if she practiced eating a donut and talking in front of a mirror.

"Not really," I said. "We owned a frame shop on Castro, so one of them ran that. The other one was more of a . . . homemaker.

"He's dead," I added, for no reason.

"Oh, I'm sorry."

"It's okay," I said, but once it was out of my mouth I realized that it wasn't okay. My father, the homemaker turned obese shut-in was dead, and when he died he most likely died alone. Maybe some boy had found him, a delivery boy, some kid turning tricks down by the ball field. Nothing about that suddenly seemed okay at all.

"Are you all right?"

"Yes," I said. I looked at her, a lovely, impeccably preserved woman with powdered sugar dusting at her upper lip, and saw, along with obvious concern, a slight discomfort.

That is what Joan sees every day, I thought. Every time she opened her mouth and a story about how she peed herself at Girl Scout camp came barreling out, this was the consequence: someone who wished her well and couldn't get away from her quickly enough.

"Well," I said. When I looked up again Adrienne Barbeau was holding out a cup of stale coffee for me.

"You're sweet," I said, and she was sweet, whether or not I'd come from her vagina; she was a sweet woman who was offering me coffee.

"You were awesome in *Creepshow*," I said.

"Oh. God. That movie. It's funny that that's the one you'd bring up. A young boy, somewhere around ten or so, just asked me for my autograph because of that movie, can you imagine? A silly movie from thirty years before he was born."

"Well, it's a classic."

"Yeah, not really, but there's no accounting for taste, I suppose."

"Nope," I said.

We nodded and sat there and drank.

I RAN INTO SALLY IN THE HALL LATER, THOUGH I COULDN'T SAY HOW much later. She was picking lint from the plaid lining of her trench, her red stockinged legs slim as fingers beneath her. Once when we'd first met I asked her how one could stay so thin and she'd spun on me and called me Fatty. When I recoiled from the name, she'd smiled in a pointy, feral way and said, "yes, that's how."

Now she was asking me for a cigarette. I didn't even pretend to not know what she was talking about. I didn't even give her one of the cloves, my clever decoys. We walked to the end of the hall together and stood there with her back wedging the front door open, smoking out into the evening.

"I met her," I said, "Adrienne Barbeau."

"Yes? How does she look?"

"Incredible," I said. "She ate the last cruller."

"Better her than you," said Sally, exhaling.

"She might be my mother."

"Yes, and so might I."

I looked at her, at the cloudy shape of her, mining maybe for some kindness, but of course there was none. She was my comic relief and also my psychiatrist, the thick calm baritone like smoke itself, asking me how I felt about things.

I would think of *MASH* in times like this, of Alan Alda and the shrink character, loudly named Sidney Freedman. I would remember things, be talked into them. I would have breakthroughs. Sally would tell me for certain the thing that I feared worst, that love did not exist, that man created God. I would write her name in large white stones and GOODBYE, a tribute seen from a helicopter, when she was far enough away.

20.

THERE WAS A SITUATION WITH MY WIKIPEDIA PAGE, WHICH I'D
actually had since the service began, as my main demographic
had always been nerds. Lately, there'd been a lot of speculation
about how I'd gotten knocked up, and very disappointingly most of
it was dead on, from meeting Harrison at the convention to
"canoodling" with him in Monterey. The sources were so good that
I began to get a little suspicious about it, then a little paranoid. I
erased the paragraph for personal life once and it popped back up
about ten days later.

*Hardwick is largely believed to be responsible for the break-
down of the eighteen-year marriage, a subject that she refuses to
comment on. Friends and family of the shocked wife have admitted
that she suffers from long-term mental disorders such as hoarding
and obsessive compulsion. The trauma of being left with nothing
caused her to be institutionalized twice, and Hardwick and Rice
currently have temporary custody of his two children, ages two and
fifteen.*

Reading that, both times, had been a terrible and sweaty-
palmed few moments; one of my hands brushed against my thigh and
I jumped, so completely out of and unaware of my body. I erased it
again, and again it came back, this time four days later. Again it came
back, like a rash or a stain. I began to think that it never really left,
that even when it seemed gone you could still make out its outline, a
coy and amoeba-like thing, undulating.

Sally called after I erased it for the third time, as I sat there
staring at the computer, waiting for the words to reappear with all

their angry magic, the shake and sparkle in their indignation. I jumped again.

I blurted it out, too stricken to lie or play the situation down, and she laughed and said that was just business.

"Whose business?" I asked.

"No, it's THE BUSINESS. This is the part that's hard, idiot, not the part where you get fucking swag-bags from the Spike Awards. People will hate you for succeeding. That's what you've earned. It has to do with people's self-hatred, really, it has absolutely nothing to do with you personally."

"Yes, but that's my point, actually, I think this is personal. I think it's Joan or one of her friends. Maybe her mom. It knows everything. And then I erase it and it comes back with more."

"Don't be a paranoid shit," said Sally, punctuated by the metallic scrape of a key in a lock. "And who cares? Who cares? It's not hurting your popularity any."

"It's just . . . so mean," I said. I wanted to say more but it all sounded so stupid, stupider even than what I'd already said.

"You need to develop a thicker skin and some perspective. No one has to like you, and fuck them anyway; they're not worth your time. And you're rich. You got rich from pretending to be a space whore. If I weren't richer for knowing you, I'd hate you too. Yes, I said it. I'd go on your Wiki and tell everyone you gave me gonorrhea."

"But I didn't really give you gonorrhea. I really did meet Harrison on Cool News, talking about a shark and zombie movie."

"Well, if I were you I would try not to think about it. People are pretty stupid, and pretty out there. They're way more likely to believe that you gave someone a disease than they are to believe you're a regular nerd like everyone else. It doesn't mean anything."

"Right," I said, starting to feel a bit foolish about the whole thing.

"Go someplace nice," said Sally. "Take a couple days off. You never got to have a Babymoon."

Ah, the Babymoon. I'd read about this trend in both of the two copies of *Fit Pregnancy* that I'd stolen. Somewhere between the sixth and eighth month of pregnancy, the mom and dad slag off and go to a resort or something and slop around in themselves for one last time before they have to become responsible parents. I'd seen lots of colorful pictures of this—husband and wife mani-pedis, and the like. Huge ladies drinking cranberry juice out of margarita glasses (I knew that it was cranberry juice because it was actually listed at the bottom of the page by asterisk in a slightly hysterical way, lest anyone think that this woman was putting her child in danger by even holding an alcoholic beverage). And of course everyone as far as the eye could see was wearing a fluffy white terrycloth robe and kissing. It was depressing, these young, attractive people having one last hurrah before their babies arrived to ruin their lives, and I could understand the desire to simply never have children. If you never had children you wouldn't have to symbolically gulp your last meal in that way, all robes and palm trees swaying, you wouldn't have to accept your chastity sighing, handing over your thongs and receiving your Bjorns. Perhaps the Babymoon was the first step to the actual divorce. Perhaps in hoarding the things that you once loved, in gorging yourselves with them for a single last lost weekend, you were also acknowledging the fact that happiness was a selfish thing, and that you needed to fuck it out of your system completely. Just like any future groom at his bachelor party. A group of his closest friends were enlisted to show him everything, make him feel and drink and have everything all in one debauched night so that he might wake up the next morning a good and simple man who expected nothing.

"I don't have a white robe," I muttered, and Sally laughed. It was one of those times where I didn't know if she got the joke or if I was just funny to her in general.

"Whatever, then," she said. "Stay off Wikipedia. Even though you won't. Even though you're probably looking at it right now."

"I'm not," I said, but I was. I'd never turned it off in the first place.

JOAN GOT A JOB. EVERYONE SEEMED TO THINK IT WAS A SUPER GOOD idea. Mostly Dr. Chew, who said that it would help Joan regain her self-confidence. I didn't say anything but I didn't understand how working in a call center would do anything good for anyone. Joan was selling fruit from a catalog, mostly pears but also apples and really expensive desserts made from figs and cheeses. It made her act pretty uppity, actually, like selling pears to people who could leave their houses, walk a block and fucking buy a pear in person was a totally big deal. Dr. Chew tried to explain that having a job was more important than whatever the job was, which sounded lame and patronizing, but if it got Joan out of the house then I didn't care, since it was taking all of my mental and physical energy to try and breast-feed two massive infants at once. There was something called a *football hold* that I was supposed to use, but it had many strikes against it, not the least of which was that it didn't work. My babies were not footballs, they were more like locusts. Any suggestion that compared them to footballs only made them ornery and combative.

One evening I heard Joan and Harrison having a loudly quiet argument in the front hallway when Joan came home from work. This was noteworthy mainly because Joan and Harrison never spoke, let alone had a conversation. I went forward from the kitchen carefully, and the closer I got the more I could make out.

> JOAN: . . . have been as patient as a person can possibly be.
> HARRISON: . . . out of your mind? Who in their right mind would . . .
> JOAN: . . . patronize me. They are my children. Do not forget that they are my children.
> HARRISON: This is not the time, and you know that. Later . . . divorce
> JOAN: . . . divorce! Who is even talking about divorce?

Then I could see them, Harrison's arms in the air and Joan standing there with her long coat still on, an orange scarf draped around the collar. They both turned to see me at the same time and stopped, like fighting parents caught by a child.

"Well," said Joan tightly, and Harrison looked away.

"Is this about my surprise birthday party?" I asked.

"She's very funny," said Joan, to Harrison, "I understand what you see in her."

She flung one end of the orange scarf rakishly around her neck and opened the front door and said, "Tell my kids that I love them," and left.

"What in the actual fuck?" I said.

"She's got a place now," said Harrison. "It's closer to the call center."

"Wait, why is that bad? Isn't that kind of awesome?"

"In theory, yes. In theory, it kicks ass. But she wants the kids to live with her. She was asking for them just now. No, asking is the wrong word. It was more like she was just demanding that I give her the kids right then."

"Did you tell her to bite your ass?"

"Yeah, pretty much. I tried to tell her that after a while she could get more custody, after a long while of her not being crazy, but now that she has a job and a place she thinks she's Thurgood Marshall all of a sudden. Like, how dare I question her! How dare I question a woman who's had a job at a call center for a week!"

"Oh, she'll cool down," I said. It was too much for me to be frustrated or suspicious, I was so delighted by the prospect of a Joan-free home with no awkward silences or eye daggers or pained sighs when I interacted with Jamie or Sab.

"The fact that you underestimate her gives her great power," said Harrison, all *Star Wars*-like, and it made me want him to make me pregnant again.

A day later Joan's cowboy dad, Bill Hutt, showed up to move her shit out of the house. Harrison helped him because he kept going on and on about his old back. Joan stood next to her father's truck smoking and watching.

"You all both look just like your Daddy, don't you?" Bill asked to the babies, side by side in their belted-in oscillating seats.

"Does Joan want to say hi to Jamie and Sab?" I asked. He himself had already said hi to them and given them a clock radio to share.

"Nah," he said, smiling at the babies. "There'll be time for that."

"Really?" I asked, not understanding. "How long do you think this will take?"

He looked at me in a confused and then sad way but he didn't answer. He shrugged a little and went back to making faces at the babies.

21.

I GOT THE CALL FROM DCF THE EVENING OF THE SAME DAY THAT THE twins started eating rice cereal, so when I answered the phone of course I too was covered in rice cereal, from my fingernails up to my hairline. The woman was very kind but had blades in her voice. Her name was Tonya. She spoke to me at first as though I would understand what she was talking about. She talked about evidence, a picture, and the baby's mother. All I could think about were the twins when I heard the word baby. I was the babies' mother. It was me, silly.

By the time I knew that she was talking about James, Harrison was already in the room with Wanda on his hip, mouthing to me 'who is it?' and I just kept shaking my head and saying oh, my god. I said it until it became a sort of mantra or prayer, and until it was the only thing holding me up and I had to give the phone to Harrison, who took up where I left off saying oh, my god.

JOAN WOULDN'T TALK TO US DIRECTLY. SHE ASKED US TO CALL HER lawyer and she gave us a number, but of course it was the middle of the evening by then so we'd have to stew in this all night: a picture of a bruised thigh, a report to DCF, a question of the child's safety while in the care of a third party.

"We took her in," I said, when I could say anything.

"And you think that means anything to anyone," said Harrison, who was pacing very hard, like something caged. "All you did was give her ammo. She's not a human, she's an opportunist. She knows what scares people, and she knows how to lean on other people and she doesn't stop. She'll never stop."

I will admit that I thought about my career before I thought about the twins, but it wasn't very long before. I thought about my mild fame suddenly escalating because of a horrible scandal that involved children, and I thought about the other mildly famous people who were involved in horrible scandals that also involved children. The comedian Paula Poundstone, for one. I went to bed thinking about Paula Poundstone and the things that had been said about her and taken from her—I was not certain of any of these things, just a floating sense of unease which had attached itself to her name. Had she been guilty? Had it mattered? I seemed to remember that Rosie O'Donnell had stopped having her on her show, and I remembered vaguely a press conference in which she looked bad enough that Lisa had wondered whether or not she was retarded.

Sab would have nothing to do with her mother, even less than before. Before, at least, there had been some modicum of kindness from Sab, the way that someone who does not particularly like children will try awkwardly to be kind to a lost or frightened child. Harrison reported that Sabrina had cut her mother off completely, and had even referred to her mother as a turncoat, which I'm sure appealed to her in a dramatically teenaged manner, much in the way that I once wept over the trichinosis section of my horribly outdated tenth grade science textbook after Pops had forced me to eat pork chops. I told Harrison that he should talk to her and he said, "Talk to who? Sabby? Whatever. It's her business."

"Not at her age. She doesn't understand. She can't see any further than right now."

"Well, neither can I, actually, and I understand completely. Let that bitch feel the heat, as far as I'm concerned. Fuck her."

I started to say something, but I didn't. That was a time when I started to say a lot of things that I never actually ended up saying, ever.

N

I MOVED OUT FOR A WHILE. WE GOT A LAWYER AND SHE TOLD ME TO move out.

"Five thousand dollar retainer and this is the advice we get?" said Harrison.

It was good advice, I thought, or at least I thought that it made sense. It was important to us that Jamie and Sab stay with their father, and not with their grandparents—who'd recently made a bid for them in a drunken late night phone call—or God knew whatever other distant relative Joan might have. For me, these phantom kin brought up images of toothless, overall-wearing moonshine junkies, which was probably unfair, but whatever. I'd earned the right to be a little unfair.

There was that motel called Monte Carlo under the highway; it was pretty awful. I didn't have the heart to rent a place. I didn't want to talk to anyone. I didn't want to look at anyone or explain anything. What I wanted was to slide a check in an envelope under a door every week. I wanted a room with thin walls and a shag carpet and I wanted to hear my neighbors cry and laugh and snore. I wanted to hear the cheerful background music of the TVs mounted to their walls. I am on hiatus, I would say, every minute like the last minute before sleep. I am on hiatus.

I tried having the babies over, and it went poorly. Their shiny scrubbed soft baby skin was not used to smoke and filth and synthetic fibers, and they cried in the dank of my room and reached out with their little starfish hands to leave. My neighbors, unmoved by the tears of actual babies, were also quite keen for them to leave, and the whole experiment ended up lasting about five hours before Harrison came and brought them back to the house.

Harrison quit his job, and we set up a little routine where Jamie would spend a few hours every weekday morning at a daycare, at which time I could come over to the house and be with the babies. At first they were thrilled to see me, but as time went on the experience became stranger and sadder for them, and they were fidgeting and confused. It reminded me of a guy getting a lap dance who doesn't know where to look or what to do with his hands. Harrison wouldn't tell me that they thought Sabrina was their mother but he didn't have to. The babies told me. They pointed at her school picture, framed on the mantel, and made M noises. They were so happy that I couldn't even bring myself to correct them. I smiled and nodded, again and again.

Nighttime was the worst because that was when my body remembered the babies the most. We'd slept with the twins in our giant bed—baby, adult, adult, baby so that Harrison and I could still lie beside one another. Often we lay back-to-back curled around a baby, and in that position it was very easy to imagine that baby still inside of me. The stillness of that, of being someone else's armor. At the Monte Carlo I would sleep and be fooled into that feeling, only to be woken up by a fight in the next room over aluminum siding.

I pumped every two hours, then every hour, but the milk in my breasts dried up and wouldn't come back, not even with medication. It was the stress, the doctor said. To me it felt as though my motherhood was being stripped from me piece by piece. No babies, no milk. I didn't really even have stretch marks. I expected to wake up one morning in jail or on the bench at a bus station and everything I'd known would have become a dream, the kids, Harrison, everything. A kind of falling apart of a life, a collapse.

At night I would think about the three ghosts that Sabrina had warned me about, the ones that dragged ass after Joan, invisible to all who were not deep, true, and sixteen. I would picture them and their slanting, horrifying expressions, pat as masks. Maybe they had come into my room at night, maybe they watched me feeding the babies and holding them and staring at them as though they weren't real, as though they couldn't be real, as though nothing as beautiful and good and pure and perfect as they could be real. Maybe the ghosts had taken notes, conferred with one another, and wandered back out to Joan's room to whisper in her ear. I wished most of all that I had accepted the protection from Sabrina, any protection, whatever she had offered me.

At the small pharmacy in town I bought a large green candle and two squat white ones, the way she'd suggested, and while they were burning I imagined that nothing could find me, and that nothing else could be taken.

I dreamed of ghosts that stole and plotted; I dreamed of ghosts and women who wanted me to suffer.

AT THE END OF THE FIRST TEN DAYS I TOOK A LONG DRIVE OUT OF Oregon to visit my father and stepmother. I called and didn't wait to be invited, and of course Lisa was too polite to act as shocked as she must've been, and I pictured her spending the rest of the afternoon fluffing pillows, filling the basket in the bathroom with tiny sailboat-shaped soaps and shaking out clean sheets to put on the guest room bed.

Dad and Lisa hadn't lived in San Francisco since having the kids, which was sad but understandable, I guess. Most of Lisa's psychics had told them to move, seeing as the West Coast was going underwater, or whatever, anyway, so I guess they assumed that living underwater might be a bad environment for raising children. They were still in California, though. I understood that, too. California is not so much a place on a map as it is a chemical in your brain. As much as I loved Oregon and Troubadour, there was something really experimental about that love, as though it was an affair that I understood to be an affair. Being back in California, even in the strangely dry, flat, high school football-y Vacaville, CA where Dad and Lisa had settled I felt such a surge of beating love in my chest, such a sureness and pride from being there. I had been told from childhood from various well-meaning self-important do-gooders that I was lucky to have been born in America, which is maybe true but also kind of missing the point so far as I was concerned. At that moment I felt lucky to have been born in California.

Dad and Lisa lived in this awesome '70s style ranch house that housed all of these fantastic things on its property: a kidney-shaped swimming pool, a stuffed marlin over the living room couch, an in-law, a velvet painting of a stalking tiger in the hallway, a barn, and several alpacas. Also a koi pond. Sometimes in the summer if you got up early enough you could walk out on the patio and see, like, a fucking egret standing there in the koi pond trying to catch a fish. And there were always tons of animals hanging around, three-legged cats and possums and turtles that would dive off the diving board. And Dad kept big tanks of saltwater fish in the dining room, except they all got eaten by this one huge bass-looking fish called Oscar. I'd witnessed Dad catch a grasshopper and rip off its legs and put it in the tank with Oscar. I'd seen him sit in his little hammock chair and do it while he was talking to me about something, maybe baseball.

The minute I got there I wished I'd been able to bring the kids.

And Lisa got on me, of course, for not bringing the kids. My sister and brother climbed on me even though they barely knew anything about me; they wanted to play and show me all their toys very excitedly, as though, in the showing, the toys became new.

Lisa looked great, and it occurred to me then that she always looked great, that it was in some way her job to look great.

I told her she looked great and the greatest of reliefs transformed her face. She thanked me and hugged me and told me she loved me, everything, while genuine, was still somehow tied up in her gratefulness. She was quick to tell me what she'd had done—boobs, Botox, neck—and even quicker to tell me what she was doing—boxing, cardio funk, Pilates—and it occurred to me suddenly that she was Joan's age. Joan with her button-down denim shirts, with her love of humorous refrigerator magnets and Erma Bombeck.

"How did you manage?" I asked.

"What?" said Lisa, still singing the praises of cardio funk.

"How did you stop being the other woman?"

"Oh. Jesus. Well. First of all, be the only woman. First of all, be the only vagina in town."

"Do you ever feel like it's a thing that will forever precede you? Because I do. I put a lot of work in, into being a good person. I feel like . . . how many hands do I have to shake? When do people forget, when does it stop being a thing?"

I think that I half expected her to act as though she didn't know what I was talking about, and I thought that that would be kind of nice to have it just be my problem, a thing I had to overcome, completely in my mind. But of course she nodded, seeming a little amused, as though she couldn't believe it had taken me so long to bring it up.

"Well, it's not really what I wanted for you," she said, with irony or something, irony-light, or perhaps ironing. "But I guess we tempted fate here and there.

"I would have to imagine that I got away with a lot more than you have, just because of the dynamic of the thing. A lot of people would actually end up thinking more highly of me after they found out that I broke a gay couple up. A lot of people shook my hand and at least one guy told me that I'd done God's work. That was pretty bad. It's that feeling like, yeah, everyone accepts you but then they're all horrible people themselves."

She sat down at the table with me and grasped at her ceramic mug of herbal tea. I noticed how pretty and unchipped her nails were, and this really nice rosy nude color. She could not have done them herself. Some small woman had bent and labored over those nails. Those nails had required multiple processes.

"If you were a first wife, would your nails look as good as they do?" I asked. I don't know if I meant to or if I was just so carried away by their beauty and symmetry. It was not often that I was so taken aback by a nail, or a set of them.

"I am a first wife," said Lisa, and it was half-straightforward and half-shitty. And in the shitty half there was also some fraction of sadness, and of defensiveness, and of course after she said it, she apologized.

"I hope that they would," she said, after staring into her cup for a long while. "I mean, look, you know who I am and who I was. You know how I made my money. All of it has always been based on real, um . . . tangible things. A good face, a good body. I'm not a systems analyst, you know that. I'm not an idiot, I just depend on the things that work for me."

"That makes sense to me," I said, and Lisa smiled in a relieved, slightly hysterical way. "That's not unreasonable to me. But I wonder a lot about how people see us. Women like us."

"Well, I mean, to sort of roll around in that, in the cliché of being 'the other woman' seems really decadent to me. We have kids. You just blow your whole wad the minute you walk in a room if you feel that self-conscious about it."

I could tell that she didn't appreciate me lumping her in with me in my whole "women like us" spiel.

"Remember when you told me that you weren't a systems analyst?" I said. "That was awesome."

LISA AND DAD LOOKED AS THOUGH THEY WERE ON PERMANENT VACA-tion from life and I guess they kind of actually were. I mean, Lisa sold some kind of door-to-door body and face care line, an Avon-y kind of thing, but she mostly just bought the shit for herself with her employee discount. What a life they had, all stuffed marlins and discounted body creams. I tried to borrow money from them once, when I lost my job from *ICFB!* the first time. Dad got really uptight about it and kept going on about the economy and the financial climate and the European markets.

"Oh!" I'd said, "Don't get me STARTED on the European markets!" It was then that I realized that there was a part of me that would always be an asshole, even when I was asking for money.

They got me on the patio with an imported beer in a hammock chair and the Giants on the outdoor waterproof TV just in the background like conversation or a song and I told them that Joan said I was a child endanger-er. My sister was in my lap when I said it, braiding the hair of a black Barbie.

"Oh, Jesus," said Lisa. Her forehead didn't move when she said it.

"That's not . . . can she do that?" said Dad.

"Well, she did do it," I said. I told her about the bruise on Jamie's thigh, and how she took a picture of it and how that started the investigation.

"Oh my god, kids get bruises all the time," said Lisa. "You should see these two. Oh my god."

"And how did he get the bruise in the first place?" asked Dad, and I didn't even get to tell him that I didn't know because Lisa was already angry at him for asking.

"Don't ask her that, like she did anything wrong!" she said.

"I know she didn't do anything wrong, I just want to know what happened."

"Nothing had to happen for a kid to get a bruise. Kids are constantly getting bruised."

"Well, the fact that they got bruised means that something happened, Lisa. It's not fucking stigmata."

"Kids fall . . ."

"I don't know how it happened," I said, and Dad and Lisa both looked at each other in quietly victorious ways. "I knew about it when the Department of Children and Families called me."

"Is the child still in the house?" asked Dad.

"Yeah, but I'm not," I said. I told them about the Monte Carlo motel under the highway and they both gasped. Lisa took the baby from my lap and set her down a few feet away with her brother in this sort of gated pit with colorful balls that played music.

"I don't want her to hear," said Lisa, after a moment of realizing that she'd taken her daughter from the lap of an accused child beater. "That's all that that was."

"Was that mandated?" asked Dad, "You leaving?"

"No, it was voluntary," I said. "Our lawyer said it would be a good idea until the investigation was through, and that way Sab and Jamie can stay with their father. The twins are with me a lot of the time, um, but a lot of the time not, as well. It's hard. It's a hard situation."

"That's disgusting," said Lisa. "That makes me want to spit."

"I wanted you to know," I said, dumbly. "I guess I could've called."

"You need to be around your step-mommy and Dad right now!" said Lisa. "This is where you need to be!"

And she was half-right, I guess. I needed to be someplace where food was put in front of me and where I wouldn't have to do the dishes after I ate, a place with a clean bathroom and lots of new products that I could use, that I was welcome to use, but I also needed to be in California, I needed the balm of that, a place that remembered me as young and strong, and was happy to see me, the familiar tributaries of its highways and streets still there and there for me.

I wanted to tell her so badly that I'd gotten away with nothing, and that maybe she hadn't, either. It was shocking the way ideas would cluster in my skull, opposite things managing to happen concurrently, the way I could live in a place where I would gladly lay flowers at the grave of Harrison and Joan's marriage and also take some dark, never to be mentioned pleasure at having bested the woman in some way. And "never to be mentioned" seemed to sum up the forecast for all my future happiness with Harrison, with the babies and Jamie and Sabrina. I could love my life, the outcome of having taken a man from another woman, I could be grateful for it, but I couldn't fucking talk about it. I couldn't include it in my Christmas newsletter, if I ever wrote a Christmas newsletter. There would always be a sad, empty place in the margins of that luckless, hypothetical letter where a recipient could doodle in my many shortcomings, the also-ran that was my karma, and the horrible kinds of things that would happen to me as the years went on, all of which, of course, I would deserve.

"Those bitches need for something bad to happen to you, I get that," said Lisa. "I feel like . . . there's a part of the brain, of their brains, that couldn't function if they weren't constantly telling them these little stories, little parables, all that 'good is good and bad is bad' shit. It's not that they want for something bad to happen to you personally, much in the way that they don't want something bad to happen to like, fucking Muslims, personally. They just can't live if they think that people like you will go unpunished."

"People like us."

"Us. You, me, whatever. If someone hates you without knowing you, or if they hate me, it just means that they're scared. Like the end of *The Fog*, okay? Like the last part of that movie *The Fog*, where the radio DJ goes on the air and says that bit about what happens if all that zombie sailor shit wasn't a bad dream and the townspeople don't wake up safe in their beds, that the fog could come again. You and me are The Fog. Maybe we aren't satisfied with the men that we stole, maybe we want more. Maybe we want a new man. So these terrified women, what else can they do? Not admit that they're fucking scared and that maybe their marriages need some examination. It's on us. It about what we did and what we could do again."

"*The Fog*." I said. "Why would you use *The Fog* as an example?"

"I don't know. It was on last month on AMC. And we saw the remake not too long ago. It was pretty bad."

"You know. Don't you?"

"What? What do I know?"

"That Adrienne Barbeau is my mother."

Lisa glanced up from her beautiful nails and looked at me for a very long time.

"Oh, honey," she said.

MY MOTHER WAS AN EGG DONOR. I WAS CARRIED FOR NINE MONTHS IN the womb of a surrogate. Lisa told me in the kitchen, a little off-handedly, that there were existing pictures of the surrogate taken while she was pregnant with me. She stayed with my fathers the entire nine months, I guess. She slept in the room that I guess became my room. I considered big leather photo albums hidden somewhere filled with pictures of this random pregnant woman, all roly-poly in bib overalls and head scarfs. Close shots on her big belly, with me hidden inside like a candy-center, chilling in my rented apartment. It was this sense of disconnect like nothing I'd ever felt before; I replayed Adrienne Barbeau's concerned face while deflecting my bonding maneuvers, and shuddered.

"Why would they . . . ?" I said, and after the first bit was out of my mouth I realized that there was no end to the question. All that was left was why they would, and how could they, and just like that I was a nobody from nowhere.

"It's slightly more complex than that," said Lisa. "You know, the sperm."

"THE SPERM?" I said, at first joking hysterical but feeling authentically more hysterical all the time. "THE SPERM?"

"I'm going to make you that cup of tea now."

"Is it Darth Vader's sperm? No, he's actually famous. Can I just tell people that it was Darth Vader's sperm?"

"What's all the clucking about, you little hens?" asked Dad, leaning on the door jamb, half-in and half-out of the kitchen. It was a little Marlon Brando-y, his stance; there was a lot of swagger in him but also some caution, like a small bird ruffling itself out to seem bigger, or a bigger small bird holding a handgun.

"We're talking about the sperm in question," I said. Once I'd seen him there in the doorway, standing all fluttery and handgun-y I looked to the table before me and didn't look back.

"She really thought Adrienne Barbeau was her mother," said Lisa. The silence that followed contained the pained, obvious gaze between them. It was not enough for me to be well-to-do, successful, a good mother. I had found a way to be crazy in a really unique way, a way that seemed destined to destroy everyone as handily as any tsunami or kraken.

"Well, her name was Adrienne," said Dad. Having to tell a hard truth had made him especially lackadaisical but in a somehow Southern way, as though the warm weather was such and had been for so long that it had somehow bled into his personality. He'd adapted to it as easily as any lizard or muskrat; I half expected him to randomly switch the leg he was standing on to get some relief from the sweltering desert sands. Instead he walked (sauntered?) over, flipped a chair around, and sat down beside me like a guidance counselor. He put his hand on my back. His hand was shaking.

"I feel as though you should be calling me in the middle of the night," I said to the table.

"Tell her," said Lisa. "Just tell her."

"Well, it's complicated," he said. "She's not a kid. It's . . . uh . . . complex."

"Certainly not more complex than her gay father leaving her gay father for a woman, right? She's been through enough lately to handle something like this, you know that."

"Then you tell her, Lisa. You tell her."

"Don't get mad at me. We're not fighting here. Don't fight with me. I just don't think we should lie to her."

"Who's lying, Lisa? I'm just trying to take my time with a sensitive issue, okay? Is that okay with you?"

"You know what? Maybe I shouldn't even be here? Maybe

this isn't even any of my business, right? Maybe I should just go bake a fucking pie or something."

"This is not . . . please don't find a way to make this about you, Lisa. Maybe someone else would like to be insecure for a while, did you ever think of that?"

"Guys," I said, and it seemed to disarm the situation to some extent, the smoke of it faded and wafted, and after a moment I'd gotten used to it enough to not really notice at all. I was focusing mainly on the table, which was really nice, and wondering what it was made of and how much it had cost them. Oak, maybe, or cherry. It was too nice of a piece of furniture to have in a house with small kids, is what I was thinking. There were some deep scratches filled in with kiddie substances, mashed vegetables, modeling clay, any other sort of orange-y colored caulk substance.

Lisa's voice, a cool front, materialized above me, "can we just . . ."

Dad, "It's fine."

Lisa, "Kid? Hey, Kiddo?"

"Yep," I answered. Sweet potatoes? Carrots? Hungarian goulash?

"Your Pops was the father. It was Chad."

Chad. For some reason the name had seemed perfectly serviceable as the name of an adoptive parent, and yet from a newly biological point of view there was something really unsettling about it. Just the realization that I'd come from the loins of a Chad, the diminutive of a name that never existed. That combined with the fact that my talk show-mentored stepmother had chosen to reveal the fact to me in a strange third person, a la *The Maury Povich Show*.

"Why not you?" I said to Dad. "I have so much fucking more in common with you."

And I did—I was a hot, happily married cheater, not a fat guy who'd died in his own fat filth, surrounded by Asian men.

"He was adamant that it be his," Dad said sadly. "It didn't matter to me as much. He wanted to be the one to . . . do the whole thing. Go through the whole process. All the appointments, you know. It was a different time, we didn't have any rights. I mean, the birth certificate . . . I'm not even on the birth certificate. We got this letter from Mayor Moscone . . . it was addressed to Chad and Adrienne."

"I didn't know that your name wasn't on the birth certificate," said Lisa. Her hand was on his arm. They never fought for long periods of time, and the physical displays of affection that followed often put the actual fight to shame anyway. I couldn't figure out on the periphery of everything if that was irritating or comforting.

"Well, it just wasn't an issue."

"So why didn't Chad just automatically get her when you guys broke up?"

"He wanted her to be able to choose," said Dad.

And that seemed pretty unkind, seeing as I did choose and that I chose not to be with him. And I didn't know. I didn't know what to say. He was hard to be around and having his blood in me didn't make him any easier to be around. I guess letting me choose whether or not I wanted to be around his fat ass kind of put a shine on him in death, but it seemed symbolic at best. I knew for sure that, had I been given a second chance, I would not spend one extra second with the man, and the fact of that just made me feel mean.

I tried again with, "but Jim Nabors said . . ." and still there was nowhere left to go.

22.

OUR LAWYER WAS NAMED TABITHA JONES, AND WE CALLED HER TJ. She was tiny and mean and wore her skirts to mid-calf. She was from New York and somehow in knowing that, her brusqueness became acceptable, even admirable.

Joan's lawyer was Attorney Thomas, an older man with a terrible, humorous toupee. We all stared at him, even TJ, waiting for that goddamn thing to tip off like a toy boat down a bathtub drain. We all met in TJ's office for what she kept referring to as a five-way, as much as Harrison and I kept asking her to refer to it as a "sit down," a phrase we found to be much less sexual. Joan was wearing an ugly suit that was actually very strategically ugly, as TJ would later explain. If Joan looked bad enough, I guess, people would feel sorrier for her, this also combined with the fact that her children and husband had been stolen by a Hollywood star who had also beaten and possibly molested her baby son. A bad suit could go a really long way toward winning a trial, or at least that's the way it was explained to me.

She didn't speak very much, Joan. She sat there next to her lawyer like a child. It reminded me of these old interviews I'd seen with Twiggy, where she was just standing so placidly next to her manager or whomever and the manager was doing all the talking, I guess because Twiggy was too sensitive and frail to field questions without a buffer. I didn't know Joan to be either sensitive or frail, so it was interesting to see. It made me angry, but in a really tired sort of way.

TJ got right in there, as was her way, asking her questions rapid-fire as though knowing that the answers would be too trivial to wait for. She wanted to know what Thomas would give us, what Joan would concede.

"This is a very difficult time for Joan, as I'm sure you can appreciate," said Attorney Thomas in his old-timey lemonade on the porch sort of way. "She's trying so hard to rehabilitate and also come to terms with the way that her life was ripped apart just earlier this year. She's not averse to working with your clients, of course, she just needs time to think. She is very cognizant of making a decision in the heat of the moment, and she understands that that would be very disruptive to the children."

"Is she aware that what she's claimed is also slanderous to my client, who is a public figure and stands to lose countless revenue from this . . . witch hunt?"

"The safety of the children is the only thing that concerns my client right now, I'm sure that you'll appreciate that. We have gone to great lengths to not spill this story to the media."

"To the extent that my client lives under the highway in a motel? Do you appreciate that?"

"We . . . are all making sacrifices in the best interests of the children, Tabitha. Joan has had to accept quite a lot of money from her parents in the past few months, and that has been very traumatizing for her, as she is partially estranged from them . . ."

"Which is why she came to live with us in the first place," said Harrison. We all jumped at his voice, a strange deep spike in all of the flat, lawyerly notes.

"And she appreciates that," said Attorney Thomas, smiling.

"Do you, Joan?" asked Harrison. "Do you appreciate that?"

Joan lifted her eyes briefly and looked at him, her face unmoving as my stepmother's.

"Joan understands all of what has been done for her," said Thomas. "But that does not negate the seriousness of these claims."

"You know that Easy never laid a finger on him," said Harrison, still talking to Joan. "You're JEALOUS. You're jealous that I chose her and you're jealous that the kids like her better. I knew you were bat-shit before but this blows everything else away. How do you sleep at night, you horrible cunt? How do you look yourself in the mirror?"

"Who's open for a break?" asked TJ. "Anyone?"

"I could use some air, myself," said Attorney Thomas. He stood but Joan did not stand with him.

"I would like to speak with Easy, please," she said, eyes to the floor.

"Then speak," said Harrison. "Go ahead."

"Alone."

"Fuck that."

"I would like to speak with Easy, just she and I together, please," said Joan in the same even, quiet tone, like Twiggy asking her manager for a piece of chocolate.

"Are you sure that's a good idea?" asked Attorney Thomas, and Joan shrugged off his light fingertips at her arm.

"It's fine. It's what I want."

"It's okay," I said, and Harrison made some eyes at me which maybe meant I was crazy or stupid or both, and I shook my head.

"Well!" said TJ, with a mean, cheerful strangeness. "Then the three of us will take five."

"Please make it more like fifteen," said Joan, looking at nothing.

When we were alone, she said, "Did I ever tell you that I once beat a dog to death with my bare hands?"

"No," I said. I did not pull any friendly, uncomfortable faces, I did not rub my face or scratch the back of my neck. I had heard too many stories about shower curtains and bars and Loch Ness Monsters and Fruit Roll-Ups and getting lost time and time again at the big box stores. They all seemed so sinister now, the lot of them, a feeble-seeming veil for a wicked and plotting brain. The thing that I said was *no*, and I meant it. She had never told me about the time she beat a dog to death with her bare hands.

"Sabrina was a baby," she said. "No, not a baby but the kind of overgrown toddler that everyone still calls a baby because they are the only baby in the house. Maybe we would have called her a baby forever, had Jamie never been born, but he was finally, from my last living egg, streaking out across my uterus like a little star. In the end, Jamie was the thing that saved Sabrina from being a baby forever."

I wanted to look away at something. I wanted there to be something worthy of studying at length. The books in TJ's office were all thick and foreboding, the kind of books that would line the shelves of a false bookcase in a haunted house, weathered and heavy with dust. The plants were plastic and tall, surrounding long tables filled with pictures of people in suits standing very close and smiling. How would they feel to know that they would remain captured in that mild happy way forever, subject to the various butt-hurt scrapes that went on between angry exes and angrier siblings, and the children, angriest of all? My head and body hurt. I sat there and felt age on me like a swarm of something, a plague of something. It would devour me and leave a slumped and apologetic skeleton connected by spiderwebs to the chair and walls like something out of MAD magazine, a guy who waited too long at the DMV, a woman in a hospital waiting room surrounded by old *Redbooks* and cigarette butts.

"I didn't leave the house much," said Joan, "when she was a baby. I didn't drive. We had our little routine. Mostly what we did was wait for Harrison to come home. We didn't . . . really exist without him. I mean, if we did exist, there was certainly no documentation of it. We haunted that house. We lived by the TV schedule. The cartoons, mostly, and we ate the same terrible things—white bread toast with butter. Off-brand sugary cereals. And popcorn. Sometimes when she was hungry I would make the big plastic white bowl with microwave popcorn and I would give her a sippy cup of Diet Coke. Amazing. Amazingly and so casually abusive. I don't know. It was like that part in the movie *Poltergeist*? The part where the ghost psychologist is talking to the little boy at night and trying to explain ghosts to him, and she's whispering that thing about people who have passed on and don't know they are even dead, and they're just sitting around getting sadder and more frustrated. That was me and Sab. That was the life we had.

"After a while Harrison took notice of it and he started trying to get me to go places, first around the block, then to a park, then to a doctor. And I was hurt and embarrassed, and we fought, and he would ask me what kind of life I wanted, and what kind of life I wanted for my daughter. It ended really badly every time, and then we'd forget about it, and then we'd fight again about the same thing a few weeks later. We just, you know, hated each other. Eventually, he got the dog. I guess he assumed I wouldn't let an animal shit in the house all day, and we didn't have a yard, so. So, yeah, he got the dog."

"And you killed it with your bare hands," I said. "And then you learned something about yourself. And grew as a person. And that's why you said what you said about me, and why I deserved it, because you killed a fucking dog."

"I never laid a finger on Jack," said Joan, horrified in her ugly suit. She was so horrified that she actually did a comical look-around, as though concerned that someone might have overheard the terrible untrue thing I'd said about her killing Jack. The dog was Jack, I guess. I didn't ask what kind he was, but she mentioned he was small and brown, and so from then on out I pictured him as a Jack Russell Terrier. The details to most things existed in my mind as a kind of joyless teleplay, with costumes and spit takes and ethnic housekeepers, as though I'd painted the world with my feet while watching Nick at Nite.

"He was a WONDERFUL animal," said Joan. "All he wanted to do was be with our family. Harrison got him from the shelter. He'd been a rescue, and he was wonderful. A wonderful family dog. Wonderful with the baby."

"Wonderful."

"Fine, be a shit, but this was a good dog, and Harrison was right, after the first time I didn't let him crap in the house. I would get the baby in her stroller and we'd take the dog for a walk together. I was fearful. I had a lot of apprehension for that walk, and when it was done for the day I would feel such relief, immediately followed by apprehension for the next day's walk. Would it rain? Would the stairs have wet leaves on them? Would I fall? And I could imagine falling with the baby holding my hand and the dog's leash all wrapped around my legs and the slow-motion awfulness of that. And the ground and the pain and the blood! And the sounds that would come out of me, all guttural and primal, and the baby screaming and crying the way babies do when they are really, genuinely hurt and not just scared or tired. The great sucking in of breath and the wailing. It was always with me, every minute. And I couldn't tell anyone, not Harrison or anyone. I was just so careful, and I just held on to Sab and the rail so tight every time. And every time we would somehow make it back into the house alive.

"I took him afternoon and evening. Harrison would take him before work and then for his last little pee to the corner. And I had . . . my goodness, by the end I had exhausted every possibility I thought of the bad things that could happen. It was a very busy street that we lived on for one thing, so, I don't know, I had these visions of, like, a car jumping up on the curb and creaming us. It was very easy for my brain to create that scenario, like a movie. The whole grill of the car, the headlights, just right there. I've always been really good at seeing these things. Not positive things, mind you, just horrible things. So, I made it a point not to even cross any streets, not even the really baby streets. I just made a big cube—just a big square, and gave Jack enough time to poop and sniff and then it was done. It was a ten minute deal, and that's not even me being conservative. It was ten minutes at the outside, really."

"I don't have the stomach for this right now, Joan," is what came out of my mouth, and it surprised me a little. I felt meaner than that.

"I want you to know me," said Joan. "I want you to understand where I'm coming from," and I looked at her and didn't say anything for a while so finally she added, "of course I don't expect you to be on my side about this."

"There was a new family at the corner, at one of the corners," she said. "Right at the corner before you got to the very busy street with the curb-jumping cars. Well, they weren't that new, but they had a new dog, a female, a mutt. A yellow-colored dog. She was always barking but not in the usual way that a dog will bark, not just like a dog defending its territory. She barked all the time—they muzzled her when they walked her and they barely walked her, so she was bored and angry and the barking was more like screaming. Very fierce. They kept her in the yard, mostly, and the only thing that separated the yard from the sidewalk was a chain-link fence. The crazy part was that this family had kids, small kids but still older than Sabrina, a small girl and an even smaller boy. The yard was actually nice. Big. They had a wooden structure out there for the kids, a nice one. A kind of professional one where you have to actually pour concrete in the base to keep it stable. The dog—her name was Izzy, I know this because the male owner would stand there and scream her name to no avail—would put her front paws up on the fence and just go apeshit on anyone. Not just if you had a dog, of course, but especially if you had a dog. Izzy would stand there in her yard with her front paws up on the fence and bark at another dog like she wanted to kill it.

"Everyone knew. The owners, in their defense, I guess, they always behaved in a pretty chagrined way, as though they could shrug and smile their killer dog into being something anecdotal, or even neighborly, but everyone on the block still knew. Once I saw a youngish mother with her baby in one of those front-carriers, and Izzy of course went bonkers when they walked by and the male owner was just there tinkering with the garbage can lids and the young mother said to him, 'that dog is going to kill someone one day,' just like that. Really matter of factly. It reminded me of that part in *The Exorcist* when the little girl comes downstairs during the party and tells the astronaut that he's going to die and then she pees all over the living room rug. The owner's face was weird; it was angry and shocked and embarrassed and it didn't know which to be first. He sort of bristled out a response that was more like a jumble of indignant sounds than anything. It sounded like when someone insults a millionaire at a party in a cartoon."

Then, Joan said, he'd tried to make a kind of conspiratorial face with her, like what a kook, right? And Joan had looked away. She'd envied the mother in a way, the unangry telling of a thing that was hard, much like the way that my Dad once told a used car salesman that his blackened thumbnail was going to fall off while the man was handing him a complimentary pen. Joan also longed to tell the owner that his dog was out of control, and not exercised enough, and should be put down in the most humane of ways, with its family surrounding it, on its sleeping blanket, perhaps with a well-loved stuffie nearby. But this was not a thing that most young mothers did, especially not ones who had yet to shed their baby weight and felt very conspicuous and open to the cruel taunts of others. Perhaps if she herself had been wearing a stylish knit cap and peacoat and skinny dark wash jeans that made her legs a mile long she might have been more open to sharing her feelings in that way, but she was a young mother of the regular sort, wearing whatever did not have baby vomit on it, and she wanted to be done with her afternoon walk for the day.

"It wasn't a thing I thought about every day, oddly," said Joan. "I was way more preoccupied with things that would never happen, like the car thing. Or teenagers. Evil, roving packs of teenage boys who wanted to hurt the baby and make fun of me. It didn't occur to me as much to fear a thing that was so destined to happen."

She didn't have Sab in the stroller that day, she said. Sab was getting bigger and liked having the choice between a ride and a short walk, it seemed to appeal to her growing sense of independence in a small, adorable way. It had gotten to the point where she only wanted to take the stroller when she'd brought a toy or when she was eating something. The rest of the time she was happy to jump off low stoops and shuffle through the crunchy piles of leaves.

"The strange thing is that Izzy didn't start out barking. Had she just been barking the entire time I could've crossed the street at least. Even Jack was surprised. She was just there all of a sudden up against the fence screaming at us, and I backed up and right into the baby and she went back off the curb onto her bum. And then that dog was up and over that fence so fast. I guess, I guess she wanted Jack. I'd dropped his lead and he was near the baby, that's the kind of dog he was. She was crying and scared and he went to her. But that's not where my mind was. All I saw was Izzy and Sabrina, and Sabrina crying.

"I saw the collar, it was red, the collar, and I got a hold of it and pulled hard and I was on this dog, the dog was down on her side and I was on top of her, holding her, pulling her away from my baby. And this dog was gagging and snarling and its eyes were rolling and red and there was this white foaming spit and I could see that this dog wanted to kill my baby and while I was lying there I could see the dog killing my baby. I could see the dog's mouth on my baby and it shaking her head back and forth the way that they do. And all of my weight was on this animal and I was . . . I made a fist like this and the thing that was in my head was the way they say that you're supposed to punch a shark in its muzzle to make it go away, or else poke it in its eyes, and I hit the dog with my fist at the side of its head. It kind of yelped but it wasn't stopping, it was still wild, it still wanted to hurt someone, and I punched it again and this time there was blood and more white spit but I couldn't attribute the blood to this animal; I felt as though it could be my blood, or Sabrina's blood, and I kept . . . I couldn't stop hitting this animal. If I stopped hitting her, she would overpower me, I thought. I thought she would get up and she'd be even angrier, and I couldn't let that happen. I felt so calm inside. I can't remember it in any other way. I can't remember my heart beating, or if I was breathing or sweating, but I remember this animal's face coming apart beneath me. I remember that at one point my hand went into the dog's mouth and I thought that it bit me, but it couldn't bite me, it was maybe not even alive then. It hurt because my fist went right through the dog's jaws and hit the concrete and it opened a few knuckles. There was blood everywhere. On the baby. I saw it on the baby and I started screaming but it was the dog's blood, Izzy's blood. The baby was fine. Jack was beside her and they were watching me. Sabrina had that one face babies make when they're too afraid to cry; it's a horrible face, it's horrible when you know that you're the reason the baby is making it."

Joan said that the owner appeared then, that he'd actually probably always been there, and that for some reason she remembered him wearing a white starched shirt and overalls.

"No pitchfork?" I said.

"I know, right? It's amazing what the mind can do after so many years. I have no idea why I would align him, and that moment, with farming. And not just farming but play-farming, like a farmer from a cartoon or a children's book. He just started yelling, no words but yelling, just disembodied sounds coming really oddly from his throat like he was just learning to yodel and he was also angry at the same time. Did I mention the scarf, that I was wearing this pink scarf with a really wide weave and it was just, like, lolling out in the dog blood like a tongue?"

I shook my head.

"I don't remember how I got home, though. I don't remember showering or changing clothes, but it's not really as though I blacked out, either. It was something else. I don't know if that's a thing, remembering the horrible part of a story perfectly and then blocking out the really mundane parts. I actually would like to remember those parts. There were a lot of old people in that neighborhood, and a lot of flags. American flags of course and then that other kind of flag that you change every season, you know, one has a Jack-o'-lantern and then it's a horn of plenty and then a Christmas tree or Santa or whatever. And I do remember an old lady coming out and seeing the blood and screaming and saying that she'd known all along that that dog was a killer. She hadn't seen. All she saw was the blood and the baby and all of us down on the ground like that. She didn't know.

"It was a bad scene. The owner had seen everything and he was acting like I was some kind of a . . . well, he was acting as though he were the victim in all of that, that his dog had only wanted to play with my dog. He began crying, which was awesome. None of us were crying by that point, but he was. He was holding the body of the dog, and, you know, she looked so much smaller there in his arms, and he was crying. He was calling me a monster. Me, the mother. He was saying he didn't know how he would tell two people, a boy's name and a girl's name, I guess the kids. I guess that he was talking about the kids.

"Nobody fucking questioned me, you know? It was self-defense. The guy . . . I don't even remember his last name, he was very loud on the block for a while, I guess, but everyone hated him already, everyone had hated that dog, except for its family. I saw the mother a few times after I killed Izzy. She was very pale and drawn, the kind of woman who always seemed to be wearing a winter coat even when it was very warm. I guess they got another dog immediately, another rescue, but really old. An old Basset mix. It always wore a coat, too, or maybe it was a bulletproof vest. I never saw the kids after that. And they moved, finally, the lot of them. They were just there and gone one day, like a smell. They just drifted out of the neighborhood."

"And then you were fearless," I said.

"No," said Joan. "God, no. I was more scared then, and then I had a reason to be, so Harrison didn't give me such a hard time about it. He started coming home earlier and he came home for lunch, too, so I never took Jack out again. He was hit by a car a year or so later. He got out and got hit by a car. It was for the best."

"It doesn't sound as though it was the best for Jack."

"Well, yeah, I guess not. I know that it wasn't a drawn-out process. He was just smushed, just a mash of animal, like a squirrel or a cat. Roadkill. We didn't have to take him to the emergency room or anything. I'm pretty sure that the driver of the car didn't even know it hit him. They didn't stop, in any case."

It was weird, the way she told a story, what time did while she was talking. I'd seen a *Nova* a few months before about space and time, about how everything started with the Big Bang, actually a very organized thing, and became quicker and more disorganized, and how it was to blame for every erratic thing that happened, every time you broke a glass or fell in the street. It said that time went slower if you were moving forward, but that the way we moved on this planet was so slow to begin with that you couldn't really tell at all. When Joan told a story it made you forget about any kind of time, at least it did when you stopped being uncomfortable and just gave in to it. In the middle of it I wouldn't have been surprised to walk out of the room and run into myself walking in to begin hearing the story. I had a visual on that. I was always much better looking in that visual, more pulled together. I think it would have broken the heart of my brain to accept that I looked old or tired. But if I was defying natural laws anyway I wanted to believe that I still looked like a kid.

"What I want you to know about me, is that I am a mother before I am anything else. Maybe I'm appealing to you, I don't know. Maybe I feel as though I owe you more of an explanation now that you are a mother yourself. In that second, in the second that I saw that dog headed for Sabrina, I knew how far I would go. I am not . . . I am a fearful person by nature, I don't think that that's a secret, but I found something that I would die for, and that was the baby. It didn't have to be a dog, it could have been a man, or a fire, or anything. It was danger, and I didn't think about it, I just went forward. I didn't think about it."

"I could lose my babies," is what I said. "If you get your way, I could lose the twins."

"And how does that feel?"

"You suck."

"It's a bad situation, I want you to know that I understand that. And I don't want that, for you to lose those babies. I just don't want to lose mine, right? I want all of us to keep our babies. It's fair. All I want from this is what's fair."

There was a rustling against the door, and then the door opened a crack and part of TJ's face was there.

"Knock, knock."

"We're all set," I said.

TJ walked into the room with a kind of careful hopefulness.

"Wonderful," she said, her mouth still a straight line across. "And was this little chat a productive one?"

"It was about a dog," I said, and that was all I said. I stood up and walked out of the office and the building and to my car with everyone behind me, saying my name.

23.

THE CALL CAME AT NIGHT, OF COURSE. I HADN'T BEEN SLEEPING, NOR had the men who lived to the right and left to me. One was watching a boxing match on the television, and from the screaming and swearing I assumed it was a fight on which he had a great deal of money, and the other was making some sort of loud love to something, to another person or to himself. There seemed to be no second voice in his room in any case, but by then I had trained myself to think the best of these people so perhaps it was a mute woman he was having sex with, or a mute man.

It was TJ on the phone. My ringtone for her was *Everybody Hurts*.

"It's over," she said, the kind of thing you want to believe but won't let yourself, like summer vacation or a plane landing safely.

"What is over?"

"Everything. Didn't I tell you? Didn't I tell you that a person can't be that crazy for that long without something happening?"

Actually, I had no memory of her ever saying such a thing, but I didn't say it aloud. I said, "What is over?" again, and it made TJ laugh.

"Bitch tried to kill her father. Tried to set him on fire."

"Joan?"

"The one and only," said TJ. "Attorney Thomas is being very vague. At first all he would say is that there had been an altercation. Then it started to come out. Nail polish remover, my god. What a nutcase."

"Did anyone get hurt?" I asked. I thought of Joan's father in his cowboy hat with his case of soup, and shuddered.

"Everyone is fine. It was probably more for show than any-thing, not that that matters. She's going away for a long time."

"You sound like Commissioner Gordon," I said.

"I don't follow."

"After Batman catches a villain, in the cartoons or the comics or whatever, they always get the guy in cuffs and then Commissioner Gordon says, 'you're going away for a long time.'"

"Oh."

Or maybe I was thinking about Scooby-Doo.

"Where is she going?" I asked.

"Same place for right now, on suicide watch. We'll know more later. She's not getting her hands on those kids, though, that's for sure. Sabrina will be of age by the time it's even a question."

"And what about me?"

"You? You get to sleep in your bed tonight, is what. You living away isn't a courtesy that anyone is concerned with now, believe me. Certainly not Attorney Thomas with his tail between his legs. The investigation will be dropped. It's not a thing."

"But DCF and Joan are two different things, you're the one who told me that."

"Will you relax and listen to me now? No one is following up, nothing new is coming forward, and your accuser is in the hatch. It's not a thing. And even if it were a thing, they've had too many budget cuts down there to keep a handle on any of this piddling shit."

"So, budget cuts are the reason that I'm off the hook," I said.

"If you want to be literal," said TJ. "But no one is asking you to be."

I DROVE HOME IN MY UNDERWEAR RIGHT THEN. I LEFT EVERYTHING I'D brought to the motel at the motel except for my wallet and shoes and keys and when I pulled up I remembered that I didn't have my house key anymore, that I'd given it to TJ as a gesture of something, of good-will or something, so I stood on an overturned flower pot and squeezed in through the bathroom window. The seat was up and one of my feet went right into the toilet and I dragged my one wet foot behind me through the house like Igor. The house sounded like sleeping babies.

Harrison was on his side in bed. The babies were together on one side of him, on their backs and seeming to be holding hands like a small, sweet Hansel and Gretel. And Harrison startled when I wedged in behind him. A small startle, not the full-on karate move that some men do when you surprise them. He asked me if he was dreaming, and I told him no and not to wake the babies and that Joan had tried to set her father on fire.

"Oh, Jesus," said Harrison.

"She wasn't successful."

"Is that why you're here?"

"Yes," I said, into his neck, "also, budget cuts."

24.

WITH SO MUCH WISHING THAT EVERYTHING COULD HAVE JUST been a bad dream, having the whole business wash away like a bad dream seemed ominous, like that one period in a slasher film where the masked killer is presumed dead but is really just hanging out in the sewer plotting his revenge. I got one phone call from Dr. Chew offering me a free consultation, and by then I was so keen to repress everything I couldn't even imagine what she would consult me on. Hardwood flooring?

There was some talk of a lawsuit, but I don't really know who was talking about it. TJ? I remember telling her that there was no money there and her getting so angry and saying, "I'll tell you where the money is!"

My Wikipedia page once again collapsed into boring facts and small, comforting lies, one of which suggested that my true birth mother was Suzanne Somers.

I sat with Jamie and the babies, mostly, and watched cooking shows on BBC America. Everyone wanted to sit on my lap. Everyone wanted me to be their mother.

I took a walk into downtown Troubadour by myself one afternoon while Harrison stayed with the kids, a walk in the slushy, almost-snow. I thought I might see a movie but I'd seen everything, even if it had just come out. The previous month had given me a kind of horrible, boring gift of premonition. I could guess the next line out of any actor's mouth regardless of the circumstances and it made me feel strange and sick. So instead I walked to Forfeit Valley Medical to see my Aunt Jane.

It had been a while; I fumbled through the directory looking for her office number. There was a Dr. Haken in room 85, but the name had three strikes through it and, written beside it in my aunt's small, neat print: *Dr. Swift*. She was leaving for the day. I came up the hall to see her locking her door.

"Dr. Haken isn't here anymore," she said, not looking up. I stood and waited until she did. She smiled in the way she always did, something forever lost in translation.

"Ah," she said. "Hi, kid."

SHE LOOKED GOOD. HER HAIR WAS VERY SHORT, LIKE MIA FARROW short, and I asked her about it, was it hard to do. She said that it wasn't, because what was hair.

"Vanity," she said, around her cigarette. She was staying at the Monte Carlo.

"I was just there," I said.

"Why?"

"It's complicated."

"Okay."

She wanted to buy me a drink. We walked to the hotel mainly in silence, although I asked about my cousin Avery and she said he was well. In school, she said, but she didn't say where or for what. She mentioned that he was spending winter break with Keith. At first I didn't know if she was implying something or if she just thought that I was already aware of something, but then I figured out that she was just saying the facts, that Avery was spending his winter break with Keith, the tired deposition of her life.

We drank gin and tonics in the Monte Carlo Bar, which was plush and raspberry-colored and a little sticky, like a thrift store stuffed animal. I asked her how she liked Troubadour, and she seemed to shrug with her whole body.

"Oh," she said, "I hate people."

"This isn't really the place to find anything," I said.

"It's the same as any place. I should know; I've been every-where. Avery and I were in Kunduz not too long ago."

"Kunduz."

"Afghanistan."

"Of course."

"Yeah, it's all the same. Every place."

"Troubadour is the same as Afghanistan?"

"Yes, but worse," said Aunt Jane. "Troubadour is worse somehow."

"I understand."

Once when I was thirteen, I stayed with her and Avery for a summer and at times we were joined by a man named John who'd suffered deep third-degree burns when his wife, a woman named Lydia, had set him on fire. They were still together, the man and his wife. She was in jail at the time, but they were still together. John would go places with us, to the store, to the movies, whatever. Once at a restaurant a waitress had stared at him for forty-five minutes and when he left to use the men's room she'd rushed over and asked Aunt Jane how he'd been burned.

"In a fire," said Aunt Jane, not raising her eyes from her newspaper. Maybe that was the only way you could live, I thought, by knowing that every place and everyone was the same.

"This is more tonic than gin," she said, peering into her glass.

I said, "I know about it. I know about Pops."

"What? What about him?"

"That he is my biological father."

Aunt Jane stared blankly for a moment; it was enough for me to ask if she'd even known in the first place.

"I knew," she said. "I think I knew. I must've known."

"It was shocking."

"Well. You seem to have lived through it."

I wanted her to say something about blood and about our family, about the things that had been passed to me like a baton. Maybe even a curse. A family curse to liven things up a bit. Aunt Jane looked into her glass some more.

"You look like my grandmother, man," is what she said. "Your great grandmother. Her name was Anise. She was all right, not like that frigid bitch Rose. The same face and mouth." She made a straight line with her hand and held it against the tip of her nose. "Everything from here down."

"I guess I knew," she said, drinking. Once, as a kid, Avery and I went to meet her at the hospital, to eat lunch with her at the commissary—grilled cheese sandwiches and butterscotch pudding. As we walked down the hall, a red-faced man grabbed her arm hard, as though for balance. His whole life was in his face—what he was worth, what he would sacrifice, maybe even the reason he'd been born, and he'd said, "You're telling me . . . you're telling me forty percent? You're telling me that there's a forty percent chance he'll die?"

Aunt Jane, impervious to Avery and I cowering behind her, had looked into the man's face, not at her arm or his digging grip, and said, "No, there's a one hundred percent chance he'll die. I'm saying there's a forty percent chance that it's the burns that will kill him." I asked her if she remembered John and Lydia and she nodded without thinking. I asked her if they were still together.

"Oh, of course," she said. "Of course they are. Who else would have them?"

"That's something," I said. "That seems like something, to go through all that and to still be together, no matter what people think."

"Oh," said Aunt Jane. It was all she said for a long while, and I could tell that she wanted to be kind. Maybe kind was not the word.

She said, "So often people will confuse survival with goodness or with purity, when it is just what our bodies know how to do. I think that it is . . . *unwise* to not make that distinction."

"I am probably pregnant again," I said. I'm not sure why, but sitting there in the sunken bar of the Monte Carlo, my half-drank gin and tonic in my hand, I felt very strongly that another little swimmer had gotten through. I pictured it, a sperm in a top hat and bow tie and holding a bouquet of roses like the illustrations in *Where Did I Come From?*

"Again?"

"I gave birth to twins in October."

"Oh," she didn't say congratulations or anything. I really appreciated that.

"Irish triplets," I said. I meant to laugh afterward, but it came out like a gasp, all gurgling like a man who'd just been shot in the throat.

On the way back home I found two magnet letters pushed up into the frozen earth, an H and an R. I pried them from the earth and walked home.

In a fire, I thought, the way in which we all were burned.

JUST AFTER THANKSGIVING, HARRISON AND I DROVE THE KIDS TO SAN Francisco for a weekend. Six hours in a minivan with twin babies, a three-year-old, and a teenager. We took advantage of a lot of rest stops.

I took the family on the sad tour of my life: *Here is the frame shop where Papa met Mimi. Here is the frame shop where Papa left Pop-Pop for Mimi. Here is the flat on Douglass Street where Pop-Pop ate himself to death.* We went to the beach—too dangerous and cold for swimming, just fine for a Pronto Pup and a walk with the stroller. Sabrina and I went shopping in Union Square; we ate chowder out of bread bowls on Fisherman's Wharf.

"How could you ever leave a place like this?" asked Sab, over hot chocolates at Ghirardelli Square.

"There are other places," I said, and she rolled her eyes.

Right before we drove home, we stopped at the aquarium in Golden Gate Park.

"Any great whites?" asked Harrison.

I told him about the time, years ago, when that aquarium was the first to keep a great white in captivity. Her name was Sandy. After less than four days she stopped swimming and they released her back into the ocean. Not far from where Mimi lived, I told the kids.

And once, about ten years after that, they had a dead great white on display in a big frozen glass case right inside the main entrance. It had gotten caught in some fisherman's net and died, and the fisherman had kept it on ice until he got back home because that's what you do, you hoist around your frozen sharksicle like the ultimate trophy, like an oversized novelty check or love. Pops took me to see it; I wore acid-washed jeans and a Harley Davidson t-shirt. We stood there and stared at this rigid thing, its reflectionless eyes and frost-bitten dorsal fins. It was more than dead, somehow; it seemed impossible that it ever could have lived. Behind us the vague images of people, the flashing of their cameras, saying, "wouldn't want to come across that guy in the water."

"Sounds depressing," said Harrison.

"It was," I said. "It's the kind of thing you have to see with your own eyes to know it's for real. A real thing. Not a frozen husk that used to be a shark. Not a fish that gives up and stops swimming."

"Our shark could not be contained," said Harrison.

"Ours was one hell of a shark," I said.

His hand found mine and held.

I DROVE SAB TO TWO NORTH TO SEE HER MOTHER ON CHRISTMAS EVE. It was late afternoon and snowing, and all of Troubadour was alight with that kind of false, tinsel-y goodwill that would evaporate in less than forty-eight hours when it was time for people to start punching each other in the faces over bath towels at the After Christmas Sales. For now all was quietly harmonious. Even the soul station was playing the standard carols, albeit sung by Boyz II Men and Gerald Levert. Sab was wearing long purple and black striped gloves with the fingers cut out, and a wooly hat that looked like a tiger with long ear flaps. She was biting her nails.

"You don't have to be worried," I said.

"I'm not," said Sabrina. "I mean, there's a difference between being worried about something important and just dreading some really awkward shit."

"How do you know it will be awkward?"

"How could it not be awkward? What is she going to say to me? I love you? I want you to be happy? I've missed you?"

"Yes," I said. "Probably all of that."

"And what would that mean to me, any of it?"

"Well, she is still your mother."

"That's what everyone has been saying to me for eight

months, like it's an excuse for anything. But she doesn't change. She doesn't stick to anything. She acts out of selfishness and hurt feelings and she doesn't change, and I'm supposed to love her because I came out of her vagina? I wish I'd come out of your vagina! If I'd had a choice I would have come out of YOUR vagina!"

"That's . . . very sweet," I said.

"People just . . . they tell you this bullshit about how you can make your own family or that there's not just one way to make a family, but then they get caught up in where your blood is and where you came from and it doesn't make any sense. It's not fair. It's a lie."

"Well."

"Just like going to see her on Christmas is a lie. I don't even believe in God. Maybe she doesn't either. So why do we have to act like we like each other? And what is this?"

"A sweater."

"I know it's a sweater, but why did we have to buy it for her? Because we're supposed to? Why would you buy her a sweater after what she said you did to Jamie?"

"I don't know," I said. "Because she's your mother."

"Well, I hate her. I fucking hate her."

"So, what? Do you just want to go and get ice cream instead? We're already here."

Sab's face, pale and cat-eyed beneath her tiger hat, went mean. "Can I tell her I hate her? Can I throw the sweater at her?"

"I guess you can. If that's what you have to do to feel okay."

"I don't even know if I'm one of those people who can feel okay anymore."

"Well," I said, "I guess you'd better throw that sweater at your mom and find out, then."

Sab got out of the car quick, the package in both hands like a machine gun, and I had to run to keep up with her, grasping at her shoulder and collar so she wouldn't slip on the ice. The waiting room was empty. The nurse in the snowman sweater at the desk offered us a molasses cookie from a wooden hatbox and told us, in barely more than a whisper that Joan wanted to see the both of us.

"Why?" I asked.

"Oh, who knows?" said the nurse, too cheerfully, and it made me wonder how hard the eggnog was flowing in the break room.

Joan was not behind glass, the way I'd imagined, or masked on a dolly like Hannibal Lecter. She was sitting on the edge of a narrow bed in a black hoodie and black sweatpants with little red bootie slippers on her feet. She was very thin, I noticed, and there was more gray in her hair than there had been the last time I'd seen her, when she was sitting in my lawyer's office telling me about the time she'd killed a dog. She and Sab didn't embrace. Sab bent down a little and Joan patted the back of her shoulder with an open palm and their faces grazed each other's a bit, it seemed. Sab sat across from her mother in a hard-backed chair. I stood.

"That's for me?" said Joan.

Sab was still gripping the present in her lap. She looked at me, and then held the gift out toward her mother.

"Thank you," said Joan, setting it on the bed beside her. "You shouldn't have."

She looked up at me then, her smile placid and unnatural, "How are the babies?"

"Big," I said.

"And how is Jamie?"

"Bigger."

"Is he excited about Christmas?"

"Yes."

"Excited for Santa to come?"

"Uh-huh."

"That's wonderful," said Joan in a dazed sort of way, as though she knew that something was wonderful but she couldn't for the life of her remember what that thing was. She had a new kind of lizard stare, like a lizard staring at something that it wanted. She turned it on Sab again and asked her how school was going.

"I'm on vacation," said Sab. "My grades are good."

"Yes? You like your classes?"

"Yes. But I'm on vacation."

"Yes. Any boys you like? Boys at school?"

"I don't know," said Sabrina.

"That's wonderful. You look wonderful."

"You don't even have any idea where you are," said Sabrina. She was breathing hard. It was cold in Joan's room; I could see Sab's breath.

Joan just smiled.

"I want you to say something to me," said Sab. I put my hand on her shoulder. "I need for you to say something to me about my life."

"Of course," said Joan. "Anything."

I watched Sabrina's mouth moving. Maybe she was asking what mattered, whatever mattered. Maybe she was going to ask her mother why she'd done the things that she'd done, or why she'd left or why the chemicals in her brain were unbalanced or why it mattered that her mother was still her mother in the end. In the end, though, she started crying, a crying that started with a shaking and became a sobbing and she bent forward in her chair and wept. I crouched beside her. Joan, still sitting there on her bed, looked shocked, but really more shocked in a curious way, as though the things that were happening around her were happening too quickly for her to absorb.

"Hold your kid," I said, and she blinked once and then nodded. She reached out a tentative hand toward Sab's shoulder.

"No," I said, "Hold her," and I took the hand she was holding out and eased her gently to the floor until she was kneeling in front of Sabrina. She put stiff arms around her and Sabrina cried harder, and the harder Sabrina cried the tighter Joan held her.

"It's okay," said Joan, maybe another lie, who could tell. It was what Sabrina needed right then, though, and it was all one could ask from Joan, to kneel there and tell her kid that it was okay.

"I'm so tired!" wailed Sabrina, and we all felt it, we were all so tired. We all wanted to hibernate and forget, we all wanted to lie down in the snow, to be very cold and then very warm and then just to sleep. I wandered over to the window and looked out at the white blanketed parking lot, at my own little van, in the snow a humped, solid doghouse-looking thing, and I knew what I wanted right then: a bucket of fried chicken.

I wanted to bring a bucket of fried chicken home through the snow to my family.

"It will be all right," said Joan, her hand stiff against Sabrina's tiger hat.

I have always found that people who believe that it will be all right sleep better than people who don't, so why would you fight it? Maybe you believe it enough and sleep and maybe somewhere in that there is happiness. And why would you fight that? Why would you fight that if you knew better all along?

It snowed all Christmas. Lisa and Dad called from Vacaville and during my conversation with my stepmother she mentioned that the koi pond had frozen over, and that if you looked closely you could see the orange bodies of the fish beneath the ice like a cluster of little hearts. Some would be lost, of course, she said. They would have to wait until the spring to see what had survived.

ACKNOWLEDGMENTS

UNDYING GRATITUDE TO THE SEVEN LITTLE RYANS AND PAM; TO MY awesome early reader, Rusty Barnes; to my savior, Sarah, and Allyson, the coolest girl in the world; to my darlings, Sue, Rachel, Helen, and Lisa; to my sweetheart web support, Tori; to Kelly, the first love of my life and confidante for all things pointless; for healthy cynicism from Nick Barnes; to Lara; to my brilliant photographer, James Yeater; to my dad, Richard Asuncion—had I had a more normal childhood, I certainly never would have had a career in the arts; to John and Molly Doyle for teaching me the meaning of the word *neighbors*; and, lastly, to my mother, Michele Asuncion, who never, ever, ever thought for a minute that it could be any other way.